KAT'S

CONUNDRUM

RAVEN AND HUMMINGBIRD

BOOK THREE

NIKKI BROADWELL

AIRMID PUBLISHING
TUCSON, ARIZONA

Kat's Conundrum

ISBN: 978-1-7326173-5-3

This is a work of fiction. All places, names, characters and events presented here are a product of the author's imagination.

Formatting by: Polgarus Studio
Cover design by: Daniela Colleo—www.stunningbookcovers.com

OTHER BOOKS BY NIKKI:

A Witch in Time Saves Nine
The moon in Her Eyes

The Last Keeper of the Light

Rosemary for Remembrance

Burning Night

Siobhan's Secret—book 1 of
Raven and Hummingbird series
Dagda's Daughter—book 2 of
Raven and Hummingbird series

~The divine feminine is alive and magic is afoot~

PROLOGUE

Bones rattled as the witch shook the bag and muttered her questions. She pulled the drawstring open and let them scatter across the dirt floor, the action causing the candle to flicker and nearly go out. "It is as I thought," she mumbled, her gaze moving from the bones to the shadow on the cave wall. "I will make you whole again, and when I do, you will assist me."

She moved the candle in its holder and examined the bones again, gnarled fingers running through her matted gray hair. "They tell me that I am the one who will bring down the world. Once I am finished the world will reflect what I, and others like me, want." She rose from where she kneeled. "But first I must stop the girl who has come from the god's loins. She is my nemesis and my trial. If she succeeds, I will fail." She glanced down again. "And I cannot fail." She bent to gather the bones together, replacing them in the velvet bag. Turning, she placed her hand on the wall where the shadow hovered. "Soon, my love. We will be together very soon." Outside the cave the wind came up, howling like wild dogs. The candle blew out, plunging the cave into darkness.

The note said:

My dearest Katel,
My time on earth has abruptly been brought to a close and
I have gone home to the Underworld and the duties I left
behind. Do not seek me there; if you do it will be at your
own peril. Your father has been stripped of his powers and
locked away where he can never again do damage. The
borders have closed, the worlds of gods and humans
separated forever. I have no insight left to impart, only that
you must listen to your own heart and the wisdom of the
forest. Use the gifts given you.

Kat stared at the square of white left on the bare counter of what had been Cerridwen's Cosmetic Cauldron. She'd been working here off and on for over two years and trying her best to learn what it meant to be a demi-goddess. Airmid, her teacher in the fine arts of goddess powers, had left months before, heading home to Otherworld to fight the darkness that had crept through the opening between worlds. The shelves were empty now, with no remnant of the creams and essential oils Cerridwen had concocted from the herbs and seeds Kat had collected in the forest. All that was left was dust.

A sinking sensation entered her, anxiety making its way into the pit of her stomach. She hadn't realized how much this woman's presence had soothed her, how the work had kept her mind off disturbing events and buoyed her moods. Why hadn't the crone goddess mentioned her impending departure? Or for that matter, the terrible news that Bran would not be allowed to return. Her mother and baby brother were thousands of miles away, and from what the note said, the love of her life might be banned from ever coming back.

Her thoughts turned to her immediate plight, the weighty sense that it was up to her to get rid of the Dubh and stop whatever was creeping over the land. According to Gwen, it was her destiny. But without the support of Gwen and Airmid, she felt lost, especially since Dagda was no longer around to piss her off and bring out what was lurking beneath the surface. Her powers seemed to arrive unbidden when she was around him, fury with her father sparking them.

Anger rose up at the damage that had been done to her, the goddesses' decision to have Bran live with her as a teenage boy, his disappearance into the nether realms of the Norse world to find himself again. If it hadn't been for her, Bran would be dead now. The loss of his presence in her life was worse than any of the others. She was now utterly alone.

Kat walked out of the empty shop, her troubled gaze going to the smoke rising from the forest in the distance, the blank faces of those walking by, and the proselytizers carrying signs with messages about repenting and the end of days. The lead-up to all this had taken many months, months in which she'd been missing Bran and waiting impatiently for his return. The Dubh were here, their amorphous shapes wafting by in the increasingly gray world. They looked like ghosts, with their pale ever-changing bodies, but that was not what they were; ghosts did not suck the life out of the world, leaving it cold and dead. According to Cerridwen they were not the problem, they were merely a symptom. If they weren't the problem, what was? In Kat's mind leaching the color out of everything alive was no small thing.

Many of the people she saw were numbed out and blank. The temperatures had dropped, the days shortened and the nights so cold that no amount of heat could keep out the chill. Those who were resistant to the Dubh were the ones carrying signs and seeing evil everywhere. And the others had apparently lost their senses. Was there something more malevolent waiting at the edges of the world to wreak even more havoc?

Last time Kat had spoken with her, Cerridwen had feigned innocence when asked what was happening in Otherworld—how the trial of Dagda, Kat's father, was going. Considering her own intervention, Kat had assumed that things would work out for her father; she'd made a special trip to Otherworld to plead his case, citing his love for her mother as the reason to be lenient. If it wasn't for her newfound ability to shift into a hummingbird, she would not have found her way to Otherworld, some small kernel of knowing arising once she was in bird form.

"He did what a god would do faced with a life on earth," she'd told the group of gods and goddesses she addressed. "He fell in love with a human woman and lost his wits in the process, embracing the greed of money and power that has become the main purpose of life on earth." Kat remembered the shocked faces when they heard about what earth was like, their expressions saying that they all had power but they did not wield it for personal gain. When Kat went on, they watched her, their eyes wide with interest. "But he changed and he's been wracked with guilt," she'd told them, "not to mention heartbroken over having to leave the love of his life and two half god children."

That last statement had sent murmurs rushing through the group as they discussed her message. Kat had waited for questions but none were asked. But she'd left out one important detail—the real reason for her father's guilt and shame had been caused by her mother rejecting him.

Later, when she was back on earth and Bran had been called upon to participate in her father's trial and sentencing, she'd assumed he would be gone a week or possibly two. When a month went by and then another, she'd felt his absence keenly, but with this news, anxiety came rushing to the surface. If the border was really closed, she might never see him again. As Hummingbird she'd made it there once, why not try again? She nodded to herself. It was the only idea that made any sense.

Kat's tiny gossamer wings beat against the invisible barrier, her hummingbird heart racing. There was no getting through whatever this was, and in her current state she had no alternatives other than to return to earth. When she reached the ground and turned back to human form, the seriousness of the situation penetrated. She had been so sure that as a demi-goddess she could pass through into Otherworld—she'd done it before in bird form. But now she realized that what Cerridwen had said in her note was the truth. The worlds of gods and humans was separated forever.

It was dark by the time she reached her apartment, her body like lead as she took one slow step after another. At home she pulled the crumpled note out of her pocket, the words blurring through her tears. When the paper grew hot and caught fire, she dropped it, staring in horror at the pile of ash on the floor at her feet. She lay on her bed and gave herself over to grief, finally falling into a stupor-like sleep.

Kat woke to gray light, the words of Cerridwen's note emblazoned in her mind: *listen to your own heart and the wisdom of the forest.* She grabbed a jacket and ran from the apartment, ignoring the cold wind that blasted her in the face as she skimmed the distance at a run. The trees taunted her as she entered the woods; the towering leafless gray limbs seemed like a testament to futility. Kat picked her way over burned stumps, skirting around trees that looked ready to topple over, following a former deer path deeper into the forest. There had to be some green left somewhere, some area that the Dubh had missed in their greedy search. What they wanted was beyond her understanding. She'd never had any personal dealings with them, but they eyed her from time to time, their eyes empty as they wafted by.

In the distance she spotted a few old growth trees, their trunks gray but the branches at the top still green. She hurried toward them, allowing her scattered thoughts to drift away. Communicating with trees was a tricky business, one that required a clear mind and a ton of patience. Trees were ancient, and what they had absorbed over their years was not readily given.

She slowed her steps as she approached the gnarled trunks, bowing her head in respect. These beings had been here for hundreds of years and would be here for a hundred more, barring fires or hurricanes or tornados uprooting them. Would the Dubh finally be the ones to kill them? Some had already burned, scars lining the trunks, but they persisted, despite it all.

As she asked for guidance, the pointlessness settled into her. Her approach had to be in keeping with what they were. Trees didn't think in human terms, nor were they conscious of the puny dealings of what went on in the world of humans. They communicated amongst themselves, keeping away pests by sending out scents, drawing helpful predators to them in the same way, and filling their leaves with toxins to fend off unwanted insects and leaf-eaters of all kinds. They bloomed at the same time to widen the gene pool, and 'moved' south or north depending on the warming or chilling of the environment around them. They exchanged information and nutrients with help from fungi, and worked with whatever foraged on their leaves and roots, communicating with others of their species through the web of their roots. Kat was awed by their size and age and how they functioned.

She sat on the ground next to a particularly enormous cedar, one that she viewed as the sentinel; its crown rose higher than all the others, an aura of age and wisdom emanating from it. When she placed her hand on the gnarled bark, she could feel the energy coursing through it. It was very much alive.

She breathed in and out, waiting. The sky turned dark, the silence of the forest and the smell of dead leaves and burned wood settling into her. Hours moved slowly by, her crossed legs going numb as her mind opened and cleared. When her mother appeared in her mind with an expression of fear on her face, Kat's eyes flew open. Something was amiss. She didn't know if this vision had come from the trees or not, only that she was needed. Her knees ached when she rose from the ground, her hands going together to thank the trees before she sprinted away.

Dagda had accepted his punishment, ready to be imprisoned inside the tower for all eternity. It was what he deserved. So, when he was told that instead of that, his powers would be stripped and he would be sent back to earth as a human, he argued. "I want to stay here as a god. You can put me anywhere, I don't care, just please don't take my powers."

Forseti, the judge, scoffed. "And how can we keep you locked in a tower if you have powers, Dagda?"

"You can…bind them."

Forseti shook his head. "Your daughter has convinced us of your love for this earth woman. We are giving you a second chance."

"I don't want a second chance! What I did down there…I would rather die than go back." But no amount of pleading would change their minds. And so, the borders were opened to expel him from Otherworld onto an earth depleted of color.

He was heartsick, disgusted with himself and angry with his fate. At first, he wandered aimlessly, hoping he would simply die. Sleeping on park benches, and in doorways was not only uncomfortable, but also led to several bad confrontations with those who saw him as a bum. He wanted to argue, wanted to turn them into toads or send them sprawling, but when he lifted his hand, nothing happened.

He caught a cold and coughed for weeks, his lungs burning as though they were on fire. His head was hot but he felt chilled to the bone, shivering as he was rousted by the police. When he questioned them about his symptoms, wondering what it meant, they laughed at him.

After a month of this, when he became so emaciated that he could barely get around, he searched out his former property, surprised to find it brimming with color. The rest of his street had turned a dull gray, and many of the people had simply vacated their houses. Maybe it was his former power still infused into the land that kept it alive, or maybe Kat had been here and worked her magic. It was an oasis in a world that held nothing for him.

The next day he began the slow assembling of scrap wood into a shack to protect him from the elements. A god who had never experienced cold was now shivering through the night. And the hunger that turned his belly into a beast was even worse.

As the endless days passed by his body turned into a mass of pain, his hands blistered and bleeding from carrying the rough wood. Being forced to rely on muscle and will was new to him and not at all welcome, emptiness seeping around the corners of his mind. He'd stolen tools from a house close by, also making off with some scraps he found in a shed behind one of the beautiful mansions so like the one he'd created as a god. He found moldy bread and canned goods in the houses that had been abandoned, his hunger finally at bay.

The ashes still remained from the fire he'd set that night. The beautiful house that he'd conjured for Siobhan was gone as though it had never been. He wondered how humans could stand all the pain they went through—not only the hunger and the constant aching, but also the emotions that he was fraught with every moment of every day. It was nearly unbearable. One minute he'd be working and in the next he was overcome with a hopelessness that hung off him like sticky vines. He'd begun to drink, his forays to the local bar made easier once he learned how to beg for loose change. How far he'd fallen.

Days turned into months as he fought for control. But no amount of wishing could change the fact of what he was now—an old broken-down man with no way out of here. *Why didn't you kill me?* he asked every night before he dropped into a nightmare filled sleep. He'd tried to kill himself with pills he'd stolen when he broke into a house close by, but he'd come to in the morning with only a pounding headache, and the violent need to empty his stomach. Was that another part of his punishment—to be stuck here until he died of old age or one of the horrible disease's humans were prone to?

When he thought of Siobhan it made things even worse, the idea of her seeing him like this taking what little self-worth he had and throwing it into the ever-increasing garbage heap in his yard. He hated his life and he hated himself.

A security cop had rousted him early one morning, asking what he was doing on the property. For some reason the man had believed him when Dagda said he was the former owner who had fallen on hard times.

"So, does the current owner know you're here?" the cop had asked.

"The current owner is my daughter and she would never throw me off this piece of land."

The man had nodded, as if this information was enough to allow him to squat there for as long as he wanted. "Just make sure you dispose of your garbage," he said before he left, watching a rat scurry across the yard.

There was pity in his eyes, an emotion that would have made the former Dagda livid. But this Dagda only nodded and got back to the slow work of putting a shelter together. Why he bothered, he didn't know. As far as disposing of his garbage, he had no way to do that. And besides, the rats made good companions.

3

Siobhan answered the door, her eyes widening in surprise. She pulled Kat into her arms. "Why haven't you visited sooner? I've been so worried! At the very least you could have called." Mior clung to Siobhan's legs, his large dark eyes regarding Kat solemnly. A moment later he was off, playing with his toys on the floor and ignoring them.

"I lost my cell phone and I haven't had the energy to get another one." Kat gazed around her mother's small apartment, the one she hadn't been in since the day Dagda left for Otherworld. The aroma of essential oils wafted in the air from the diffusers her mom had set up, a comfy couch and chair adding to the cozy feeling. Crystals caught the light from the windows, casting rainbow shadows on the walls. On the porch windchimes moved in the breeze, musical tones echoing. Her mom was still a hippy at heart. "I had a vision of you looking worried. Are you okay?"

Siobhan sighed. "I feel as though something terrible is going to happen. When I was with your father, I never felt like this. He was such a protector, you know?"

"That's my job now. Now tell me about this premonition."
Siobhan shook her head. "Kat, you have your own life.
You can't be expected to watch out for me. I'm a grown
woman." Siobhan led the way to couch. "Now tell me how
you've been."

"Mostly I've been waiting for Bran to come home, but…"

"Bran left months ago. Your father's trial couldn't
possibly take this long."

Kat let out a heavy sigh, not sure if she wanted to share
the bad news. She flopped onto the couch. "The border is
closed, Mom. I tried to get into Otherworld but now there's
an invisible barrier that I couldn't get through."

Siobhan sat next to her. "But you're a half-goddess—
they can't keep *you* out, can they?"

"Apparently they can. I worry that Bran didn't come
back because…" Kat looked up, gazing into her mother's
concerned eyes. "Because I didn't tell him I went to
Otherworld to defend Dad."

"Pish tosh, Katel. That would never stop him. He loves
you to distraction."

Kat's eyes filled. "You really think so?"

"Yes, I do. Now tell me everything. Do you know what
happened to your father?"

Kat shrugged. "I thought I might have done some good,
but the note Cerridwen left for me seemed to suggest
otherwise. She said Dagda has been stripped of his god
powers and locked away."

Siobhan nodded sadly, her gaze going to the small boy
who was now playing with blocks next to where they sat.
"Can you say hello to your sister, sweetheart?"

Kat leaned forward, giving Mior her best smile. "You've

grown so much since I was here. You're a big boy now."

Mior gave her a shy smile, his deep blue eyes reminding Kat of her father. "You look like your daddy," she whispered, taking his proffered hand.

Siobhan stifled a sob. "He reminds me so much of Dag. It just breaks my heart. I miss him so."

"I miss him too, but I miss Bran more. I have to find a way to reach Otherworld. I can't think until I find him and discover why he didn't come back."

"Your father's behavior must have caused this. If only he'd repented earlier, we'd all be together."

Kat thought about her mother's death and resurrection. She wouldn't mention how wrong it had all been. As glad as she was to have her mom, she knew that Dagda raising her from the dead and then conceiving a child with her should never have come to pass. "I should know what to do," she muttered. "Some demi-goddess, I am. The world's in trouble and all I can think about is the man I love."

Siobhan gazed into the distance, thinking. "Is the Norse realm also closed?"

"I haven't checked."

"I was there, you know. Mior was born in Odin's castle. Seems like a lifetime ago. Perhaps from there you can breach Otherworld's barrier?"

"Hmm…I was there once too, when Bran went missing the last time. Remember?" She let out a humorless laugh. "What's with his disappearing acts? That time he was on some kind of walk-a-about that ended up with him nearly dying."

"He's temperamental, isn't he?"

Kat scoffed. "And yet he lived with the homeless here

for months. He's a walking contradiction." Kat was making light of what had been a terrible time. She knew that Bran's sojourn in the bleak regions of the Norse realm was due to his utter desolation. Her father had taken away all of Kat's memories of him, and Bran had finally lost it.

"As I remember, you're the one who saved him."

Kat looked up. "I'm not sure I remember how to find it again."

"How did you do it before?"

"I..." She paused, retracing that horrible trip. "The hummingbird found the way."

"You mean you as hummingbird knows how to get there."

"Well, yes, I guess that's true." Kat remembered the visions she'd had on that trip, she and Bran riding side by side as warriors heading to battle. It had seemed like a past or future life, or maybe it was the imaginings of a woman about to die. "My powers have disappeared."

Siobhan frowned. "What are you saying? You mean your half goddess abilities are gone? Have you tried?"

Kat nodded as she moved to sit on the floor next to her brother. "I can't shoot sparks out of my fingertips, I can't make anything invisible, and I can't move fast, other than when I'm a hummingbird. I was also able to affect the weather, but now..."

Siobhan's canny gaze met hers. "I wonder if it's your father's absence that's causing it. Or perhaps it's the barrier between the worlds?"

Kat glanced up from where she was stacking blocks. "I hadn't thought of that. But the hummingbird..."

"That must be part of your own unique nature. Let's

hope you still have that, Kat, because without it you'll…"

"I know—I'll be stuck here unable to do one thing to help the disintegration of this planet."

Siobhan laughed. "I wouldn't go that far—it's only a few trees."

Kat stared at her mother, wondering if she'd lost her wits. The gray pall had taken over so much by now, the evidence of the Dubh nearly everywhere. "Mom, have you been into town?"

"Well, no, but I go to the market down the street, and sometimes I meet up with Brody, although…" her voice trailed off.

"Are you and Brody still together?"

Siobhan gave a shaky laugh. "No. That last bit with your father was enough for me. My ability to love another man is gone for good."

Siobhan had suffered greatly at the hands of Dagda. It was a testament to forgiveness that her mother had any feelings for him left. Dagda's depression had touched Siobhan's heart, her kindness overcoming her anger. Just before Dagda left earth to face his punishment, she'd begged him to stay. But in the end, he couldn't face what he'd done, or the possibility that she might reject him again. He'd been so fragile those last few days. "But, Mom, he's not coming back this time. I think you should do what makes you happy."

Siobhan's eyes shone with tears. "You don't know that for sure."

But she did know. Otherworld would never release her father. And now that the barriers were in place it was even more unlikely. She turned away to play with Mior, trying to keep her own tears from joining her mom's. They were both in love with men they might never see again. "Something really bad is happening to the planet, Mom. It isn't just the trees and it isn't just in this country. The newspapers are full of it."

"Really? I don't get the news. It's too depressing."

Kat shook her head and looked away. Her mom seemed to prefer being in a bubble. Maybe she'd never recovered from Dagda's meddling with her mind. Kat turned to the window to watch the ghosts of the Dubh drifting along the street, their large eyes like holes of pain.

"Ghosts," Mior said, pointing. "I don't like them."

"I don't like them either," Kat said. The people walking by either wore earbuds, cutting themselves off from anything except what they were hearing, or they were as blank as the sky. Without powers she was as helpless as they were.

"How am I supposed to do anything about this?" she muttered.

"About what, dear? Are you talking about the world or Bran?"

Kat shrugged, tears pricking her eyes. A few short months ago she'd been certain of her path, knew that it was her destiny to save the planet. Airmid had trained her for it, and Cerridwen had imparted what she knew about Kat's future. Now she had no powers at all, aside from being able to turn into a tiny bird. "I had a destiny, Mom. But without powers I can't fulfill it. What should I do?"

"Didn't you just tell me that it's Bran you seek? I suggest concentrating on that first. If you can make it to Otherworld perhaps your abilities will be restored." Her mom stood and pulled her to her feet. "Go to the forest and meditate."

In the forest far above town Kat allowed the grief to take her over. She missed Bran like an ache around her heart. He would know what to do, and if he didn't, the two of them would form a plan.

She could hear the tree sprites chattering in the trees, their language indecipherable. She hadn't seen them the last time she was here. "Are you here because of the Dubh?" she asked, but she got no answer from them. A moment later they all disappeared. *Even the sprites want nothing to do with me.*

Her fingers wrapped around the Celtic pendant she wore around her neck, the buzz and hum of it tingling as she held it tight. It had come to her from her mother, had been made more real by the nearly identical one Bran wore around his neck. They were linked by these two pendants, but since the barriers had gone up, she'd had no contact from him, either through the pendant or any other way. She tried to imagine him, to see him through the linked lockets, but when nothing happened, she let the heavy silver drop to its place in the hollow between her breasts.

She was staring at the ground when she noticed the shadowy opening beneath the tree. "Okay—I guess you're trying to tell me something," she muttered, looking up at the branches moving in the breeze. She loved this particular forest and felt a special connection to this tall and stately tree. Even without powers it had spoken to her.

Kat dug away the debris and stared down into the void. *Should I, or shouldn't I?* The words flashed across her mind before she made her decision. Signs were meant to be followed. She descended into darkness, her feet finding purchase on small roots and rocks lodged against the sides of whatever this was. There were moments when she lost her footing, scrabbling to hang on to an errant root in order to keep from tumbling headlong into what seemed an endless tunnel leading straight down. She didn't think, didn't ponder where or why, just followed her instincts and what she knew the tree had intended for her.

At some point she changed into her hummingbird self, tiny wings allowing her to drop more slowly and see what was all around her. Her mind went into bird mode, colors shifting and changing as she passed by lightened areas. Where the light came from didn't interest her, only the colors themselves and what her brain registered when she saw them.

When she reverted back to human form, she was on solid ground, her mind cloudy and fuzzy. She didn't know how long she'd been heading downward, nor did she have any sense of why she'd decided to climb into the hole to begin with.

When she stood, her legs wobbled, dizziness making her sway as she reached for something to grab onto. It was too dark to determine what it was she held, but when her eyes adjusted, she let out a horrified scream. A skeleton stared back at her out of empty eye sockets. Backing away she began to race along a horizontal tunnel that headed into inky blackness. As she ran, she heard screaming in the distance. People, many of them, sobbed and cried out as though in terrible pain.

She stopped to catch her breath, afraid of what she

might find around the next turning. *Shall I keep going or turn back?* But there was nothing behind her but the skeleton and the hole she'd climbed down. Climbing back up would be impossible, unless...unless there was another way out that she'd missed in her hell-bent flight away from the bones—the person had obviously died down here. *Like I will*, she thought as her mind cleared. Light shone in the distance, shadows flickering along the tunnel walls. Fire. Something was burning.

The acrid smell burned her eyes, the screaming growing louder the closer she got. When she emerged into an enormous cave what met her eyes was a lot worse than the skele ton she'd left moldering behind her. People danced around what looked like a bonfire, but this was no ordinary fire. It was supernatural, filled with images of demons and devils with wide-open mouths and eyes that burned like smoldering embers. The dance was unnatural too, wild terror on the faces of the humans who seemed unable to stop or look away. Their arms waved in the air, their movements random and off balance. The screaming filled her ears until she found herself screaming too. She was sucked into their midst, horror suffusing her with the realization that this was her destiny—to stare into these flames and dance for eternity.

How long she'd been there when she heard the voice she didn't know. It could have been an hour or a day. Her body was limp with the effort, her mind scoured and lost in the sea of wailing. She was covered in sweat, her clothes sticking to her, her hair in damp tendrils around her face. *Kat!* The voice was familiar but she didn't have the energy to turn her head to see where it was coming from. *Kat...come to me! Now!*

When Kat tried to turn, she was shoved to her knees, her body trampled as she attempted to stand. She whimpered in pain and fear until she felt strong arms pulling her free. Cool air blew from somewhere as she was dragged and tugged away from the fire.

"I warned you not to come here—why are you here?" Cerridwen demanded.

But this Cerridwen was not the one she knew. Instead of the white haired, older woman, this goddess was young and shapely, her hair a deep rich brown, a dress of periwinkle blue that matched her eyes hugging her breasts and hanging in velvet folds to her bare feet. If it hadn't been for the familiar voice, she never would have recognized her.

Angry eyes met Kat's. "Do not tell me the trees sent you down here. They would never do such a stupid thing."

An enormous cauldron bubbled over a small fire, misty herbal odors billowing up from the contents. The screaming could no longer be heard. "Where am I?"

"This is the Underworld. Do you not recall the note I left? This is where I live, Kat. It is no place for you."

"But the people back there…they…"

"What did you see? Everyone sees something different when they enter this realm."

"I saw what looked like demons, or…"

Cerridwen gave a laugh. "The worst things you could conjure. I am sorry for that. Now tell me why you are here."

"I'm lost, Gwen. I have no powers and I can't do anything about what's destroying the world. And I have to find Bran!"

Cerridwen pulled her shawl off and placed it around Kat's shaking shoulders, helping her to a flat boulder close to the cauldron, and pushing her gently down. The air had dried her sweat and now she shivered, her nerves like tiny wires lit up from within.

"Bran is not in the Underworld."

"I know that, but you are. Can you bring him back to earth?"

Gwen shook her head sadly. "This is my realm—I do not move between worlds."

"You...you can't go to Otherworld?"

Cerridwen placed a hand on Kat's arm. "I have my life here."

"But what do I do? I can't get to Otherworld, and my destiny..."

"Your destiny is to find your way, Kat. It isn't about a specific outcome. I thought we talked about all that."

"And when you were still at the shop in town you told me it was up to me now. How can it be my destiny to save the world when I'm no longer half goddess?"

"You're what you've always been. That has not changed. What has changed is the path you must take."

Kat sighed, her gaze going to the mists arising from the cauldron. "Can you help me figure that out? Everything is turning gray."

The goddess gazed into the middle distance. "The Dubh are merely hungry—it is only sustenance they seek. They live in the in-between place, which has now been invaded, just as they have invaded your world. They flee what is coming. You will not be able to save it, Kat. The darkness that is the baser nature of human beings encircles your world in an invisible cloud, gathering strength with every moment. It feeds on itself and grows, bringing darkness

23

from other realms. When I look into the future, I see the destruction of everything. I know you think it is your destiny to save the earth, but one person alone will not be able to stop this. Drink. It will restore you and perhaps clarify what I'm trying to tell you." Cerridwen dipped an earthenware cup into the cauldron and handed it to her.

Scents of rose, peppermint and the tang of other herbs Kat couldn't identify wafted from the steaming cup as she brought it to her lips. The first sip jolted her out of her fear, warmth infusing her with energy. "Oh…" she gasped. "I feel…"

"You just drank from the cauldron of wisdom and inspiration."

Kat smiled for the first time, a feeling of vitality and power pulsing through her. "Did the cauldron give me back my powers?"

Cerridwen frowned and shook her head. "That is not its purpose."

"But…I feel so strong!"

Cerridwen touched her hand. "You must listen to me. Ragnarok is coming. Every realm will close their borders. You have a long road ahead of you, Kat. I fear for you."

"Ragnarok? But that's a Norse myth about the destruction of the universe!"

Cerridwen nodded. "You may call it what you will, but no one will escape."

Kat stared at her. Perhaps this was all an elaborate dream. The voice was right but her face was not, nor was her manner. The Cerridwen she knew would reassure her about the future. And what was with the cauldron? Inspiration and wisdom? After the immediate rush of energy, she didn't feel any different. "What am I supposed to do if I can't stop it?"

"You must accept the truth and simply follow your path. You have many lessons to learn." Cerridwen waved her hands in the air and the goddess, the cauldron, and the fire all disappeared.

4

K at woke in her bed, her head fuzzy as though she'd had too much to drink the night before. Sunlight filtered through the shade on her window and she heard birds singing. The dream seemed real. The most important thing she recalled from it was that Ragnarok was coming. She gave a shaky laugh and swung her legs out of bed, her feet hitting the cold floor. Her toes were covered in mud, and when she glanced in the mirror in the bathroom, her hair was filled with bits of roots and moss.

She stared at her bloodshot eyes in the mirror. If it wasn't a dream why would Cerridwen send her back so abruptly? They'd been right in the middle of a conversation. She laughed again—of course it was a dream. But then how had her hair turned into a tangle of roots and moss, and why were her toes muddy? She didn't sleep-walk, so that explanation was off the table. And there was something at the back of her mind, bits and pieces that she couldn't remember, as though they'd been shoved into the deeper recesses of her brain.

I fear for you. Cerridwen's words repeated in her mind,

sending a shiver slithering down her spine. And then she remembered the only advice Cerridwen had bothered imparting. *Follow your path.* Was her path about attempting to get to Asgard? She let out a sigh and turned away from her frightened eyes and pale face. Bran. She had to find him and discover what came next. *Is that path enough for you?* she whispered, anger toward Cerridwen galvanizing her into action.

By the time she left the apartment, the sky had filled with dark clouds. Even if she could turn into a hummingbird, the weather looked very bad for a creature so tiny and fragile. She let out a heavy sigh, watching the clouds shift and bump, the air crackling from distant lightning. Summer was coming to a close and storms were upon them. Imagining her bird self, she waited. A second later she was covered in tiny feathers, her wings beating so fast she couldn't see them as she rose straight up into the air.

The wind caught her and took her off course as she struggled to find her way. But once she was high enough, the blustery air died down. She'd been this way before, knew where she was going, some inner knowing that pointed her in the right direction. No confusing thoughts marred the trajectory she took, and no wondering took her mind in zillions of different directions. It was dark now, with no light to guide her and no warmth to keep her tiny wings going. She knew she had to stop, but something inside her tiny brain kept her going. This was important.

When she fell, she was barely conscious, her bird mind shutting down completely as her wings stilled.

Kat heard muffled voices, felt pressure on her back and arms as she was lifted. She let out a cry as pain surged through her. And when she tried to open her eyes, they were stuck shut. Panic set in.

"We are trying to help you, Katel!" a woman's voice pleaded as she struggled.

Whoever it was knew her name at least, but where was she?

"You're in the Norse realm. Your eyes are injured, and until we can determine the cause, you must allow them to rest."

"Who are you?" Kat whispered.

"I am Frigg, who you have met, and Freya is with me."

Kat relaxed. Odin's wife, Frigg, had healed Bran. She had yet to meet Freya, but she knew her to be the goddess of love. "How...where...?"

"We found you unconscious. Do you remember how you came to be here?"

The last thing Kat remembered was a dream that featured Cerridwen as a young and beautiful goddess. Cerridwen had told her something... "Am I still dreaming?"

"This is no dream. If we hadn't found you when we did, you would have died," Freya's deeper voice intoned.

A door screeched open and warmth washed over her as they carried her into what she assumed was the castle.

"What is *this*?" a booming male voice asked. "Do not

tell me this woman is Dagda's daughter."

"Yes, Odin, it is Katel, but surely you do not blame the child for her father's transgressions."

"She was instrumental in his pardon, Frigg. I'm surprised he hasn't shown up here demanding something outrageous."

"Keep your voice down," Freya whispered. "Katel is severely injured and needs quiet."

Kat tried desperately to open her eyes, Frigg's and Odin's raised voices following her as Freya whisked her away. "Dagda has no powers!" she heard Frigg yell. "You have no reason to be jealous or even…" A door opened and she heard the crackle of a fire, the conversation fading. "My father was pardoned?"

Freya helped her onto a soft surface and smoothed the hair back from her forehead. "This is not the time to worry about anything other than getting better." Fingers brushed over her closed eyes. "Sleep now."

Kat's thoughts disappeared like birds taking flight, a cocoon of warmth enveloping her. She slept.

When Kat woke again everything was dark. She assumed it was night until she heard Frigg's lilting voice. "You are awake!"

When Kat tried to sit up, she was gently pushed back. Her fingers went to her wide-open eyes. "Why can't I see?"

There was a moment of silence and then a sigh. "Something has happened to your sight, Katel, something that neither Freya nor I know how to rectify. Can you recall the moments that led up to the trip here? Perhaps something happened that has kept you from wanting to see."

Kat shook her head. "I would never want to be blind," she whispered.

"Sometimes these sorts of injuries are psychic in nature. Perhaps there is a part of you that wishes to be in the dark."

Kat let out a sob. These goddesses couldn't fix this? "Cerridwen, she…"

"What about Cerridwen?" Freya asked.

"I dreamed I was in the Underworld and she had this cauldron that I drank from."

There was an intake of breath. "You drank from the cauldron?"

Kat nodded, wiping tears from her unseeing eyes. "Only a few sips—but that was a dream, wasn't it?"

"Why were you there? What did the goddess tell you?"

"She only told me about Ragnarok. Are you saying I wasn't dreaming?"

"This Ragnarok, when is it to begin?"

"She didn't say, only that I can't stop it." Kat heard the two goddesses whispering in a language she couldn't decipher. The energy was different now, as though a window had blown open and cold air was absorbing all the warmth. She shivered, willing her eyes to work, but they remained stubbornly dark. "And the borders between Earth and Otherworld are blocked," she continued, hoping to quell the terror building inside her.

"Yes, well, Otherworld has always been quick to react when there's the slightest disturbance. But as you found out, our borders are open. There is nothing amiss."

"I thought I was to have a role in saving earth. I'm a

demi-goddess and I used to have powers, but..."

"If you do not have powers how did you find your way to Asgard?" Before Kat could reply, Frigg said, "Freya and I will now leave you to rest while we fix you a meal."

She heard the swish of fabric and then the sound of the door opening and closing. The terror she'd been holding at bay closed in. She lay flat on her back, her mind whirling with her inability to do anything until her eyesight was restored. What if she was permanently blind? The thought took her breath, her chest constricting. She pushed herself up to sitting, but when she attempted to get out of bed, she landed flat on her back on the floor.

"My dear girl, didn't I explain that you needed to rest?" Freya asked, helping her back to bed.

When had *she* arrived back in the room? Kat felt like a prisoner instead of in the care of two healing goddesses. She shivered and huddled deeper under the quilt. "What about seidr?" she heard herself ask, remembering her father's accounts of what the two goddesses had done to save her mother when she was giving birth to Mior.

"Seidr—well, yes, sorcery is a possibility, although it can exact a heavy toll."

"But you used it on my mother, Siobhan. You saved her life."

"And she nearly died in the process. It is a dangerous and risky magic."

Kat was quiet after that, her thoughts setting off in several different directions. Finally, she said, "I give you my permission to use seidr. I'd rather have you try iffy magic than stay blind like this."

"You have no understanding of what seidr means or

how it works. I will talk it over with Frigg once she gets back."

"Where's Frigg?"

"She's engaged elsewhere at the moment."

Kat felt a little blip in her heartbeat, her palms going sweaty. "I wish I could see," she muttered, rubbing her eyes.

"Do not do that!" Freya's hands were on hers, pulling them away. "It is important that you let your eyes rest."

"Why aren't they getting better?"

"It is still undetermined, Katel. As I mentioned, it could have many causes, even the loss of your goddess powers. I have brought your breakfast and I will feed it to you unless you think you can manage on your own."

The idea of the goddess feeding her made her feel slightly ill. "What is it?"

"Porridge and bread and tea."

"If you show me where the spoon is, and the dishes, I can manage."

After Kat was sure the room was empty, she picked up the spoon and proceeded to eat. As she chewed and swallowed, thoughts ran around her head like angry snakes, setting her teeth on edge and making her stomach hurt. She sensed that something was off about Freya. She had to get out of here, blind or not.

Later that evening Freya came again, her fingers smoothing Kat's hair and lulling her into a twilight sleep. She heard an incantation, envisioned dark shadows circling around her. Her eyes fluttered open on a darkened room, a candle flickering in the breeze coming from the open window. Why could she see now when she couldn't before? Perhaps she was dreaming.

The goddess who bent over her was wizened and old, and wearing a tattered black gown that hung to the floor. Onyx eyes peered at Kat as her gnarled hands moved across her body. "Before we start, tell me why you are here."

Before she could think, Kat's mouth opened and the words poured forth. "I lost my goddess powers and I thought if I reached Odin's castle I could get from here to Otherworld where Bran is. I'm sure they will be restored once I'm there. I have a destiny, a…"

"And what is your destiny?"

"It was to save the world, but without my powers I can't even think about that…as soon as they're restored, I'll know for sure what to do. I'm sure stopping Ragnarok is involved in my destiny, even though Cerridwen said it isn't."

"Ah," the goddess said, a smile landing on her hideous face. "Now tell me what else Cerridwen told you."

"She said I had to follow my path, whatever that means. She said there was darkness around me and that she feared for me."

"That's very good to hear," the goddess whispered. "Now we can get to work and find out what more you have to tell me."

A second later Kat couldn't move. When she tried to cry out the sound stuck in her throat.

"Do not struggle," the goddess whispered hoarsely. "It will only tire you. It won't take long to draw out the secrets that are hiding behind this blindness."

Kat's terror intensified as her mind's eye showed her the

goddess's claw-like hands, the magic that sizzled around her. She wanted to scream, but no sound came out of her mouth. Icy fingers touched her, pain searing through her head as they moved in circles on her temples. *No*, Kat screamed inwardly, dizziness closing down her mind. She fell into a black void, her eyes shutting on the terrible face and the excruciating pain. It felt like her brain was being split apart, its contents lying open for anyone to see.

"Yes...yes..." the goddess whispered greedily. "Now that wasn't so terrible, was it?"er eyes fluttered open upon a scene so terrifying that she shut them again, a cry rising up from her throat.

The next morning Kat had no memory of anything, aside from the feeling that she'd been violated, and the headache that pounded in her temples. When she heard Freya come into the room, she shrank back against the headboard, not sure why the goddess frightened her so much.

"Good morning! I hope you slept well."

Kat felt cold fingers on her temples, the murmur of words she didn't understand.

"Now that's better, isn't it?"

Kat nodded as the headache dissipated. "Thank you," she murmured.

Days passed and Kat's other senses heightened, her hearing so acute she was aware of conversations going on down the hall. She heard Odin's deeper tones, the anger that he bit back every time he spoke Kat's name. Freya seemed adamant about keeping Kat there, her voice going shrill as she argued with Odin. "She needs to give me what I want before I release her. Until then she will remain in the castle."

Odin was anxious for Frigg to come back, something in his voice betraying how much he counted on her. His voice had an edge to it, laced with fear. "I know exactly what you're up to, make no mistake about it."

"And yet you are powerless to stop me." Freya let out a hoarse laugh. "Your wife is important to you, is she not? Once this is over, she will be allowed to return. Until then you will put up with my presence." Overall Freya was dismissive and arrogant, her tone of voice disrespectful and nasty. No one spoke to the chief of the Aesir and the king of Asgard like that. Odin was the god of thunder, the most powerful Norse god there was.

Kat felt Odin's dismay, his inability to throw Freya out of the castle or reclaim his wife. With every minute that passed, Kat grew more afraid. All her senses were on high alert. She felt a malevolent presence that seemed to be waiting and watching. She wanted out of here. "Why aren't my eyes getting better?" she asked when Freya arrived with another tray of food. "It's been many days now."

The goddess laughed nastily. "You are concerned about days? This could take moons, Katel. It is up to you to heal yourself."

"Heal myself? What are you talking about?"

"It is you who has caused this, and you who must find a way through it. I have done everything I can."

"How can you say that? You've barely treated me and I'm sure I didn't cause myself to go blind!"

"An accident did bring on the original problem, most likely the fall you took. But there is no physical reason for why it lingers."

"But, I…" Before she could complete the sentence, she felt a wave of air and her thoughts careened away. She lay back against the pillows, her energy spent as though she'd been running.

"Why would I choose to hurt you?" Freya asked in silken tones.

"Did I say you were trying to hurt me? I just don't get why I'm still blind. When will Frigg be back?"

"Did you know that Frigg and your father were lovers? Perhaps that's why you feel closer to her. She betrayed her husband for a god who cares nothing for anyone but himself. I would never have allowed myself to be seduced by Dagda," she spat.

Kat reeled with this news. "Did Siobhan know?"

"Your mother may have suspected but she was in thrall to Dagda, just as Frigg was. Your father is a pig and deserves whatever has happened to him. I hope you didn't inherit his traits."

"No wonder Odin doesn't like me."

"Yes, and he does not forgive easily. It is why I am here and Frigg is not. But I see him growing restive as her return is delayed."

"Where did she go?"

"That is not your business."

"Odin misses her."

"And how do you know that? Have you been

eavesdropping? Concentrate on
getting well and stop thinking about castle politics."

"I need to get out here. Lying in this bed is obviously
not doing my eyes any good."

"And where would you go? You are *blind*, Katel. Why
did you come here in the first place?"

Kat had a moment of panic. "I can't remember now. I
knew why a few days ago."

There was a lengthy silence and then a relaxed sigh. "The
cauldron has taken your memories. It was wrong of
Cerridwen to allow you to drink—this may be the explanation
for why you are blind."

"The contents of the cauldron of wisdom and inspiration
causes blindness?"

"It can if the person drinking from it is not prepared for
what they see. But I have taken care of all that. You will not
be plagued with any more disturbing memories."

Kat did feel as though something had been taken from
her, whether her worries, thoughts, or some other essential
piece of her being. Simple details, like why she was here. "I
don't remember much of anything about the cauldron or
what Cerridwen told me. I flew here, didn't I?"

"Flew? Are you saying you can shape-shift?"

Kat was suddenly worried that she'd mentioned it.
"I…"

Freya's fingers went to Kat's temples, pressing painfully.
"The cat's out of the bag now, little one. Tell me everything."

Kat tried hard not to speak, but it was as though she had
no will of her own. She blurted out her abilities, going into
detail about how she'd found the Norse realm and why she
fell.

There was a long silence when she finished. "Well, it's a good thing we found you," Freya said, removing her cold fingers from Kat's temples.

Kat listened to Freya's bare feet move toward the door, the swish of air as the door opened and the clunk as it settled back into the frame. She felt invaded and helpless. Something was terribly wrong.

It was deep in the night when she heard Freya return. She went cold all over as

the woman moved close. "Now that we've opened you up, let's see what else you have to tell me," Freya whispered.

"I don't know anything—what is it you want?"

"My dear, you have no idea what you learned from the cauldron. It is everything I need in order to follow through with my plans."

"What plans?"

"Quiet now. Go to sleep and let me get to work. When you wake you will have no memory of what I've said or what I've done here tonight."

When Freya touched her, Kat's thoughts coalesced and drifted away, her heartbeat slowing until she barely knew if she was alive or dead. When she tried to move, she was unable to lift a finger, terror sending her heart into an uneven rhythm.

Freya mumbled strange words as she bent over her. In her mind's eye Kat could see the creature with her, a monstrous bloated thing that she held out as she mumbled to it in an encouraging tone. When a tongue came out and slid across her skin, Kat blacked out, a dream replacing the terrifying scene. *She was in the dark by the cauldron, Cerridwen urging her to drink. "This holds the secrets of the universe," the goddess told her as she took a sip. "To keep you safe it will be hidden in the deepest recesses of your mind until the moment when you need it."*

Kat woke with the overwhelming urge to leave. An unnamed fear had taken over her, her hands shaking as she tried to make sense of it. Nightmare images came and went, as though she'd had the most terrifying dream ever. She was still blind and she knew that Freya was not trying to heal her. Frigg would have helped, she was sure of it, but Frigg was gone.

It was very early morning—she could smell it and taste it on her tongue. She listened, letting a moment or two go by before she placed her feet on the floor and stood, bracing her hands on the bed to steady herself. Without her eyesight she felt dizzy and disoriented as she felt her way along the wall to the window. This room was the one in which Bran had convalesced. She knew every nook and cranny of it, including how far it was from the window opening to the ground below.

5

Dagda stretched and glanced out the little window he'd managed to install. It was one he'd found at a junkyard, the panes surprisingly still intact. It was astounding the things humans threw out. The dump was a source of much of his building materials, discarded planks and even a pot-bellied stove that someone had left. He'd also found a few plastic plates, a metal teapot and an ice chest. Luckily, he'd run into Daniel, his faithful driver who was happy to help as long as he got paid. Dagda had money now, dug up from where he'd stashed it in his garden. Good thing he'd remembered where he buried the metal box. It was humiliating to have the man see him this way, but he needed him.

Instead of the flowers in his former garden he was building raised beds, hoping to grow vegetables. Winter was on the way and he had to plant what would make it through the cold weather. He'd made friends with a man at the nursery down the road who sold him a few starts that he assured him would grow, despite the inclement weather and the gray pall that lay across everything. "Just make sure you fertilize and keep them covered if it freezes." The man was a fount of information.

"I can set you up with electricity," Daniel said when he came by early the next day. "Give me a couple of days and I'll rig it up for you."

"Thanks, Daniel," Dagda said, trying to exude his former power.

"You're a pathetic old man now, aren't you?" The driver said with a laugh. "What happened?"

"I got kicked out of heaven," Dagda quipped.

Daniel laughed. "You were heading that way the last time I saw you, but now...now you're just..."

"Don't say it."

Daniel chuckled and turned away. "I'll be back soon. It won't be *too* expensive," he said, waving his hand.

Dagda watched him leave, wondering if it had been a good idea to resurrect this particular relationship. He felt humiliated enough without Daniel reminding him of his weakness every day. But he did need electricity. And having a car at his disposal was invaluable with all the supplies he still needed. Goddamn this human body and its frailties.

A second later he was overcome with shame, the memory of the horrible things he'd carried out here as a god rolling over him. He'd nearly destroyed Siobhan, not to mention what he'd done to his daughter. And then he thought of Mior, tears welling and streaming down his ravaged face. His son who he would more than likely never see again. "Fuck this!" he shouted, waving his fist ineffectually. And then he was on the ground, doubled over with a pain in his gut so severe he thought he might be dying.

He spent the next hour in the bushes, attempting to stop what was happening in his intestines and failing miserably. When it was over, he lay spent and shivering, wondering how to prevent it from happening again. And all the while his mind screamed in agony, the memories of what he'd been, assailing him. He wanted his powers back. He wouldn't fall prey to evil ever again. Just *please* let him have the powers back and stop this body from turning on him.

6

The ground seemed farther away than Kat expected, time slowing as she sailed through the frigid air before landing flat on her back. She gasped for breath, scanning inwardly for any broken bones or sprains. The decision to jump had taken a while, her thought processes going around and round in a circle as she weighed her options. But a part of her knew that Freya would never heal her, that the goddess's intentions were something else altogether. In the end it seemed wiser to follow her intuition and get out of here, blind or not.

As she pushed herself up, she was glad she was wearing the clothing she found in the chest against the wall. The warm scarf around her neck, the leather pants that she'd had to roll up and belt with the strip of leather, and the enormous wool sweater that hung to her knees, kept her from being instantly frozen as the wind hit her full in the face, whining around her like a pack of wild animals. She pressed forward against it, hurrying in what she hoped was the direction of the front gate. But this was Asgard, not one of the realms where ice prevailed—why was it so freaking cold?

When she ran smack into the iron gate, her questions disappeared, voices in the distance making her frantic to get the gate open. When she heard someone call her name she was already through and sprinting, hoping her memories were accurate about the open terrain between here and the large forest that covered the hillside and stretched endlessly toward the sea. Her only thought at this moment was to find cover and get out of the wind.

By the time Kat reached the trees her legs felt like rubber, her ungloved hands aching with cold. She'd stolen boots from the same place where she'd found the clothing, but they were men's boots, too big for her, her feet and legs chafed and blistered from the effort of keeping them on. Her blindness had not lifted, her headlong run with her arms held out in front of her, tiring her even more.

The forest welcomed her as she sank down, the trees solidness and the whisper of tree spirits lifting her dark mood. So far, she had not formed a plan, other than getting away from Odin's castle. But now that she was still, her mind careened from one scenario to another. Why had she felt compelled to leave the castle? And why was she here in the first place? Freya had told her in no uncertain terms that Ragnarok was not happening. And what about the theory Freya had come up with to explain her blindness? Could what she'd learned from her few sips from the cauldron of inspiration and wisdom have affected her so much that she couldn't face what she'd seen? In truth she didn't remember seeing much of anything.

She pulled out the scarf she'd filled with bread and cheese from the midday meal Freya had left the day before, and untied it, taking care not to eat too much. Once that was gone, she would have to find another form of sustenance. What that might be, she didn't know. Should she chance turning into a hummingbird or continue like this? *You need to go home*, a stern voice said inside her head. *A blind person can't help anything*. But already she was able to see things inside her mind that she'd never seen before—spirits who normally were invisible to the naked eye, and colors that only her hummingbird persona could discern. The magic of the place sang to her even if she couldn't see it with her eyes.

The trees loomed up around her, dark and silent, colors drifting off them as they breathed in and out. They called to her, their voices filled with ancient magic. She felt them around her like long lost friends. Sounds were amplified a hundredfold now, scuffling animals, a leaf coming loose and floating, an acorn dropping, the scrape of a twig against a branch, the chirp of a bird, even the movements of caterpillars and other insects under the leaves and pine needles. That coupled with the aromas of decay, animals, mushrooms, and green things growing, were like a cacophony inside her brain. It was almost too much to process.

When she tried to think about her present circumstances it was as though a curtain had come down, memories of the past gone as she attempted to make sense of things. She had no idea why she'd come here in the first place, so how could she make a decision about what to do or where to go? Her mind felt scoured, cleaned out, and as empty as her eyesight. She was exhausted from trying to make her mind work, finally wrapping her arms around her shivering body. Despite the

terror that every alien sound sent coursing through her, she
drowsed and then fell asleep.

Kat woke to rain and a shrill shrieking that seemed to come
from all around her. In her half-awake state she'd forgotten
that her eyesight was gone, panic setting in until she
remembered. She plugged her ears, reducing the sound.
Now she could discern different tones to the noise, as
though insects were being driven from their homes by
some horrible unseen force. But it wasn't insects.

When the rain stopped the sound stopped with it, a
purple haze filling her mind's eye as she grappled with the
realization that the rain was emitting a chemical that hurt
the trees—hence the screaming. In her mind she could see
the tree spirits, could hear the audible sigh of relief as the
passing shower moved by. And then she smelled the
smoke; it was as though the rain had heralded the opposite
of what it was. Fire tore through the forest, filling her lungs
with its toxins and sending birds and creatures skittering.
Instead of the shrieking, a silence descended, the trees and
their spirits seeming to give in to this new assault. She
reached out to them mentally, dismayed that she could do
nothing for them.

Heat finally forced her to her feet. In her mind she could
see and hear the swish and sweep of flames moving up the
hill in a red-yellow tide, animals and birds fleeing as it
progressed. She ran blindly, heart hammering in her chest
as she struggled through brambles, scratching her arms and
legs in her haste to get away. She was running with her arms
held out in front of her when she heard the snap of twigs
and a heavy footfall.

"Hello," a male voice called. "Where are you going in such a hurry?"

Kat stopped dead in her tracks, her fast beating heart skipping a beat. She knew she should run, but for some reason she couldn't seem to move. There was magic here, a powerful force that couldn't be denied. She jerked away when a hand came down on her shoulder.

"What...are you blind?"

Kat nodded, trying not to cry. She was terrified of whoever this might be, and without being able to judge with her eyes, she felt completely vulnerable.

The leaf detritus rustled as he moved closer, warm fingers touching her cheek. "You are covered in seed heads and mud."

He smelled of sunlight, cold air and grass, and his breath on her cheek was warm and filled with spice. Her fingers went to her face, brushing away the bits of debris that had settled into the salt of her tears.

"Your eyes are wide open and yet you cannot see? Are you unable to speak as well?"

"I can speak," she murmured shakily.

"Do not be afraid of me. I am Val and you are on my land."

"Val...are you a god?"

Val let out a roar of laughter, startling her so much that she stumbled back. That is until he caught her elbow to steady her. "And who are you, if I might ask? And why are you here on my land?"

"I'm Katel, daughter of Dagda." At least she could remember that much.

"Ah, the scandalous daughter who has brought tragedy

down on the world of gods."

"I didn't do anything," she said hotly.

"It is well known that you were instrumental in the release of your father."

"I...I only just heard about this, but I don't know what it means."

"It means that the judges have taken the word of a demigoddess over their own kind. This ruling has taken all the realms by surprise."

Kat felt weak, her hands beginning to shake. "I can't stay here."

"And why is that?"

"I don't belong here—I don't know why I came. I live on Earth."

"All borders are secured."

Kat felt the sudden need to sit down, her legs giving way. "But...I got here somehow."

"When was that? The borders have only recently shut."

"I...I don't know how long I've been here."

"Where have you been? Certainly not here in my forest."

"I was at the castle—Odin's castle."

"Ah. Visiting, or for another reason?"

"Not visiting. I came...I came because...I can't remember," she ended, tears beginning.

"Would you like me to escort you back?"

"NO!"

He chuckled. "Well then, it seems you are to be my guest." He helped her to her feet and took hold of her hand.

Kat moved as if in a dream, her sightless eyes making things up as they moved across a field of grass that brushed against her legs and down a steep hill.

Val was utterly silent as they progressed, his hand holding her steady when she stumbled. They entered what seemed to be a thicket of berry bushes.

"Can you heal my eyes?" she asked, pulling against the thorny bushes.

"It depends on what is wrong with them. Why did you leave Odin's castle? It seems it wasn't on good terms?"

"Freya, wasn't helping me. I didn't trust her."

"You did not trust the goddess of love?" He let out a low chuckle.

"She...something seemed off...the way she was talking to Odin was disrespectful."

Val didn't respond, his breath the only thing she could hear aside from the tug of vegetation against her heavy wool sweater. When he finally spoke again, she'd forgotten what they'd been talking about.

"From what I know of Freya, she would never be disrespectful to Odin. Perhaps there was sorcery involved. Was Frigg at the castle?"

"She was there at the beginning and then she was gone."

"Hmm...it does sound odd from what you've told me."

By the time they reached his castle, or whatever it was, Kat had exhausted herself with terrifying scenarios. He let go of her hand and she heard a door creak open before he led her inside a hall that smelled of damp stone and spent fire. "Sit here," he ordered, pushing her down on a bench. As she slid along the narrow wood, she heard him stride away, his voice echoing as he spoke to someone presumably in the kitchens.

Kat attempted to think, but nerves had turned her brain

to mush. She could barely remember her own name. She heard him return sometime later, the scents of warm food making her mouth water.

"You are my guest," he told her placing a spoon into her hand. "While you are here, I will attempt to heal your eyes. You do not have to fear me."

"But who are you?"

"I am Val, as I said. I am not a sorcerer, but I am adept at magic."

She heard the scuff of a chair, the heavy sound as he sat. He scraped the wooden spoon along the side of the dish, the crunch of his chewing loud in her ears. She wanted to refuse the food, but her stomach had other ideas. She tucked into the gamey stew, trying to ignore the proximity of this god she couldn't see. Sometime later he took hold of her hand and guided her up a set of stairs and into a room that smelled of lavender. He helped her out of the heavy sweater and leather pants and tucked her into bed. "Sleep well, little bird."

Kat woke abruptly, her eyes opening on darkness. Her sleep had been interrupted by fragments of memories from the past. Or at least she thought that's what they were. A man with mossy eyes, a woman who cautioned her about things she now couldn't remember, a hummingbird who seemed to represent her in some way, but she didn't know how or why. She didn't move for several moments, letting her senses reach out. The air coming through the window was cool but not cold. Rain was coming. The caw of a raven echoed, reminding her of someone and making her heart beat a little faster. Shouts rang out from somewhere below. She heard the stomp and whinny of horses, the clang of metal, the bray of hounds. She jumped up from the cozy bed and located the clothes hanging over a chair, hurrying to dress.

When she heard the door open, she quickly turned away to pull on the leather pants.

"Better fitting clothes for milady," a woman's voice announced, soft footsteps coming toward her. A second later her arms were full of soft material. "Would milady like some help with these?"

Kat felt the material in her arms. There were buttons and laces that didn't make any sense. "Yes, I think I might need some," she murmured.

Deft hands slipped the silken fabric over her head, laces tightening in front to pull it closed. Kat felt her breasts push up and out, the bodice secured carefully. "The green suits you," the woman said.

"Wish I could see it," Kat muttered, her fingers moving to the low-cut top, attempting to hike it up.

"Is milady blind?" the woman asked. "No wonder milady's hair is such a mess." Kat gave a yelp as a brush pulled through her tangle.

"His lordship waits to speak with you, so come quickly," she said after securing Kat's hair on the back of her head.

"I wish I could have bathed," Kat said mostly to herself.

"Bath will come later. I will see to it personally."

Kat allowed the woman to lead her out and down the set of wide stairs she'd taken the night before, wondering if this was all part of an elaborate dream. She smelled Val before she saw him, the vision of sunlight and fresh air taking over her senses as she was led toward him.

"Ah, now you look like the goddess you are," he said. Kat felt his warm fingers on her skin as he lifted her pendant. "What is this?" he asked.

"My mother gave it to me before she died. Dagda, gave it to her before I was born."

"It's ancient magic and holds memories of times past. But these memories are yours, not your father's or your mother's."

"That doesn't seem right. It originally belonged to Dagda."

"Right or not, it is what I see. Apparently, this pendant was always intended for you." His lips grazed her fingers before he helped her to the bench. "Eat now. I have to be away for a while, but when I get back, we will see what I can do about your vision."

"Are you a healer?"

"Not a healer, but I do know herbs and I've had some luck in this field in the past."

"With blindness?"

"With this type of blindness, yes," he said enigmatically. "I must be off now. Please make yourself as comfortable as you can. Isabelle will take care of any needs you have until my return."

Kat heard his boots cross the room, the heavy thump as the door closed behind him. For a second she had the strangest sense of loss.

After Kat's breakfast of porridge and delicious cider, Isabelle returned to keep her promise of a bath. Kat didn't know where the woman took her, only that a tub was filled with warm aromatic water and her skin was washed from stem to stern, and her hair scrubbed before she was wrapped into a giant towel. "Am I dreaming?" she asked no one in particular as Isabelle re-dressed her and brushed out her hair.

Isabelle laughed. "It is a shame you cannot see yourself. His lordship…"

"His lordship? Who is he?"

"It is not my place to say," the woman murmured. "But his wife died and he has not re-wed, and…well. You would make a lovely companion for him. Would you like to take a turn around the garden before his lordship returns?"

Kat was shocked by what Isabelle said, her thoughts in turmoil as she let herself be led blindly along the paths. It seemed that the gardens were vast by how long they walked. The sun shone down on them, birds singing in the trees, the scent of roses and lavender wafting about them. She had a momentary memory of Dagda's house and a garden of roses.

A frisson of fear slid down her spine. She had so few memories since waking in her bed after her supposed trip to the Underworld, the entire time at Odin's castle, banked inside a fog. Now she was in this god's house, a man she couldn't see and didn't know whether to trust or not. She froze when she heard the clatter of the horses, the sound of men's laughter, a shout.

"The men have returned," Isabelle said, tugging her toward the noise.

Kat pulled against her. "I don't want to go back."

"You must. The master wishes it."

"But I'm not his subject or his wife. I'm a free..." But the words went unspoken as she tilted, her balance disappearing as the buzzing of a hundred bees filled her head.

"Katel, can you hear me?"

"I...yes. What happened?"

"You fainted."

Kat felt the edges of a bed with her fingers, the feel of pillows propped behind her head. Terror took her over; it was just like what she'd gone through for the past weeks. She pushed herself up—she had to get out of here.

A warm hand landed on her upper arm. "You must trust that I will not harm you, Katel. Whatever happened at Odin's castle will not happen here."

"I don't faint," she whispered, settling back.

"Well, you did today. Close your eyes. I am attempting an experiment. Now tell me what you see."

Despite her alarm, Kat did as he asked, watching the visions that played across her mind's eye. "I see a light-filled bedroom, a window that looks out on a landscape of trees, and beyond it, a hillside of waving grass. Blue mountains in the far distance. Horses grazing. The sky is very blue and everything shimmers with a mystical light."

"You are seeing what is here, Katel. Your blindness is not real."

"If it isn't real, why can't I see you?"

"Because you are afraid of what you might find out."

"Find out? About what?" she asked in a frightened

whisper. She put her hand out to touch him, feeling folds of wool. When his fingers took hers there were no knobby knuckles or warts.

He placed her hand on his face, letting her feel his cheekbones, his eyebrows, his mouth, and then turned her hand over and kissed her palm, his warm lips sending tingles up her arm. She felt his breath just before his lips brushed against hers, her heart rat-a-tatting against her ribs as his hand moved to the back of her head. Instead of pulling away, her mouth opened under his, her body melting against him as the kiss deepened.

When he released her, she gasped for breath, wanting more. But when she reached for him, he nudged her away. "That was very wrong of me. I am taking advantage of your vulnerability. You are very lovely, Katel. And I am lonely since the death of my wife. Unfortunately, you have another path to follow. Now let's see what you might remember, now that you're in my realm."

A light breeze touched her skin, colors shimmering behind her eyelids. She felt him all around her, waves of air touching the skin of her face, her chest, her arms. Suddenly her mind was strangely clear, thoughts appearing, one after the other, like they'd been standing in line and finally been allowed in.

"Better?" Val asked.

She leaned back against the pillows and took in a deep breath. "I can think now. What did you do?"

"Only a bit of repairing of what was taken. Can you tell me now why you came here?"

Her thoughts spilled out, as thought they'd been waiting to present themselves. But it wasn't at all like what had happened with Freya. She had the sense that this god was looking out for her. "I came here because…because I wanted to find a way to reach…Bran. I was in love with him, but now I can't remember much about him." She paused to take in a breath.

"Take your time," Katel. I am only testing my magic to see if it still works. It's been a long time since I've had a subject to work on." He let out a self-deprecating laugh and placed his hand on hers. "Powers need to be used, just as a singing voice unexercised will grow rusty. I hope you don't mind being the means to an end. It is all in your best interest."

Kat listened to his melodious voice, trying to see him in mind's eyes. She'd been able to see the bedroom and what lay outside, why not him? She let out a heavy sigh and continued. "I used to have powers but now I don't. And I thought it was up to me to save the world, but Cerridwen said that's impossible, that what's happening was set into motion long ago."

"Why would you feel the need to save it?"

"Because my father is responsible for the beginnings of Ragnarok."

"Did you assist him in his endeavors?"

"No, but that's why I was born. It's my destiny. And if Earth is to die because of something Dagda started—Ragnarok, that is—how can I stand by and watch it destroyed?"

His fingers twined through hers, sending chills up her arm. "You believe in determinism?"

"I…I don't know what that is. I just know what I've been told."

"And who has told you this?"

Her mind felt suddenly fuzzy and disconnected, thoughts tangling as she tried to speak. "I…Cerridwen told me it was up to me now, and Airmid was training me to control my power. But then everything changed. And when I asked Cerridwen about what she'd told me earlier, she said I need to follow my path."

"That is good advice. You and you alone have to decide what your life is to be. Sorcery has been used on you, not once but many times. It has affected how you think and it has caused your blindness. What happened just before you arrived at Odin's castle?"

"All I remember is drinking from the cauldron of wisdom and inspiration."

"That explains it. You have learned the truth, and it conflicts with what you've always believed."

Katel saw images in her peripheral vision, a world that shimmered just out of reach. A wrenching sensation went through her, as she realized that Freya had tampered with her memories. "Freya took something from me," she muttered. "I can't remember what Bran looks like, or even one conversation we ever had."

"That was not Freya—that was a practitioner of seidr—a witch. This Bran, who is he?"

"He's a god who used to love me. But he's in Otherworld now. I thought seidr was a good thing. Frigg used it to heal my mother."

"That may be true, but it is dark magic and can be used to hurt as well as heal. You just said you felt like something was taken from you. The Freya I know would never do this."

Kat's eyes swam with tears, some deep knowing trying to rise to the surface of her mind. Her eyes burned, visions coming and going like fast moving videos or time-lapse photography. A headache pounded against her temples. Her stress mounted and before she could stop it, she was a bird, gossamer wings carrying her up and toward the open window. She saw Val standing below her, his crystalline eyes wide with shock. His ears were pointed, pale hair hanging straight to his shoulders. He was beautiful and ethereal—luminous. And then she was through the window and into the world of reds oranges and pinks, her senses taking her directly to the rose bushes.

7

The hummingbird flew from one rose bush to another, sipping nectar and tasting the tiny bugs that lived inside the flowers. She hardly noticed the man following her, his tall robed form keeping pace with her through the large garden. When she rested on a low hanging tree limb the man approached, his hand extended. What did he think, that she'd just hop on his finger? She flexed her wings and rose to a higher branch. Darkness was falling when she felt something change. A cold wind came up and she fluffed out her feathers, the need to be in another form intruding on her mind. It was only a minute later that she fell, her human form caught neatly in strong arms just before she hit the ground.

"You have surprising talents."

Kat rubbed her eyes, the sight of him taking away her breath. Magic shimmered around him, crystalline eyes swirling as he gazed at her. He was gorgeous.

He placed her on her feet. "You could have flown away. Why did you not leave here?"

Kat had to look away. The glimpse of him was like

seeing the sun after years of gray. "I didn't even remember that I could change like that. Maybe my bird mind realized that if I left, I wouldn't find the array of food that lies within these walls."

He chuckled. "Yes, well, that is true enough. I have the best gardens in the realm and they bloom year-round. Now that you can see, what do you think of it?"

Kat looked around, aware of the buzz of energy wafting off Val. "It's amazing. And you—I didn't expect..."

"A member of the Elven race?"

Kat nodded, blushing. She suddenly felt clunky and ugly next to his graceful form. "Last time I looked I was in Asgard, but this is Alfheim, isn't it?"

"Yes. You must have crossed over without knowing it. The border is not marked and you were blind at the time."

Kat smiled. "It's wonderful to see again. But why can I?"

Val took her hand and led her along pebbled paths toward the house. "You have allowed the truth to surface."

She turned to stare at him. "Have I? Nothing seems different." But then Cerridwen's words flooded her mind. She stumbled, leaning into Val.

"Steady there. Are you all right?"

She sucked in breath, her mind far away as she watched him open the door leading into the wood and stone manor house. Inside lights flickered, many candles brightening the cavernous interior.

"Oh, milady!"

Kat turned to Isabelle, taking in the pointed ears, the triangular face and the sweet smile. Her hair was piled on her head in swirls, her body delicate and diminutive. "It's good to finally *see* you," Kat murmured, trying not to stare.

Isabelle curtsied and hurried away as Val gestured to the bench on one side of the long rustic table. "Have you allowed yourself to see your future?" Val asked her, setting a cup of tea in front of her.

Kat nodded slowly, not at all sure what it was that had made her so dizzy. "It's fragmented."

"Perhaps if you share, I can be of help. The cauldron's wisdom is sometimes difficult to decipher."

"Is that what you think it is?"

Val smiled. "Since the cauldron was your last true memory before you reached Odin's castle, and your subsequent dealings with the dark witch, I would have to say yes."

Kat made herself look at him. Her cheeks heated as she remembered the feel of his lips. "When I drank from the cauldron, I had a vision of the future and the past, as though time had no meaning. It seemed like it was all interwoven, like a tapestry…and there was more than one of me…" Kat stopped, confusion wrapping around her like a thorny bush.

"Other lives, other times," Val said quietly. He sat on the bench next to her. "What the cauldron has to offer is all encompassing, wisdom that is intended for the gods. If Cerridwen allowed you to drink, she must have trusted you with this knowledge and found a way for you to keep it hidden. This explains your blindness and possibly why the witch performed seidr on you. She wanted the knowledge."

Kat struggled, her thoughts twisting into a knot. "The blindness was because…because…"

"What you learned was too much for your mind to take in."

"Do I need to stop Ragnarok, or…open the borders?"

Val's gaze clouded. "Is this what you saw before you fainted? If so, it is a daunting task. Have you discerned a reason for such an undertaking?"

Kat shook her head and picked up the mug of tea. Her hand shook as she took a sip. "I think it's the only way to reconnect with Bran, but there must be something else."

Val glanced at the cup in front of him on the table, his long fingers circling round it. "Perhaps it is merely this Bran you seek."

Kat sighed. "Connecting with Bran was my original plan, but now he's like a distant memory. How can that be my path?"

"If this was your original plan then you must trust it, despite your inability to remember him. Love is a powerful force and if you had deep feelings for him, it is reason enough. I suggest a period of rest to reclaim who you are. And this is the perfect place to do it."

"But if it's my path to save the world I can't just lie around here and nap!"

"Didn't we determine that saving the world was not your job? Even Cerridwen told you that. As far as Bran goes, perhaps resting will allow your memories to surface and you will remember your love for him."

Kat thought about what he'd said. She knew deep down that she had once loved Bran. "Can I reach Otherworld from here?"

"Not in the way you think, but I do know how you can get there."

"What is it?"

Val shook his head. "You need to rest before we go

further. Your mind is frazzled from the sorcery and the work I've done to repair it. It needs time to heal."

Kat gazed around at the flickering candles before landing on the man sitting next to her. Waves of energy poured off him, and she could feel the force of it entering her body. Her life before this moment seemed to be fading into the distance. "I feel...drawn to you. Part of me wants to stay here forever."

Val smiled. "The Fae world has a magnetism that's hard to escape. I will not allow you to lose yourself, Katel. Now, before I force you to take a rest, I want to see if you can remember more about this vision you received from the cauldron. I want to test what I've attempted so far, to see if my ability to heal still works."

Kat glanced at him, a frisson of nerves settling in the place where a moment before she'd felt only trust. "You mean about time having no meaning, or many lives? It's all mixed up in my mind, a jumble."

He picked up her hand, and began to massage her fingers. "What we see in a vision is often not reality. It is for us to decipher—kind of like a puzzle or a riddle. You mentioned past and future being interwoven. You said you thought perhaps you've lived other lives?"

Images Cerridwen had bestowed on her rose to the surface. She didn't really want to share them, as though she'd been entrusted with a secret. But what he was doing to her fingers calmed her nerves and took away her reluctance. "Time isn't linear, it's a ribbon that flows back and forth, weaving under and over itself," she intoned dreamily. "Lives are lived along the ribbon and the world has been destroyed before. There is a darkness that will eat up all the light. The trees…the trees…I…"

He picked up her other hand, massaging her palm and each finger joint. "What does light represent to you?"

Kat felt relaxed and dreamy, her thoughts untethered. "Spirit, magic, the unseen. The opposite of darkness."

Val nodded, glancing toward the fire now blazing. Night had fallen while they'd been talking, a chill coming into the room. Isabelle had come through to light more candles, the warm circles sending flickering shadows onto the walls and ceiling. "There is something dark working against you. You have a connection with trees and with a life you lived long ago."

Deeply relaxed, Kat listened, her eyes drooping. She wanted nothing more than to lie down and take a nap. But when his gaze met hers, she felt a jolt. "I love trees, but what life are you talking about? I only know this one. How do you know these things?"

"Because I am Fae and have seen a bit of what you are and what you've been."

Kat pulled her hand out of his. "In other words, you looked inside my mind?"

"I saw what you allowed me to see—nothing more."

Kat picked up her cup and drained it, placing it back on the table. She was fully awake now but also exhausted, as though she'd been taking a test or studying something she didn't understand. "I have to go to sleep."

"Yes, it is very late. Tomorrow we will talk again."

Kat nodded and stumbled toward the stairs, her head swirling with exhaustion.

Morning came too soon, bright sunlight waking her before she was ready. Her dreams had taken her many places during the night, none of which had been pleasant. Val had been there, but every time she reached for him, he drifted further away. And Bran—Bran had been indistinct and ethereal, a ghost. Was she even in love with him anymore? How could she know if she couldn't remember him? A terrible feeling of loss twisted inside her.

There was a quick knock before Isabelle appeared in the doorway. "Is milady ready to rise and break her fast?"

Kat let out a long sigh and climbed out of bed, allowing Isabelle to pull the thin nightgown over her head. The diminutive woman replaced it with a simple brown wool gown that fell to her ankles. Kat stood still while she pulled the laces tight in back. Kat felt the fabric, marveling at its softness. "No silk today?"

"This was his lordship's choice. It belonged to his wife."

Isabelle brushed out her hair, making her sigh with pleasure. Once the tangles were out, she braided two braids and secured them at the nape of her neck. Isabelle stood back to take a look at her handiwork before urging Kat ahead of her out the door. "His lordship is waiting."

When Kat arrived in the dining room, Val was seated, a tankard of some liquid in front of him. "Good morning," she said, sitting on the bench next to his chair at the head of the table.

He nodded to her, his gaze roving across her body. "The dress suits you," he finally said. A moment later Isabelle arrived from the kitchens with two plates, setting one down in front of Val and one in front of Kat.

Kat glanced down at the array of sausage, eggs and

thickly sliced bread, realizing how hungry she was.

"Once we've eaten, I will explain some things and then you will take a walk in the garden. After that you may go to my library and read. After lunch you will nap."

Adrenaline rushed through her. "You can't tell me what..." But the protest on the tip of her tongue disappeared when his swirling eyes met hers.

"Rest is important, little bird, if you are to fulfill any destiny. You are exhausted."

When he said the word exhausted, Kat was suddenly so tired she could barely keep her eyes open. Rest did sound wonderful. She ate, her mind drifting on waves of contentment.

Once the food was gone Val wiped his mouth carefully with a napkin and rose from his seat at the head of the table. "Come with me. I have much to impart. If you remain here much longer, I am afraid I will not be able to restrain myself."

Kat met his gaze, heat rising into her cheeks when she stared into his mesmerizing eyes. "Maybe you shouldn't try," she whispered.

Val's beautiful eyes widened. "Are you saying what I think you're saying?"

"Yes," she said before she could stop herself.

Val gazed at her for a full minute before he took hold of her hand and led her toward the stairs. His bedroom was filled with shimmering light, just like his eyes. It entered her body, every nerve tingling in anticipation as his fingers touched her face, her hair, and ran lightly over her breasts. While he unlaced her dress and removed it, she stood utterly still, like a package that needed opening. She was naked when he carried her to his bed, his mystical eyes roaming across her body as he removed his robe. He bent to kiss those parts of her that seemed waiting for his touch. And when his lips met hers, she opened to him like a flower that had been touched by the sun.

Kat was sleeping when she heard him stir, turning in time to see him before he pulled on his robe. "Wait," she called. His skin was lit up from within, pearly and translucent, his body perfect.

He stopped and turned, his eyes meeting hers. "It is time to rouse ourselves, Katel. And time for you to tell me exactly what it is you want. If it is to stay here with me, I will be happy to have you in my bed every night."

"I do love being with you like this," she murmured.

"What of this god, Bran?"

"I don't know anymore."

"And yet we've established several times that you love him."

Kat turned away, tears of shame pricking her eyes. "Being here with you…"

Val sat by her, his fingers tracing the tears that slid down her cheeks. "You needed this diversion, but you must recognize it for what it is. I would gladly continue, but I fear I would be hurt in the long run. You see I am looking for a long-term companion—a wife. I cannot take a woman who is in love with another."

Kat sat up and reached for her dress. "I'm sorry, Val."

Before she rose to dress Val lifted her pendant. "Do you think this is related to your future?"

Kat's fingers closed over his. "This pendant connects

me to Bran—or at least it used to."

"Take it off," he commanded. "There is more here that I want to explore."

When she slipped it over her head, he took it in his hands and closed his eyes. "There is something hidden here," he said. "I've established that it's ancient magic, but now I can see the link with this god. You've been together many times." He opened his eyes. "Do you have any memory of past lives?"

Kat shook her head. "I met Bran when Dagda resurrected my mother from the dead. He was sent from Otherworld to watch over me. I already told you that my mother left this to me when she died."

Val nodded, staring at it as though he could see something inside it that was invisible to Kat. "This pendant indicates a love that has continued through many lives. There is more, but it is well hidden."

"I see Bran through a haze, as though he's a ghost."

"If you allow it, I can work on you again. I did return some of what you lost, but there is more."

"Can the Fae can resurrect soul memories?"

He nodded, watching her.

Kat pondered that for a moment. Did she want to add more complications to her already confusing life?

"You are the only one who knows where your destiny lies, Katel. Anything you've heard from others, or had implanted in your mind, is folly."

"But how do I tell the difference?"

"Let me work on you and then perhaps you can answer that question for yourself."

"Now?"

He smiled. "Now is as good a time as any."

When his fingers moved lightly across her eyes, Kat closed them, her thoughts disappearing into a mist filled void. She heard him murmur words she couldn't understand, felt his fingers tracing across her skin. She was afraid, but when her body began to shake, he said, "Relax, I am only finding what you have hidden from yourself. There is magic within you that has not been tapped, powers you have yet to acquire and understand." His voice reverberated, as though she had entered an echo chamber. She couldn't hear him anymore as she walked through a foggy haze, trying to find something she'd lost.

"Katel!"

Kat opened her eyes to see him watching her worriedly. She was still on his bed. "What did you do to me?"

"I looked ahead in time."

"You mean you saw my future?"

He nodded, his expression somber. "You will be tested by the fates and your life will not be your own. It is a twisted path you have to follow, Katel. It will not be easy."

Kat frowned. "What does that mean? I'd like specifics, please."

Val rose from the bed where he'd been sitting next to her. "The future cannot be shared. I'm sorry."

"But...you said you'd help me figure out my destiny! I don't think it's right for you to know and not share it."

"The future I saw was one of many possibilities. You love this god, Bran. I have looked inside your pendant and know that this is true. Once you find him the rest will come clear."

"But if I can't remember him how will that help?"

"But you do remember that you loved him once. If it wasn't for that I would beg you to remain here with me."

When she rose, he helped her slip the dress back on, deft fingers lacing it up in back. He pulled her hair away from the back of her neck to kiss it. "I am glad for the time we have together."

But Kat felt betrayed and lost to herself. She'd hoped for clarity and all she'd gotten was more uncertainty. Her mind had been invaded twice and she wasn't at all sure whether Val was to be trusted. He seemed sincere, but was he? She'd allowed him to enter her body and her mind, and now she realized she didn't know who he really was.

As they were leaving the bedroom, he turned to her. "I can imbue you with Fae magic, Katel, but only if you give me permission."

"Fae magic—will this help me find my path?"

"It will. What I have to offer is the strongest magic in the cosmos."

Kat looked up at him. "Let me think about it."

After breakfast the following morning he pulled her with him into a tiny room off the dining room. Sunlight streamed through a bank of leaded glass windows leaving prisms across the maps spread across a square wooden table.

Kat moved to look at them, her eyes widening.

"Yggdrasil holds all the Norse worlds," Val told her. "If you wish to travel to other realms, it is the tree's roots that you must follow into Nifleheim, Muspelheim, Jotunheim and from there even farther into Helheim." His crystalline eyes met hers. "Otherworld lies in a different direction."

"But why are you telling me this? Is it something you saw in my future? Where am I *supposed* to go?"

"You must decide. I am merely giving you options."

Kat didn't answer as she glanced down at the markings on the map. There were areas marked as dangerous, with large X's, areas marked with drawings of caves or huts to indicate places of refuge, areas marked with sun and moon symbols, areas with tiny drawings of animals. The tree spread before her, circles within its wide branches to indicate the realms. She felt dizzy for a second, the complexity of it overwhelming. He must have had a reason for showing her this. It had to be the path he'd seen for her future.

Val straightened from where he'd been poring over another map. "If you take me up on my offer, you will have Fae magic at your fingertips."

Kat glanced at him. "You know something you aren't telling me. Am I destined to go to these other realms? Are you saying that with Fae magic I can open the borders? Is that my destiny?"

Val pressed his lips together. "I cannot say more than I already have. You must trust me."

Kat yawned, exhausted from the lack of sleep the night before, and the complexity of what they'd been talking about. Instead of the rest he'd promised, he'd taken her to his bed and made passionate love to her, looked into her mind to see her future, and now given her a brief history of the Norse worlds. She didn't want to think about his magic, borders, or her future. She wanted to take a nap. When Val touched her shoulder, she put her head down on the table and fell fast asleep.

In her dream a being of light led her along a dark path that wound through a forest like no forest she'd ever seen. The trees spoke to her, their voices muted, limbs bending over her as she walked beneath them. Magic shimmered all around her, her fingers leaving trails of colors as she walked. She felt powerful and strong. When she hurried forward, the being turned, his face the face of Val. He was her guide, her protector. His magic kept her safe and would allow her to do what she came to do. When he smiled and reached for her, she took his hand.

She woke with a gasp. "I do want your magic," she whispered, gazing up at Val standing next to her.

He smiled. "You will not regret it."

Kat went upstairs to nap and fell into a deep and dreamless sleep.

Val was true to his word about forcing her to rest. He plied her with delicious food, insisted that she walk in the garden and made her nap every afternoon. At night he knocked softly on her door, waiting until she gave him permission before entering her room. And even though she told herself that what she was doing was wrong, she couldn't seem to resist him.

"This is the best way to transfer my magic," he murmured when she explained her reluctance. When she looked into his eyes, she felt the pull of him, her ability to say no joining the radiance that drifted all around his body.

As the days passed Kat became obsessed with his nightly visits, her need for him almost painful. His touch was electric, his kisses burning into her. But sometimes she saw another face superimposed over his, with mossy eyes and hair the color of honey. When that happened, she would find herself in tears.

And then one morning she woke knowing it was time to go. She told Val at breakfast.

"I will be sorry to see you leave, but you have my magic now and we will always be connected because of that."

"I do? But what is it?"

"All you need to do is think of where you want to go and a door will open."

"A door...you mean an actual door?"

Val nodded.

"What else?"

"Time and space have no meaning in the Fae world. We come and go as we please. But without training this is hard to master. If you wish it, I can..."

"No, Val. I must leave today."

He gazed at her sadly and nodded.

After breakfast Kat gathered her things together.

Val walked her out, his face etched with pain. "If you ever need me, just think of me and I'll be there. I will miss you."

Kat nodded and swallowed the lump in her throat and headed for the gate. She turned once to see his tall shimmering form before she walked up a hill and entered the woods. When she glanced back, Val, the manor house, and the gardens had all disappeared into the mist. It seemed like a dream, her mind spinning with what had happened between them. This place was magical and now she had that same magic to use when she needed it. Finding Bran would be easy, and maybe when she did, her memories of him would return. But that thought did little to dispel the sadness of leaving Val behind.

She was deep in the woods when she thought *hummingbird*, her body shrinking away as feathers covered her. Her wings whirred and she lifted into the air, failing to recall that the doors wouldn't work for her in this form. But by that time, she was in bird mind and had forgotten Val and everything he'd told her.

8

"**J**esus, the man has lost himself! I wouldn't have recognized him if I hadn't happened by his former property."

Dagda huddled down in the booth where he was sitting, a flush of heat in his cheeks. Daniel was talking to the bartender about him. The conversation went on, Dagda growing more and more ashamed as he listened. Had he really been that powerful? It was becoming harder to remember that life. Apparently, they hadn't seen what he bastard he'd been, or maybe Daniel liked the strongman type, the sort who ordered everyone around and took no prisoners. Did he miss that life? Maybe he did. Maybe he could accomplish some semblance of the same as a human. There were definitely those types around. He'd been intimately connected with them. But how to go from this to that was a mystery. Without his god powers he couldn't conjure anything, nor could he stand up and be counted. He was old and frail. He just didn't have it in him.

After Daniel left the bar Dagda scuttled out the door and stumbled up the road. There were pockets of normalcy where humans still lived and then there were large swaths where the gray had taken over lives. He thought about his daughter and her mission to bring the color back. Looked like she hadn't managed it. Was this his fault? He'd messed with her just as he'd messed with Siobhan. Perhaps he'd left lasting damage to both of them.

Who was he now? The answer to that was nobody. He had no powers, no real life and no way of reclaiming anything, including Siobhan. The idea of her seeing him like this made him cringe inside, a feeling he'd never experienced. He thought of those last hours with her before he turned himself in. The way she'd begged him to stay. He could still remember the look in her eyes. He wiped at the water that came from his eyes and climbed the steep hill, trying to stop the onslaught of memories, but they continued to come.

At the end Siobhan had seen the part of him he'd turned his back on, the Dagda who'd fallen in love with her, the one who'd fathered Katel. He'd been decent then, vulnerable to her. That first time he hadn't stayed on earth long enough to be swayed by its temptations. He could feel the insidiousness of it now, seeping into him again—the greedy needs of humans, the way so many of them conducted their lives to benefit only themselves. The governments were full of them, corruption the name of the game. He'd been one of them when he lived here. Would he join their ranks again or would he hang on to the decent side of himself?

By the time he reached home he'd worn himself out with thinking and wondering. He went inside and sprawled on the mattress, trying to stop his mind, but the thoughts kept coming—his sexual needs, his desire for more, the waste of the life he was leading—all of it washed over him. Being human was the worst punishment he could ever have been given. They'd known it when they stripped him naked and sent him off. He was fucking doomed.

9

The hummingbird spun out of control, strong winds taking her tiny body and flinging it into the maelstrom. She fought it as hard as she could, but in the end, she had to let go.

Kat woke on the ground, aching and bruised. She lay on a hillside somewhere at the border of one of the Norse worlds, the thick roots of Yggdrasil snaking off in all directions. In the far distance she could see Otherworld, misty mountains rising up from a valley so green it made her eyes hurt. She'd already tried to go that direction, her collision with the invisible barrier still fresh in her mind. It had sent her careening downward to where she lay now. Her mind felt muddled and fuzzy, the hummingbird persona, slow in retreating. And when her human mind caught up with the change, she had the strangest feeling that she'd been living inside a dream, her memories of the past weeks, indistinct and murky. She felt as though she'd been in a coma.

But before she could puzzle that out, her attention was taken by shouting and a deafening roar. She pushed herself up and staggered to the edge of the hill. In the meadow far below giants played a game that looked surprisingly like lawn bowling, enormous balls smacking into one another with such force the ground rumbled. From what she could see from this distance the male giants looked to be twenty feet tall or more, their bodies just like human bodies except in size. Jotunheim, the land of the giants.

She watched them go about their game, terrified by their sheer size and the violence with which they were playing. If she ventured down there she'd be killed in an instant, either from a ball the size of a house rolling over her, or by being stepped on. But before she could make a decision about her next move, one of them spotted her, a shout going up as they all stopped what they were doing to stare up at her. She did the only thing she knew to do when terror struck— she turned into a bird.

She was beating her wings against the barrier again when she noticed the raven on the other side, his familiar gaze sending shivers along her bird body. But in her bird state there wasn't much more thought beyond that. They stared at each other for several moments before he flew away, dark wings receding toward the misty mountains. In the meantime, the giants had climbed the hill.

Kat came to consciousness sometime later. She was stuffed into a cage too small for her size, a dish of water and some bird seed scattered around her. *Hummingbirds don't eat seeds*, she thought to herself, her fingers going to the wire around her as she looked up. The scream that came out of her mouth was nothing in comparison with the roar the giant emitted. Enormous eyes regarded her, the forehead puckering as he examined her. When he opened the cage, she pressed back against the bars, but there was no escape from the hand that reached in and grabbed her.

"Name!" he bellowed.

"Katel!" she shouted, her voice tinny and small.

"Why are you here?"

Kat held her hands over her ears, trying to mitigate the pain of his voice on her eardrums. "I was trying to go to Otherworld."

"Otherworld," the giant said disdainfully. "Ugly place with little to say for itself. Too small."

"I come from Earth," she said as loudly as she could.

He cupped her in his palm, staring down at her. "Earth," he repeated.

"The borders need to be opened. Can you help?"

The giant ran a hand over his chin. "The borders must remain closed to keep Jotunheim safe. If you need guidance you must visit Mimir's well. Odin has given his eye to drink from the waters there."

Mimir's well was something she knew nothing about. "And how do I get there?"

"Not so fast, tiny human. You must sacrifice something in exchange. Are you willing to part with an eye?"

Kat thought about that for a moment, remembering her time of blindness. "No."

"What do you have to trade?"

Kat felt for her pendant. "This was a present from…"

The giant shook his head. "Merely a trinket."

She thought for a moment, wondering what she could possibly offer. "My ability to shift into a hummingbird?"

"Ah, now that would be something Mimir would appreciate. I will give you the

directions you need. But be warned, Mimir does not

consort with mere humans.

You will need to be very clever to get past his defenses."
He placed her on the ground, the wind from his hand
sending her flying.

She fell face down, scrambling to get up before he could
grab her again.

"That way!" he said, giving her a little push with his
forefinger. She rolled down a hill and into a thicket of
thorns at the bottom. "Look for the three roots!" he
bellowed.

Kat wandered aimlessly for a while—it wasn't like there
was a sign saying, 'this way to Mimir's Well'. When she
came upon several crisscrossing thick roots, she
remembered what the giant told her. But which root should
she follow? Instead of standing there undecided she shifted
into her bird self, which, for some reason, knew exactly
what root to follow.

"What have we here?"

Calloused fingers tightened, her wings held pressed against
her body as she was lifted toward an enormous face. The bird
struggled for a moment and then she transformed, legs and
arms taking the place of wings. She was quickly dropped, the
man letting out a gasp of surprise. Kat picked herself off the
ground, trying to regain her human way of thinking as she
took in the ancient bearded face, the long straggly gray hair
and the enormous well that lurked in the background. They
were in a cave, the walls slick with condensation, the smell of

algae and wet stone assailing her nostrils.

The man was average in size, his face lined and craggy. Bright eyes peered at her, wisdom shining from them. "Have you come for a drink?" his gruff voice asked. "You do know you must pay me before that happens."

Kat nodded, gazing toward the crystalline water behind him. It beckoned to her, a shimmering mist rising from it. "Will a drink help me figure out my future?"

He scoffed, running his fingers through his long beard. "You come here without knowing what my well has to offer? It holds the wisdom of the ages."

"But what about for me?"

"The water will show you what you need to know."

She hesitated for just a moment before she said, "Will you take my pendant as payment?"

He squinted at the silver hanging around her neck. "You do value the pendant, but there is something else that you value even more."

The giant had been right. Her heart seemed to shrink in on itself as she thought about giving up the one power she still retained. After several moments she whispered, "I will give you my ability to turn into a hummingbird."

His eyes brightened. "That will suffice. You must add it to my well before you drink."

"I...I don't know how to do that."

He frowned, his eyes narrowing. "Do not think you can trick me, girl. I am on to human's devious ways."

"I'm not being devious," she said hotly. "How do I give over a gift that I don't understand myself? It isn't like my pendant, or an eye, or some other talisman—it's part of me."

"You must merely decide to do it. I will test it to make sure it is in the well. It is easier with tangible items, I admit, but your gift is unusual and will benefit me greatly."

Kat tried not to cry. After this she would be bereft and lost, unable to shift if she needed to get away quickly or fly to Otherworld. In other words, she would be grounded. How could she get from here to earth if she couldn't fly?

"The well will answer all your questions."

"Will it? I want to know my future and I want to remember my past that was taken from me."

"Yes…it is the well of remembering. As to your future, you will have to search that out once you've taken in what the water gives."

Kat moved to stand close to the well. When she studied the water, she saw her face reflected, as well as the hummingbird shadow that shimmered around her. When she gazed past that, there were murky things that floated past, one of them an eyeball that seemed to stare up at her.

Mimir was so close she could feel his heavy breath on her neck. "I do not have all day to wait."

Kat watched the shimmering hummingbird, wings fluttering as she imagined it falling into the well. *You have to go*, she said silently, willing it to drop away and into the water. It took less than a minute before the shimmering bird disappeared under the surface. Kat gasped, feeling as though a part of her had been cut away. "It's done," she said as tears welled and spilled over.

"Yes, I see that it is," Mimir muttered. He grabbed a long-handled scoop from next to the well, dipped it into the water and handed it to her.

Kat took it, unsure for a second if she wanted to drink

from a pool contaminated with eyeballs and whatever else had been left behind. But when her gaze met Mimir's she knew she must. The hummingbird was gone and she had to find out how to finish what she'd begun. She put the cup to her lips and drank.

Kat woke sometime later in a dark wood, the well, Mimir, and the cave, nowhere to be seen. She'd had a dream that she'd given up the bird part of her, that she'd taken a drink from the well. *I must have been asleep and dreamed all of it,* she thought, standing to dust the leaves off her dress. And yet she didn't remember the woods she was in, or anything else about the past hours. It was dark now, no light except the stars she could vaguely make out through the heavy branches. And when she tried to shift into a bird, nothing happened.

10

The truth dawned slowly, Kat's thoughts going from murky, like the water she'd drunk from, to crystal clear. The first thing she was aware of was Bran, the memories of him surrounding her like a blanket of warmth. But then she remembered Val. The time spent with him seemed shrouded, as though seen through a veil; a strange lucid dream. Unfortunately, the dream became clear as the moments passed, their love-making coming back to her in lurid detail. Kat hugged her arms close, every part of her filled with the shame and guilt of what she'd done. Tears welled as her fingers wrapped around the silver pendant. She'd betrayed the one man she truly loved.

But what the well had to offer was far from over. Beyond the shock of the past and Val, another vision presented itself, showing her what her future held. She saw herself walking down a road made of rough stones, the world crumbling on either side of her. Birds fell screeching from a dark sky, landing dead at her feet. The sky was filled with fire and ash, smoke burning her lungs. Instead of Bran, another man walked beside her, one who she couldn't quite make out.

And there was something else, something her mind refused to reveal…she let out a shriek. Instead of being a savior she was to be a destroyer, the one who caused the end of everything. "What have I done?" she cried out to the trees standing silent all around her. But it wasn't what she'd done, it was what she would do in the future. When they whispered to her, she couldn't hear them, her thoughts careening wildly from one thing to another.

Kat hurried from the forest, her mind numb. It was just as she'd feared. Without her ability to turn into a bird she was stuck here. But as she ran, she noticed lights in the distance, heard the sound of car horns and the squeal of tires. She was no longer in the Norse world at all. She was home.

A car stopped, a middle-aged man peering out at her. "Are you all right, miss? Do you need a ride somewhere?"

Kat glanced down at the torn brown dress, her bare feet. Her fingers went to the tangle of hair filled with dirt and moss. "Where am I?"

"Just outside Pasadena. Do you have a place to go?"

Kat stared into space for a moment, everything she'd just learned circling inside her brain like a flock of crazed birds. Finally, she nodded and climbed into the car. "1440, Tanglewood Drive," she mumbled.

"So, you never found Bran, you weren't able to open the border, and you've lost your ability to shift into a hummingbird," her mother said, counting things off on her slender fingers.

"I didn't do anything I set out to do," Kat said morosely, "and now I'm stuck on earth."

"Is it really that bad, Kat? You did say your father has been released. Mior is here. Will Dagda show up, do you think?"

"I doubt it, Mom. The world is coming to an end and I'm the one who destroys it."

"Nonsense. You would never be a destroyer. Try not to be so literal in your thinking."

"How do I do that?"

"Really, Katel—a road of stone, dead birds landing at your feet, the world crumbling away? That cannot be reality. Please use your intuition." Siobhan hauled her to her feet. "Let's take Mior for a walk in the park. Some fresh air might clear your mind. Now tell me about this Val— what is he like?"

Kat burst into tears.

It was a half hour before Kat got herself under control. She'd told her mother everything, including details of the affair and her terrible guilt.

"Kat, you musn't be so hard on yourself. At the time you didn't remember Bran. And this Val seems almost too beautiful to resist. For all you know he enchanted you— you did say he was Fae. And what about the magic he gave you? Perhaps that is what will save earth."

"What magic? I have no idea what it could be, Mom. He talked about doors and stuff—it made no sense. And right now, I can't even think. One minute I was with Mimir drinking from a magical well and in the next I was here on earth. How did I get here? Was it merely an elaborate dream?"

"That dress you're wearing says no." Siobhan picked at the fabric. "It is not of this world."

"It could be a medieval costume. Who knows where I got it? Everything from the recent past seems like a dream."

Siobhan shook her head. "The fabric shimmers. Even I can see that."

Kat glanced down, watching rainbow colors dance through the threads. It gleamed with a mystical light.

"I refuse to believe that my half goddess daughter is unable to figure this out," Siobhan continued. "Now come on," she urged, tugging her with one hand as she led Mior with the other.

The park was quiet, swans circling the pond looking for bread crumbs. Mior chortled when he saw them, hurrying over with the bag of bread Siobhan had supplied. The two women watched him, lost in their own thoughts. It was Kat who spoke first, her voice piercing in the early evening silence.

"It was Mimir's well that screwed it up. That was never part of the plan."

"And yet the giant you ran into sent you that way. Fate is never a straight line, Katel. You needed to hear what the water had to say."

"And lose my ability to shift?"

Siobhan shrugged. "It would have been too simple had you retained that gift. The hero's journey requires sacrifice. And the hero is always reluctant at the beginning."

"I'm not a hero, Mom, and I'm not on some hero's journey. It was Val who kept me there too long, and the well, and…"

"Stop blaming others and think about what it all means."

Kat turned away to watch her brother running toward the pond. In the next second he had flung himself into the water and was sinking like a stone. Kat took off running.

Kat could hear Siobhan screaming as she searched the murk for Mior. When she finally found him, she let out a gasp, bubbles rising from her mouth. He smiled at her from his place on the bottom, his wide-open eyes laughing in delight. "I can breathe," he said distinctly, bubbles rising.

Kat grabbed his arm and hauled him out. When they rose to the surface several people had gathered around, and her mom had taken off her shoes and socks to wade into the shallows. "I was giving up on you!" she cried out, tears coursing down her pale cheeks.

"I can breathe under water!" Mior shouted.

The crowd looked on as Kat tucked Mior under her arm. "He's a kidder," she said as she climbed up the bank.

Siobhan took the soaking wet child from her, hugging him close. "It's so cold, Mior. Why would you think to go swimming?"

"I don't feel cold," the child said. "I'm warm as toast."

Siobhan and Kat's gaze met. "Well, I'm cold," Siobhan said. "And I'm pretty sure your sister is as well."

Kat squeezed water out of her hair and pressed her hands against the brown dress. It was completely dry.

Once Mior was in bed, Siobhan turned to Kat. "What other gifts do you think he has? Will he suddenly fly?"

"His Dad was a god, so it's hard to say."

Siobhan sighed. "I wish that man was here right now. It's hard to think of bringing up this magical being without him. If he's been released why hasn't he come back to me?"

Kat shrugged. "Borders are closed?"

Siobhan went to the refrigerator and pulled out leftover chicken and salad makings. "In all the chaos did you have an epiphany?"

Kat walked into the kitchenette behind her to help with dinner. "Not really, but the road does seem symbolic of a difficult path to tread. And the world crumbling? Maybe it's only my world."

"I have to say I noticed the changes today. Things are not right out there," her mother said, pointing toward the window. "How do we bring it back to normal?"

Kat let out a huff of exasperation. "That's what I've been trying to tell you—I have no idea! And without goddess powers I can't do a thing."

Siobhan frowned. "Tell me again what you learned from Cerridwen's cauldron. Perhaps your answers lie there."

"Something about time having no meaning and past lives. It isn't relevant. Val said sorcery was used on me."

"What you told me about Freya?"

Kat nodded, her mind turning to Val. Both he and Cerridwen had urged her to follow her own path. But what *was* her path? Nothing made any sense.

"You must calm your mind. The answers are still there. Go to the forest and meditate."

Kat let out a snort. "Everything I learned was stolen, just like my memories of Bran. I still can't remember him properly."

Siobhan put a hand on her arm. "Well, then, maybe you should relax and enjoy being here with me and Mior. Let others solve the world's problems for a change."

11

t was weeks before Kat took her mom's advice, heading out with a notepad and pencil. She decided to go to the forest she'd been in with Bran, the one uphill from where Dagda's enormous house had been—the mansion that had mysteriously burned down right before his departure for Otherworld.

When she came to the gates that opened onto her father's property, she noticed that a shack had been erected where the house had been. She'd forgotten about the property, forgotten if it was in the portfolio he'd left behind for her, but now she remembered it had never been sold. She glanced up at the enormous obsidian ravens on the columns on either side of the gate. Her father's symbol as well as Bran's. They were both able to shift into raven form, something they had in common, not that it made any difference in how they felt about each other. The little house in the middle of the lot was made of scrap wood, a tiny chimney of rusted metal emitting a thin tendril of smoke. Some homeless person was squatting. She stood there for a few more minutes, finally deciding to continue on.

In the woods she settled under a tall cedar and composed herself, letting her breathing slow. *Please help me discover how to proceed.* She'd always had a connection to trees, but now she couldn't hear them, or even feel the energy they exuded. *How am I supposed to bring magic back when I don't even have any myself?* Despite her doubts she let the thoughts drift away, allowing her mind to open.

You have my magic within you, she heard. *Remember the doors.*

Kat's eyes flew open. Val had gotten through to her from the Norse realm. But what magic was he talking about? The doors again. Kat sat there for another twenty minutes, puzzling over his words and wondering why he hadn't explained things more carefully. Or was this about her and her increasing inability to remember things?

On the way back down the hill she saw an old man moving around her father's yard. He looked ancient, with long gray hair and a beard, his back bent. His clothing was filthy and ragged. When he saw her, he hurried away, disappearing into the rustic shack. Kat wondered if she should confront him, finally deciding to let him be. He wasn't doing any harm.

"This man is living on the property?" Siobhan asked later after Kat relayed her experience.

"He built a ridiculous house made of scraps and I think he's growing vegetables. Or maybe it's marijuana—hard to tell."

Siobhan smiled. "I'm glad someone is getting something out of that beautiful place."

Kat let out a sigh, her thoughts turning to the message from Val. "I heard Val's voice when I was meditating. He said I have the magic he gave me. But what is it?"

Siobhan did a one shoulder shrug. "Didn't he explain it? Did he give you some talisman?"

Kat took off her coat and sprawled onto the couch. "No, no talisman. Maybe I forgot what he told me. Why is everything so complicated? Can I shoot fire out of my nose, or stop a speeding car, or what?"

Siobhan stared at her. "Kat, you've put on weight."

Kat sat up. "What?"

Siobhan sat next to her and placed a hand on her lower belly. "Is this what I think it is?"

Kat glanced at the bulge under her mother's fingers. "Oh my god."

Siobhan smiled. "You're pregnant."

"But...how can I be?"

Siobhan laughed. "Didn't you tell me that you and Val...?"

Kat's eyes widened. "That's what it is, Mom. That's the magic. That bastard got me pregnant."

Siobhan sat next to her. "You will have a Fae child. And from the look of things it seems you're at least three months along."

"It hasn't been three months since I was with him."

"Perhaps Fae babies gestate faster?"

"Why would he do this to me? I have to get an abortion."

Siobhan's mouth dropped open. "You would abort a magical child? How can you even consider that?"

Kat's eyes welled. "I don't know what to do. What if Bran comes back and I'm as big as a house?"

"Bran has been gone a long while now. He's a god. He will have to understand. As to why Val would do this,

93

maybe he knows something you don't. Perhaps there's need for this magical being here on earth."

"One magical being is not enough to change the energy here."

"Maybe not, but it's a start. Perhaps with this new life in your womb you will begin to reclaim your own magic."

Kat stared into the distance, her eyes welling. "This is the worst thing that could happen. Even if I find Bran, he won't want me. Why would Val think this was a good idea?" she wailed.

"From what you told me, he asked if you wanted his magic and you said yes."

"He didn't say it was a baby!"

Siobhan smiled and patted Kat's shoulder. "It's a lot to take in. Perhaps Elves don't think in the same terms we do. Maybe for him, giving you a child is merely bestowing you with a precious gift." Siobhan glanced around the small space, her gaze landing on Mior, who had toys spread across the carpet. "If you plan to stay here, I think we'll need a bigger apartment."

"I can't even think what to do!"

"You will stay here with me and have this baby."

Kat stared into her mother's shining eyes. "You're looking forward to this."

Siobhan chuckled. "Yes. Yes, I am."

Kat leapt off the couch and hurtled out the door, her mind overcome with what she'd discovered. She would have to bring this baby to term and birth it. What if it had pointed ears and glowed like Val? Why would he saddle her with this? But as she calmed and thought about it, she remembered their time together. Yes, he'd used sorcery to keep her there, but he'd also felt a deep affection for her. And, she had to admit, she'd felt the same about him. The baby was the reason he could reach her through the ether. Would this Fae child restore her goddess powers?

The days and months flew by as Siobhan and Kat found a bigger apartment, moved, and purchased baby paraphernalia. Kat's belly grew quickly, her trepidation growing with it. Mior seemed very aware of everything going on, patting her belly and crooning to the baby that swam inside her womb. "He is Arwen."

"How do you know it's a boy?" Kay asked her brother.

"He told me."

"But…he's only…maybe four months, and not even born yet!" Kat glanced at her mom who was watching them.

"Mior is special, aren't you sweetie?"

Mior smiled a knowing smile. "I want to see him."

"You'll see him soon enough," Kat said, thinking about the enormity of giving birth and what came after.

Along with the pregnancy came the awareness of the fast disintegration of the world around them. Markets were closed. Businesses shut. Despondency was tangible. Kat was desperate to help, but whenever she attempted anything, whether the sparks from her fingertips, or trying to affect the weather, nothing happened. Dispelling the forces affecting Earth was impossible.

It was a few days later that Siobhan suggested a picnic up in the woods by Dagda's property. "I love it up there and the woods are so special. You did say they were still green, didn't you? Maybe you can commune with the trees now. We should go before the weather shifts."

Kat agreed. "It looked pretty healthy that last time I was there—maybe because of Dad living there for so long."

Siobhan gazed at her. "You look nearly ready to pop. Are you sure you can make it up that hill?"

"I'm not even five months yet," Kat answered, glancing down at her enormous girth. "Maybe you're right about Elves gestating faster," she murmured nervously.

Siobhan raised her eyebrows. "Looks like it to me."

"Arwen is coming," Mior said sagely.

"When?" Kat asked him.

"Soon," he said, smiling.

"But not today, right?"

"Not today."

Kat let out a sigh. "That's good to hear. I feel surprisingly well for how fat I am."

Siobhan laughed. "I would hardly call you fat. You are a beautiful pregnant woman with a glow that can only be attributed to this baby you're carrying." Siobhan had knitted a gigantic sweater for Kat, handing it over. "You need to dress warmly."

Kat laughed when she pulled it on. "Big enough for a large man. Did you knit this for Dad?"

"No, dear. It's for you." When Siobhan attempted to pull a sweater over Mior's head he fought her, pulling away with a screech. "What's wrong, sweetie?"

"Too hot!" he yelled, running for the door.

Siobhan shook her head. "Ever since the pond incident he seems oddly immune to the cold."

"He's his father's son."

Siobhan nodded, pulling on a woolen cape.

It was nearly noon by the time they'd taken a bus to the neighborhood and climbed the hill. As they passed by Dagda's property Siobhan stopped. "Look," she said pointing at the old man Kat had seen the time before. "That's the sweater I knitted for Dag," Siobhan whispered, watching the man head into the garden. "He must have found it in the rubble."

In comparison with the rest of the houses and neighborhood, the garden had lots of color, despite the fall temperatures. The man was tending a bed, his back to them when Siobhan went pale. "That's Dag," she muttered.

"What? That's a decrepit old man."

"Is that what you see? Because I see the man I love." Siobhan pushed the gate open to slip through. A second later she was running.

Kat took hold of Mior's hand and followed at a distance, wondering if her mother had lost her mind. There was no way...and that's when the man turned, surprise in his cobalt eyes, his face as familiar as her own. He held his arms out and Siobhan hurled herself into them.

By the time Kat and Mior reached them, Dagda and her mother were in a close embrace, both of them in tears. Mior pulled away and ran for him, his arms going around the man's legs as he chanted, *Papa, Papa!* at the top of his lungs.

Kat waited until Siobhan and Dagda turned to her before she moved close, her heart beating so fast she could barely catch her breath. "Dad? How is this possible?"

Dagda gazed at her, his eyes widening in shock as he took in her girth.

Kat cupped the roundness of her belly. "It's…"

"It's Elven!" Mior yelled. "And his name is Arwen."

Dagda frowned and came close, his strong arms wrapping around her. Kat felt surrounded with his energy and love, her feelings for him rising quickly to the surface. When they pulled apart, she stood back to look at him. "You…"

He nodded, with a sad smile. "I'm human. It's my punishment."

Siobhan linked her arm through his. "I don't care what you are, Dag. How long have you been here—why didn't you come find me?"

"I did check on you, but you'd moved. And I'm ugly and old. I didn't want you to see me like this."

Kat looked him over. Yes, he'd aged. His back was not as straight as it once was, and he'd lost weight, but he still had that spark of vitality. "You built this place."

He nodded. "With my bare hands. Who knew I could do it?" He nodded toward the shack. "Want to see inside?"

They trooped after him across the garden and followed him through a narrow, rough-hewn door. A pot-bellied stove worked overtime to warm it up, a threadbare rug on the plank floor. A couch and a chair that had seen better days occupied one wall, a narrow bed on another. A sink and a small stove took over part of a short wall, with a small ancient refrigerator in the corner. "Now tell me, Katel, whose baby do you carry? I doubt it could be Bran's since he was still in Otherworld when they sent me down here."

Kat blushed to the roots of her hair. "The father's name is Val. He lives in Alfheim."

"A member of the light elves. How in the world did you come upon the Fae?"

"I was at Odin's castle. I'd gone blind and Frigg and Freya were helping me, but...Freya wasn't really Freya, and I ran away and ended up in Alfheim. Val found me and took me to his manor house. My memories of Bran were gone at the time."

Dagda laughed. "I guess they were. Probably a good thing. Bran isn't right for you—never was."

"You still think that? It isn't true," Kat said hotly. "I love him and he used to love me."

Dagda's eyes clouded. "Something has happened to him, Kat. He's not the same."

"What do you mean?"

Dagda shrugged. "He's lost his dynamism. He seems diminished."

"Probably because he can't get back to earth. Why did they close the borders?"

"You know very well why. Look around. Do you think Otherworld wants this creeping plague to infest their realm?" He turned from her to reach for Mior, lifting him into the air. "You've grown since I saw you last," he murmured, hugging the child close. Mior giggled and put his arms around Dagda's neck.

Siobhan bustled around looking for cups and a teapot, her gaze going to Dagda every few seconds. "I can't believe this," she murmured.

"I knew he'd come back," Mior crowed.

"If you knew, why didn't you say?" Siobhan demanded.

Mior looked crestfallen. "I didn't know when he was coming, Mama."

"I'm sorry, sweetheart," she said, ruffling his dark curls.

"So, Katel. This baby of yours. When will it be born?"

Kat shrugged. "I don't know. It seems soon."

Dagda nodded his agreement. "Will you take the baby back to Alfheim?"

Kat glanced out the small window. "I...I haven't thought that far ahead. I was hoping Bran would come back, but I have no idea how he'll deal with this."

Dagda shook his head. "There will be no more travel between Earth and Otherworld. How are your goddess powers, by the way?"

"Not good. They're basically gone. I think I need the borders open to receive the energy I need."

"Yes, that is what I feared. And earth is turning into a wasteland."

"But your garden is lush and beautiful," Siobhan said.

"It's the energy I left behind." He turned back to Kat. "Have you noticed anything odd about this pregnancy?"

Kat shook her head. "I've had messages from Val—nothing else."

"You will."

"What do you know, Dad?"

"I know that Elves are magical beings who are able to stop time and change reality. You should have these abilities, at least during the pregnancy. Once the baby is born, I'm not sure what will happen. Perhaps if you breast feed there will be a link that continues. If I were you, I'd test this out. We could all use some magic right about now."

"To help the world?"

"Of course, to help the world, but also to help ourselves."

Kat smirked. "There's the Dagda I know and love—the selfish one."

"Kat! That's unfair!" Siobhan yelled.

Dagda put a restraining hand on Siobhan's arm. "I was referring to getting the borders open, Katel. With closed borders this place will continue to deteriorate."

It was late when Kat suggested they head home. It was growing dark and she knew the busses stopped running after a certain hour. But her mother refused to go.

"Mior and I are staying here tonight," Siobhan said, glancing at Mior sprawled asleep on the couch.

"I guess I'll head out then," Kat said reluctantly. "When will you come back, Mom?"

Siobhan glanced at Dagda. "I plan to move in here if it's okay with your father."

Dagda looked surprised for a moment before he pulled her close. "We can collect your things tomorrow."

"What about me?" Kat asked.

"You'll have the entire apartment to yourself," her mom murmured. "Don't worry, dear, when your time comes, I'll be there to take you to the hospital."

Kat doubted it by the look of abject love on her mother's face. It would be impossible to pry these two apart anytime soon. The baby gave a kick, warning her that he was not waiting around much longer. She hugged them both and left the shack, crossing the garden to head out the gate.

The moon was full, the silvery orb lighting the way down the hill to the bus station. As she walked, she thought again about Bran, wondering how they would ever find each other. And when this baby was born it would put up another wall between them. Bran was forgiving, but tolerating her giving birth to another man's baby was plainly too much to expect.

12

agda watched Siobhan working in the garden. His heart leapt every time he looked at her. And his son too—it was almost too much for his human heart to bear. He was about to go off the rails when she arrived. She'd saved him from his plan to get into a life of crime with Daniel. With her here he couldn't follow through with it. Dagda let out a sigh, hoping that was true. Could a leopard change its spots? Better yet, could a former god, turned human, change for the better; he honestly didn't know. Kat's pregnancy had caught him off guard. The details of how that had come about were still to be discovered. Elves were the enemies of his kind, their magic not in the same league; Elves were far superior in their abilities. It would be interesting to see what became of this baby—how it would impact Kat. Dagda hoped the father would come to claim them and keep her away from Bran. Losing his powers had made his hatred of the god even more pronounced; just the idea of seeing him again sent Dagda into a rage he couldn't control.

"Come see what I've done!" Siobhan called out.

Dagda walked to the raised bed she'd planted, his attention taken by her flushed face and the disarray of her hair. Something stirred inside him that he hadn't felt in a long while. "What seeds are in there?"

"Broccoli and cauliflower. I love working in the dirt."

"And I love you," he said.

Siobhan straightened to stare at him. "You're happy to have us here, then?"

Dagda reached to wipe a smear of mud off her cheek. A few days before he wouldn't have believed he could feel like this again. Her being here had given him a reason to live. He was too choked up to answer.

"Arwen is coming!" Mior called out, tearing across the yard.

Dagda watched the interaction between his son and the woman he loved, pride swelling inside him. He glanced up at the darkening sky. "Do you need to go?"

"I think I'd better—Mior is in touch with things that I have no clue about. If he says the baby's coming, I'm sure he is."

"Mama, the baby is magic," Mior said, staring into the distance. "He…"

But by that time Siobhan was kissing Dagda good-bye and asking if he would watch Mior until she got back.

Dagda smiled and pulled her close. "Come back soon, my love," he whispered.

When Siobhan hurried away Mior came to stand with Dagda, reaching up to take his hand. "Will Mama come back?"

"She'll be back as soon as she can, Mior. But right now, she needs to be there for your sister."

Mior shook his head. "The baby knows what to do."

Dagda gazed down at the dark curls so like his own before his hair turned to gray. "Maybe so, but a woman is needed in situations like this."

13

Kat's pains began early the next morning, her
body slick with sweat as she fought for breath.
She writhed, unable to find a position where
everything didn't hurt. But as the pains worsened
something strange began to happen, as though a door had
opened and she'd walked through into another reality. Val
was there, his strong arms holding her from behind as she
struggled through the throes of childbirth. She recognized
his bedroom, the softness of his pillows propping her up.
He told her when to breathe, his whispering voice in her
ear calming her as the pains grew worse and worse. When
she cried out, he smoothed the damp hair back from her
face. "Another few pushes and he'll be here," he told her,
moving between her bent legs.

Dawn light streamed through the windows, illuminating
his perfect features as he concentrated. The last push went
on and on, her screams echoing as Val encouraged her. And
then he was there, the whoosh of fluids releasing her. She
fell back against the pillows, exhausted.

Val caught him, cut the cord and cleaned him up before

placing him at her breast. He worked on her for a few minutes before he lay down beside her and kissed her damp cheek. "He is ours. That will never change," he whispered.

Kat looked down at the baby at her breast, the pale hair that glowed with a magical fire. His tiny translucent ears were pointed. She slept.

Kat heard banging. Someone was shouting her name. When she opened her eyes, it was dark outside, the moon a bright lantern in the sky. She felt exhausted and sore in places that seemed odd—until she noticed the baby lying on her chest asleep. All of it came rushing back—the birth, Val. *Val.* He'd delivered her baby. She'd been with him in Alfheim!

"Kat! Are you okay? Please open the door!"

Kat struggled to stand, pulling a bathrobe over her nakedness. She clutched the tiny baby close as she lurched to the door to fling it open.

"Oh my god! You had him all alone?" Siobhan flung her arms around her daughter and helped her back to bed. She switched on the lamp. "I'm so sorry. I had no idea you were ready to deliver. If I'd known I never would have stayed with Dag."

"It's okay, Mom," Kat said, climbing back into bed. "Val delivered him."

"Val? What are you talking about?"

"I went to Alfheim and Val delivered the baby."

"My dearest girl, you were dreaming." Siobhan bustled around looking for bloody towels and checking the sheets. "Are you okay…down there? Was there tearing or bleeding?"

"I wasn't dreaming. Remember when Dad said Elves could change reality? I walked through a door and I was there—with him. Val delivered him." Kat began to cry as she gazed at the exquisite baby in her arms.

Her mom turned to examine him, her eyes going wide. "He has pointed ears."

"He's Elven. Didn't you believe me? Where's Mior?"

"He's with Dag. It's because of him that I'm here. I had planned to wait until tomorrow, but Mior insisted that Arwen was coming."

"Is this the same day I left you, or…"

"No, sweetheart. An entire night and day have passed. I'd planned to come earlier to pick up some things, but I couldn't stand to leave your father." Siobhan reached for the swaddled baby. "He…he glows!"

Kat smiled. "I know."

"You will have to keep him secret, Kat—look at him!"

"He can wear a hat when we go out." Kat reached for him, unable to have him away from her for even a minute. "Now I know how to get into Otherworld."

"Otherworld—why are you even thinking about this?"

"Because earth needs the barriers down in order to heal, and I have to find Bran."

"But, sweetheart, how will he respond to Arwen?"

"I don't know. If he rejects me, then so be it, but I have to try."

Siobhan nodded slowly. "This baby was given to you for a reason. Perhaps Bran will forgive you when you explain how it happened. Being bewitched is a good excuse, don't you think?"

"I hope it's enough. If he arrived with a baby he'd had

with another woman, I'd be pretty upset."

"Well, at least Val is far away. When will you go?"

"I don't know, Mom. But not today—I'm too tired."

"I would certainly hope not. You need to rest for at least a week before you embark on some trip into worlds unknown. I'm going to fix a meal and then go back and pick up Mior and your father. We can all have dinner together. Do you need anything else right now? Are you hungry?"

Kat shook her head, glancing down at the nursing baby. "He already knows exactly what to do," she murmured.

Siobhan leaned down and kissed her cheek before she headed to the kitchen.

Kat heard her humming and the sound of chopping, the whoosh of the gas burner on the stove coming on and the smell of something cooking. "I'm going now!" Siobhan called out sometime later. "We'll be back soon!"

Kat heard the thump of the door closing behind her. The baby was asleep when she got out of bed and pulled on some clothes. "I can't wait another second," she whispered, gathering the baby close. "Time to try out those doors."

All Kat had to do was think about where she wanted to go and visualize it in her mind. Otherworld was on the other side of the door she walked through, every detail crisp and beautiful. The door had opened just beyond where Earth ended and Otherworld began. Through the trees she could see the translucent sky. The sun was high now, tendrils of color sending rainbows dancing through the air. Kat was weak from the birth, but not too weak to walk slowly along the path and appreciate the beauty all around her.

When she turned her attention to the path again, Bran was walking toward her, his gaze on the ground. She balked and hid behind a tree, wondering what in the world she'd been thinking. She had a brand new baby in her arms and she'd betrayed him not once, but many times. There was no way to defend what she'd done.

He was dressed in the indigo tunic that revealed his upper chest, long honey colored hair tied back from his face. The silver of his pendant caught the light, blinding her for a second. When she was able to look again, he was closer, and every bit as beautiful as Val. She'd forgotten him, forgotten how she felt when she was with him and how much she loved him. She sucked in a breath; her legs were wobbly. What would she say—how could she possibly explain?

Before she could puzzle that out, he'd seen her, his expression one of wonderment. He hurried toward her and when he reached her his arms went tight around her to pull her close. When the baby let out a tiny squeal, Kat pulled away.

Bran glanced down. "And who is this little fellow?"

Kat stared into the green eyes she knew so well, unable to breathe for a second. "He's…Arwen's my baby."

Bran frowned. "*Your* baby? Who's the father?"

"Val from Alfheim." Tears arrived and she wiped them away. "I'm sorry, Bran. I couldn't remember you, and you were gone so long, and…"

Bran's arms went around her. "Shush, Kat. It's all right. You're here now, with me." He bent to kiss her.

It was an hour before she'd caught him up on what had happened, her stuttering explanations frustrating her as she attempted to defend her behavior. In the middle of it she had to stop to feed the baby, an embarrassing action considering the fact that this wasn't even his child. But he seemed to take it all in stride. Once the baby was fed, Bran led them onto a narrow path.

"We need privacy," he told her as he steered her down one twisting trail after another. When they reached a tiny dwelling deep in the woods, he took her inside, showing her to a soft pallet on the floor. "You need rest, Kat. Once you've slept, we will talk again. In the meantime, I'm going to fix something to eat."

Kat lay down and closed her eyes, falling immediately into a deep and dreamless sleep.

When Kat woke, Bran was sitting next to her, a plate of bread, cheese and cut up apple between them. The baby was in his arms. "He woke up," he explained.

Kat pushed herself up to sitting. "I can't believe I'm here. It's Arwen who allowed me to do it, Bran. He's Elven. "

"I gathered that from his ears. They can walk from one reality to another."

Kat nodded, taking the baby from him to place him at her breast. "I didn't think we'd ever see each other again."

Bran smiled. "I knew you'd find a way—you always do."

"Dagda's with Mom. He's human."

Bran nodded. "I was there when they stripped him of his powers and sent him down. It was not a pretty sight, believe me."

Kat thought of her father and his arrogance, the broken man he was after leaving earth the last time in order to turn himself in for his crimes. "I can imagine. He looks so old now. But Mom's ecstatic." She glanced at the baby in her arms. "I thought you'd decided you didn't love me and that's why you didn't come back," she whispered.

"Why would you ever think that?"

When Kat saw the love that shone from his eyes, she wondered the same thing. "I thought you were mad at me because I went to Otherworld to plead Dad's case."

"Kat, I would never begrudge your feelings for the man. He's your father. Just because I don't get along with him doesn't mean I can't understand how you feel."

A second later Kat was in overwhelm, her hiccupping sobs echoing around the walls of the tiny round stone house they were in. The baby let out a little cry, his wide-open eyes showing an awareness that he shouldn't have. Bran grabbed him away from her and held him close. "He's very aware, isn't he?"

That made Kat cry harder, her sobs muffled when she pressed a scarf to her mouth. "I'm sorry, I can't help it— everything is so…"

"My gods, Kat. You just gave birth. Your hormones are all over the place." Bran slid an arm around her hunched shoulders.

"I wasn't sure how you'd respond to this…to him," Kat muttered, gesturing to Arwen. "I was so freaked out about it. It all feels like a dream." Kat moved close, snuggling into his warmth. "Pinch me."

Bran chuckled. "I'll kiss you instead.

Kat and Bran remained in the little shelter, giving her the time to recover from the birth. Every day they visited a forest pool to bathe, washing each other's hair and relaxing with the baby to float in the dappled shadows. At night they slept snug inside the small stone house. They ate nuts and fruits from the forest, an occasional rabbit making its way into the stew Bran prepared. For Kat it was the most relaxed she'd felt in months.

It was six weeks before they were able to make love for the first time. It was a tender and careful coupling that led into questions from Bran regarding what had happened between Val and Kat.

"I don't...I mean, I didn't love him," Kat began hesitantly. "But we were attracted to each other. He wanted me to stay."

Bran pushed himself up onto his elbow, watching her. "Why didn't you?"

"Even though I couldn't remember you, I knew I loved you. When he said he'd given me his magic, I didn't know it was a baby. I would never have wanted that. I considered an abortion."

Bran glanced at the sleeping child. "And yet if it wasn't for Arwen you wouldn't be here. Perhaps Val knew."

Kat touched the pendant around his neck. "He said my

pendant held an ancient magic, Bran. He said we've been together before."

Bran glanced at her pendant. "Have you gotten anything from it?"

"No, and Val didn't elaborate. What do you think he meant?"

"Maybe that we've lived in other realms in other times? I don't know."

"What other realms are there?"

"The galaxy is filled with unexplored worlds, Kat."

Kat snuggled closer, letting go of his pendant to run her fingers lightly across his chest.

Bran's breath quickened. "If you keep doing that, I…" A moment later he'd rolled on top of her, the gentleness of their first time replaced with an urgency neither one could ignore.

The baby woke her sometime later. Kat pulled him to her to feed him.

"You seem to be a natural at that," Bran said, watching her.

"I wish he was yours," Kat murmured.

Bran shook his head. "Don't say that. Arwen was meant to be. He's special and I have no regrets about him. I don't even feel jealous about you and Val. It was something that had to happen in order for us to find each other again."

With his words, Kat's heart expanded with love. "Do you remember seeing me as a hummingbird at the boundary between the Norse world and Otherworld?"

Bran nodded. "I knew as Raven we would find each other—but I didn't know how it would happen."

"Bran, I should have my powers now. I'm in Otherworld!"

Bran grinned. "So, Arwen's magic and your own? What can you do?"

Kat stared down at her fingers, willing them to spark. "I used to be able to start fires this way." She looked at Bran. "It isn't happening."

"What about the wind, the rain? Weren't you able to affect weather?"

Kat nodded and waved her hands around, visualizing dark clouds and thunder. When nothing happened, she frowned, glancing at the sleeping baby. "Maybe Arwen's magic is overpowering mine."

Bran nodded. "As I said, Fae magic is potent stuff."

Kat stared at the baby. The idea that a child this young, could take over her powers, left her feeling odd, to say the least. "I thought that…"

Bran took hold of her hands, pressing them between his. "You have Arwen. We don't need anything else, do we?"

"We could in the future. We have no idea what might happen."

Bran scoffed. "No point in worrying about it, Kat."

As the weeks passed the baby filled out, growing quickly, his knowing gaze taking everything in as Bran and Kat forged for nuts and mushrooms. Kat carried him in a shawl looped over her shoulder. She and Bran had covered every topic, all the months they'd been apart, explored and dissected.

And then everything changed. It happened early in the morning. They were unprepared.

14

Bran and Kat were walking back from the forest pool when they ran into Airmid, her eyes brimming with fury.

"What are you doing here?" she shrieked at Kat.

Bran moved protectively in front of Kat, his eyes narrowing. "What the fuck are *you* doing here? And how is this any of your business?"

Airmid glared at him. "I'm a goddess, as you are a god. This woman is nothing aside from Dagda's daughter, who has been stripped of his powers. She shouldn't be here." She stared at Arwen, her eyes widening. "That is an Elven baby! Do you have any idea the havoc that can wreak?"

"The baby is hers, Airmid. It's how Kat got here."

"Ah—so she gives birth to someone else's child and you welcome her with open arms? How stupid are you?"

Bran frowned. "You have no right to cast judgement. You have no idea what Kat has gone through these past months."

"You're an idiot if you trust her, Bran. Her father's behavior is testament to what kind of a person she is."

"Why are you saying that?" Kat asked, moving from

behind Bran. "I thought you were my friend."

"I was, until you decided to ignore what I was trying to teach you. You're arrogant, just like your father."

Kat stared at the goddess open-mouthed. "And you thought I was nothing and had no powers. I heard you and Gwen talking behind my back."

Airmid sneered. "And what powers *do* you have?"

"Well, I…I don't know because I haven't tested them lately," she lied.

"Just as I thought. You lost them in your unholy quest to save your father."

"Not true. I lost the last one when I gave it up to Mimir in order to discover my future. The others were cut off by the closed borders between Otherworld and Earth."

"And what *is* your future? Do you have some mission to save the world, or is it purely selfish, like getting back together with this god who you think can restore your gifts?"

"I resent that," Bran said in a low growl. "You are being an utter bitch, Airmid. What exactly is your problem?"

"I don't have a problem, but you do. As soon as I tell the higher ups that *she's* here and what she has with her, you'll discover what happens when you disobey the rules."

"We didn't do anything wrong."

"If that were true why have you been hiding out? Half humans are no longer allowed in Otherworld, nor are Elven babies. I found your secret tryst spot. I watched the two of you."

"Why would you do that?" Kat cried out. "What is *wrong* with you?"

"She's jealous," Bran muttered. "We had a moment a while back."

"You didn't tell me that," Kat said, gazing at Bran in surprise.

Airmid let out a humorless laugh. "It was only a moment and a dull one at that. I guess he has a few secrets that he keeps from you."

"Get out of here," Bran ordered, advancing on her.

Airmid backed a safe distance away. "If she isn't gone by tomorrow, I will let the council know." With that statement she stalked under the trees and disappeared into the shadows.

"What the hell, Bran?"

Bran let out a heavy sigh. "I did have sex with her. But it meant nothing. She's been after me for years. I let my guard down when I was feeling vulnerable and she took advantage of it."

"Don't blame it on her. You're capable of saying no."

"Says the woman holding another man's baby."

Kat let out a huff. "So, now we get down to it, Mr. 'I'm not jealous'?"

Bran gazed at her, his expression troubled. "We're letting her come between us, Kat. Can you see that?"

Kat looked down. "You're right—I'm sorry."

"What we need to do is figure out how to deal with this."

"Why is me being here a problem?"

Bran chuckled. "It isn't for me."

"I'm glad you feel that way, but seriously—what's the deal? Was what she said true about Arwen causing a problem here?"

Bran glanced at the baby. He nodded.

"Tell me."

Bran lifted Arwen out of the shawl and placed him carefully on some moss before he took hold of her arm and led her under the trees. "The Fae are strictly forbidden here. They have powers that are far superior to ours. The gods and goddesses in Otherworld do not trust them and consider them devious."

"Racism," Kat muttered.

"Maybe. But I've heard some hair-raising tales."

"Like what?"

Bran shook his head. "They've been referred to as soulless, caught up in their own selfish needs. They can become vicious and kill without provocation. You said Val put you under a spell in order to have sex with you—how is that loving? It sounds more like rape to me. And he never told you that you were pregnant."

He frowned, his lips pressing together. "I don't like this guy and how he treated you, Kat. He knew what he was doing and didn't say a word. Giving birth is no small thing, not to mention raising a child." He let out a heavy sigh, his fingers running through his still wet hair from their morning dip. "I'm happy that having this baby brought you back to me, but the rest of it…" He shook his head and turned away. "Airmid will follow through with her threat, and when she does, Arwen will be taken from you and more than likely killed."

Kat stared at him in shock. "They would kill a baby?"

"An Elven baby? Hell yes."

"I can walk through a door, but can you come with me?"

"No." Bran gazed at her. "And I can't be parted from you again."

Kat glanced into the distance. "After I drank from

Mimir's well, I had a dream of walking along a road made of stones and the world crumbling on either side of me. Birds fell dead from the sky and there was fire and ash all around. I was with someone—a man. But not you. Mom intimated that it was a metaphor, but I don't think so. I've been trying to figure out what it means."

Bran frowned, his gaze going to the baby still sleeping on the moss. "A road of stones is one that leads to the Pinnacle. Birds die when there's a storm. And there is a specter…it's one of the myths here. He represents the death of everything."

"The Pinnacle—where is that?"

"The highest point in Otherworld. From there you can see all the worlds. It stands far above the borders."

"But if that's true we should be able to open a conduit to earth!" Before Bran could respond Kat rushed back to pick up the baby. If her destiny was to bring down the barrier, she had to follow what the dream told her. Arwen cooed as he watched the shifting shadows cast by the leaves moving in the breeze. She picked him up and kissed him, holding him close.

Bran joined her, his arms wrapping around her from behind.

"We need to go there," she murmured.

"I was afraid you were going to say that."

15

"That girl holds the key," the witch said, watching the shadow creature on the cave wall. "I took her memories, but somehow she's gathered most of them back. And she still hides something from me. The Fae, Val, has given her magic to help her, but I cannot discern what it is. You must help me."

The far dorocha moved, his shadow drawing closer to where she stood. "I am your servant."

The witch stood with hands on hips, her face scrunched into an expression of irritation. "Well, how will you do it? She is not on Earth and *I* cannot locate her."

"What is it you need, my worship?"

The witch let out a huff of annoyance. "I want to stop her from saving the world. The world must be destroyed and it is my destiny to do so. I have sent the darkness down, but the Dubh have not done as I asked." She turned to stare into the distance, her eyes so deep and black they looked empty, a void that led into nothingness. "We must find her and destroy her."

The far dorocha nodded, the darkness of his being turning

solid as he slid from the wall. "I will do as you command, my queen." The cave shimmered with dark magic.

She glared at him, her gaze softening when he reached for her. He enfolded her into the blackness of his being, the two of them twisting together, their mating call rising into the air to dissipate into the night.

16

"I could step through and be there, Bran. It would save a lot of time. Can you meet us in raven form?"

Bran looked skeptical. "You will have to be very specific about where you want to go. These doors can open anywhere, and I might not find you."

"Give me details and I'll hold them in my mind."

Kat and Bran had been discussing this trip since the night before, trying to be gone when Airmid arrived with her posse. They were both sleep deprived and exhausted, their eyes red-rimmed and burning.

"It isn't easy. I've only been there once. And I did not make it to the top."

"In all the hundreds of years you've been in Otherworld you've only gone there one time?"

"It's not a hospitable place."

"How long will it take us if we walk?"

"A month in earth time—maybe more? I don't really know. If you had your powers, we could..."

"Don't talk about it. I have the baby and that's all I need." She glanced down at his fuzzy pale hair. "Maybe there's some other magic Arwen has we can use."

"They're time walkers, but not sure how that would help us."

"They can manipulate time? What if we go back to when the borders were open and you come to earth with me?"

Bran shook his head. "Too many variables. And it doesn't address what you saw in your vision."

"True."

"The road of stones starts in a canyon. There is gravel scattered across the flat canyon floor and there is nothing green anywhere. The path is raised from the valley floor by probably a foot. Can you picture it?"

"All too well."

"The stones are black, as are the walls. The canyon is made up of interlocking sections of obsidian and the thick walls are so tall they block out most of the light. The valley narrows as you draw closer to the base of the mountain. I want you to meet me there, where the road begins to rise. You will see two enormous boulders carved into the shape of lions. They guard the entrance to the Pinnacle. If you don't see them you are not in the right place."

Kat shivered. "It sounds forbidding."

"It's freezing cold and wind howls across the mountain. No one goes there."

"How will I protect Arwen?"

"Arwen is the least of your problems—he's Elven. It's you I worry about." Bran dug through a chest and pulled out a heavy wool cloak with a hood and a pair of socks and boots. "You should wear these."

Kat laughed. "Mom talked about the hero's quest. I guess that's what this is."

"It isn't a laughing matter. It's dangerous, especially for you in your vulnerable state."

"You mean human."

"Not just that, Kat. You've barely recovered from the birth and you're carrying a tiny baby along with you. You need at least another month to gain your strength back."

"What if I open the door to the top of the mountain?"

Bran shook his head. "There is no magic that will get you there. It's a forbidden and remote place, cut off from everything, including Otherworld."

"How far is it to the top?"

"Let's meet up first before we talk about the rest of it. I don't want to scare you."

Kat pleaded with him to tell her what he meant, but he refused.

Kat was dressed and ready when they heard the approach of horses. "Time to go," Bran muttered, his eyes meeting hers just before he shifted into Raven.

Kat watched him lift into the air before she held the vision of the road in her mind and walked through the door that appeared in front of her.

Kat clutched Arwen close as she emerged into a barren landscape. The wind blew her hood off, making her eyes tear as she struggled to find her way. She could barely see due to dust and debris whirling around her. Apparently, she was on the road of stones, judging from the jagged rocks digging into the soles of her boots. Putting up her hand to shade her eyes from the whirling dirt, she tried to determine if she was going the right direction. From where she was, she couldn't see any Pinnacle or much of anything. The baby didn't seem to mind the wind, his breathing regular as he slept against her.

Kat looked up, hoping to see the raven, but all she got for her trouble was dust- filled ice in her eyes that blinded her for several moments. Bending into the wind she struggled forward, hoping against hope she would get to the boulders before her energy gave out. Why had she thought this would be easy? At least her vision had led her to the road of stones. It was exactly as she'd seen it, except for the world around her crumbling away.

The obsidian walls on either side closed in as she walked, the valley tightening like a funnel. She was lost in a reverie of better days when she slipped and fell on the gravel. Her ankle twisted, pain radiating up her leg as she tried to put weight on it. She was still lying there when the baby began to fuss. When she pulled her clothing out of the way to feed him, she let out a gasp as her skin when numb. But Arwen didn't seem to mind, seemingly oblivious of the howling maelstrom filled with ice crystals that took Kat's breath away. Kat pulled the cape over them, shivering and wondering how to proceed. The question she'd forgotten to ask was how long it would take Raven to get here.

Once Arwen fell asleep against her, she attempted to stand, letting out a sharp cry as her ankle gave out. A second later she was on the ground again, pain so fierce her eyes teared up. Searching around her she managed to locate a stick, using it to lever herself up to stand on her one good leg.

The stick helped, but the going was excruciatingly slow. And when the light began to fade her nerves shattered into a million pieces. There was no place to shelter here, she realized, scanning from one side to the other. The rock was solid, the darkness of it sucking the meagre light. Soon it was black as pitch, and even the road disappeared under her feet. She would never find her way. After tripping on the edges and slipping off the path to cause more pain to her ankle, she lowered herself to the ground and gave herself over to full blown tears.

It was sometime later that the moon rose, a sliver of pale light through the clouds that shimmered at the edges of the walls surrounding her. When the light of it reached the top of the dark stone, the road became visible again. She struggled forward.

Hours passed before the road began to rise upward. In the distance she saw the boulders, an enormous raven sitting on one of them. She let out a cry of joy and fell face down on the jagged rocks.

"Kat, Kat…wake up!"

Bran's voice was muted and far away. The wind howled, the pain in her ankle so severe that she couldn't speak. Rocks dug into her, and when she reached for the baby he wasn't there. She bolted upright, a cry coming out of her mouth before she realized that Bran was next to her, the baby in his arms.

"He's okay," Bran said. "But you've hurt yourself badly."

"I…I fell earlier and then…"

"And then you slipped when you saw me. You won't be able to walk. Your ankle's in very bad shape." He touched her face, his fingers coming away covered with blood. "You're bleeding, but the cut isn't deep."

Kat moved her fingers to run over the wound. "What will we do?"

"I'll have to carry you."

"That isn't very hero like for me, though, is it?" Kat said, pushing herself up using the stick.

Bran gazed at her out of worried eyes. "You plan to hobble up there on your own? Do you have any idea how far it is?"

"No, but I have to do it. This is my vision, and if I let you carry me, it won't be the same."

"Just as stubborn as ever."

"I have to be. If I'm not, everyone takes over my life."

The trail was treacherous, the wind fierce. Kat was sure she saw faces in the gusts, eyes watching her in her peripheral vision. When she stopped once and asked Bran to explain what he hadn't told her, he shook his head, the look on his face betraying a fear she'd never seen there before.

The wind grew stronger with every step they took, their conversations curtailed as the sound was amplified. The baby cried nonstop, his little face red from it. It was the first time he'd been so distressed, and it had nothing to do with being hungry or wet.

Birds circled and fell dead at their feet, the sky black with them. Kat was unable to move fast enough, her ankle swollen and painful inside the boot. When the going got too much for her she allowed Bran to help, but mostly she hopped and used the stick.

"Why can't I see the Pinnacle?" she shouted.

Bran didn't answer as he pushed her ahead of him, his head down against the wind.

They'd been walking for hours when a door appeared. Kat glanced down at the baby who was watching her with knowing eyes. He wanted out of here. She grabbed Bran's coat, pointing.

"Go if you want to!" he shouted. "But I can't follow you!"

Kat sidestepped the door and continued upward, her breath coming in gasps. "How high are we?"

Bran's narrowed eyes met hers. "Beyond any sort of measurement," he shouted back.

Kat stopped for a moment, seeing spots. "I have to rest," she said, sinking down.

Bran sat beside her and helped her organize the baby to feed him. He huddled in front of her to keep out the wind, his worried gaze never leaving her face. "This was folly," he finally said. "We should never have attempted it."

"How much further?"

Bran shrugged and moved closer as she rewrapped the baby and put him into the knotted scarf she wore under the heavy wool cape.

When Kat fell asleep, he cradled her in his arms, trying to keep the worst of the weather from hitting her. She felt him there while she dreamed of summer, birds singing and the aroma of fresh cut grass. But when that dream ended another took its place.

Something called to her, something malevolent that she couldn't seem to resist. She moved upward toward it, stepping forward despite wanting to stop. Carrion birds wheeled in the sky, their harsh calls ringing out across the mountain. When she saw what waited for her at the top, she let out a scream of terror, the world going dark around her.

"It's okay," she heard Bran say, his arms tight around her.

"It isn't okay. There's something terrible up there." When her gaze met his she saw that he knew. "What is it?"

Bran refused to answer her, the expression on his face closed. What he finally said made no sense to her. "It is a force, not a thing. It is evil incarnate, a being that shapes itself according to those who glimpse it. I told you—no one comes here."

"And yet this is my path."

"Is it?"

"I dreamed this, Bran."

"And what happened when you reached the top?"

"I didn't get that far."

"You have to understand what we're up against here. The evil at the top of the Pinnacle is ancient, a force that has been left to its own devices for millennia. The gods decided long ago to leave it in peace."

"I think this is the only way to take down the border, to bring magic back to earth. Maybe this evil isn't what you think it is."

"And yet you had a terrible dream about it."

"How do you know that?"

Bran smiled sadly. "I know everything about you."

"I need to rest before we go on. Is there anywhere to shelter?"

Bran glanced around the sheer mountain they were climbing. "Stay here and I'll do some reconnaissance."

Kat dozed while he was gone, her mind stretching upward to take in the force of what she had to face. She couldn't see it through the fog, couldn't feel the power it exuded. But she knew instinctively that what she'd felt off and on for the past few months, was about this. If she didn't get this border open, Ragnarok would destroy earth.

17

Dagda rose from the small couch to stare out the window. It was raining, drops hitting the panes and sliding down like tears. He felt powerless and ineffectual, his human body filled with sensations of pain. His knuckles ached every time he bent his fingers, his knees refusing to bend when he stood. He wanted to be virile and strong for Siobhan, but it was not possible. "Where do you think Katel went?"

Siobhan thought about their trip to the apartment and the shock of finding Kat gone. "She must have walked through a door into Otherworld. She told me she could do that now that she has Arwen."

Dagda turned, letting out a sigh. "Elves can be devious, Siobhan. They are aware from the moment of their birth. That baby could hurt her."

"No, Papa. Arwen is good. He will keep her safe."

Dagda looked down at his son standing next to him. "I hope you're right about that. In my experience Elves are dangerous and unpredictable."

Siobhan rose from the couch to take Dagda's hand, her

fingers twining through his. "What can we do?"

Dagda glanced down, marveling at her smooth skin, her clear eyes and the look he saw in them. It was astonishing that this beautiful woman loved him. He brought their clasped hands to his mouth and pressed his lips there. "I wish I had my god powers. Without them I'm completely useless."

"I'm not," Mior crowed, dancing around them.

"And what can you do?" Siobhan asked her son.

"I can see Kat and a man. They are on a scary black mountain and something very bad lives at the top."

Dagda's mouth fell open. He dropped Siobhan's hand and began to pace. "They've gone to the Pinnacle," he muttered.

"What's the Pinnacle?"

"It's the end of the world," he said darkly.

"Why would they go there?"

Dagda shook his head. "It has to be Arwen's doing. He wants my daughter to be killed."

"Don't be silly, Dag. The baby relies on her for sustenance. He wouldn't hurt her. What lives there?"

"A shadow creature who the gods now fear, a force for evil that cannot be stopped. No one has ventured up that mountain since the dawn of time."

Siobhan hugged her arms around her body. "But why on earth would our daughter go *there*?"

Dagda ran his fingers through his unruly hair. "Bran probably convinced her to do this. That god has no sense at all."

"She had to go, Papa."

Dagda looked down at the boy. "Why would that be, Mior?"

"Because it is her…des…dest…" Mior glanced at his mother.

"Destiny?" Siobhan supplied.

Mior nodded.

"What destiny would make my daughter risk her life?" Dagda mumbled to himself.

Siobhan sighed. "She was talking about opening the border between worlds."

Dagda nodded slowly. "The Pinnacle is far above the borders. It's in another realm altogether. Goddamn it, I wish I had my powers." When he glanced out the window again, he noticed that the gray was encroaching across his property. It had already taken the roses and the wisteria vines. Leaves that had once been bright were now dulled and pale, whirling in the wind that had just come up.

Siobhan saw it too, her eyes going wide. "This is why she's there," she murmured.

Dagda could not sit down, some strange sensation in his body making his hands shake. "The beast is loose," he muttered. "It will destroy everything."

"What beast? Do you mean the thing that lives up on the mountain? Why would it come here?"

"The Dubh are the prelude to what comes next. It was my doing that brought them here and now I'm powerless to help."

"Dag, you're scaring me."

Dag turned to face Siobhan, his expression drawn. "I should have known about this. I should never have left here until it was fixed. Katel was trying to tell me, but in my selfishness, I ignored her. Those bastards knew when they sent me down here—they closed the border knowing that earth was about to be destroyed and that I would witness everything I loved annihilated. How can the gods be so cruel?" Dagda began to cry, his face in his hands.

Siobhan put her arms around him. "Dag, please, don't. It's not good for Mior to see you like this," she whispered.

Dagda sucked in breath, turning away from her. "Do you have any idea how I feel, Siobhan? I am responsible for the destruction of the earth. The gods closed the borders long ago. It was my being here that changed it all. Kat will die up there—there is no way a human being can survive the Pinnacle."

Siobhan shook her head. "Kat told me that it began because of imbalances created by your being here, but she said the rest of it was something called Ragnarok. She told me it wasn't your fault."

Dagda's eyebrows lifted. "Ragnarok? When did she say that?"

"She told me after she got back from the Norse realm."

Dagda shook his head, his face turning ashen. "If that's what this is, we are basically doomed."

18

hen Kat woke there was a shadowy figure beside her, a dark hood covering the face. He reached a gnarled hand out and pulled her to her feet. A moment later she was walking beside him, her hand in his. Her ankle was fine now, the pain completely gone. When she turned to look at him, all she could see was the side of the hood he wore. The wind had stopped for the moment, the silence scaring her even more than the maelstrom from before. There was something very eerie about what was going on, including her inability to stop herself from going with him. "Who are you?" she whispered.

He didn't answer.

"Bran's back there. Can't we wait for him?"

This time the man turned, a skeletal face with black holes for eyes visible inside the hood. Kat let out a shriek that echoed, hoping against hope that Bran was hurrying to catch up. And that's when she realized that the baby was no longer inside her sling.

Kat's tongue grew thick, her ability to speak disappearing in her panic. Her legs moved of their own accord, any will she had, taken over by the specter walking beside her. When she tried to ask about Arwen, a babbling litany came out of her mouth that made no sense. Tears streamed down her face, sobs making her hiccup.

It seemed she'd been walking for hours, days even, when the specter stopped. A wall rose up in front of them, as black as the night sky. A chill surged through Kat, her body shaking with cold and fear. "What is this—what do you want with me?"

"I want what you want," a hollow voice said. "An end to this."

"An end to what? I want to open the border."

"And you will get your chance to do so. You will be the one to unleash the evil that has been held back for millennia."

The words rang in her ears, the vision she'd had in which she destroyed the earth rushing across her mind. Now when she looked at him his face was fleshed out, dark eyes boring into hers. "But I want to save the world."

A raven approached, the harsh caw taking their attention upward. Kat cringed as the specter's hood fell back, revealing the terrible face covered in scars. It had been horribly burned at some time in the past. The raven closed its wings tight and dive-bombed, scattering blue-black feathers everywhere. Kat screamed and stumbled backward. A storm arose so fast the air crackled with it, wind churning as lightning struck. Kat could no longer see the raven or the creature, a thin wail coming from her as she realized that her baby had been left behind.

When a strike landed by her, the ground sizzled, electricity coiling like snakes around her feet. As she jumped away the wall of black began to open. Kat fought against the power that pulled her toward it, her screaming shredded by the wind. She could do nothing about it. The last thing she saw was the raven, wings spread, his dark beak covered in blood, before the door swung closed with a resounding boom.

Kat couldn't see anything through the dense blackness. Had she gone blind again? She felt her way along the wall, trying to find a way out.

"Do not waste your energy," a deep voice said, seeming to arise from all around her.

"Who are you—what is this place?"

"It is the Pinnacle and I am the Pinnacle's keeper. Has no one explained this?" the reverberating voice asked.

Kat's heart pounded. This was the creature who had been described as evil incarnate. She took in a deep breath. "I heard you were ancient and that the god's decided to leave you alone."

There was a mirthless laugh. "I have been alone here since the dawn of time. The gods forced this on me."

"I…I only want to open the border between Earth and Otherworld."

"This cannot happen. It is my punishment to see that it is never opened."

"Your punishment? Why?"

"The gods turned their backs on earth long ago because humans no longer believed in them or in the magic they wielded. But recently there was a schism, an unauthorized opening between the two worlds. It caused an uprising here."

Kat had an inkling what this schism might have been. "Was the schism your fault?"

"It was the fault of one of the gods, but I got the blame for it. They accused me of allowing the conduit I guard to send energy back and forth between the two worlds."

"It was my father, the Dagda, who did this."

"Ah—so that is why you have come. You wish to heap more blame on me. It will do you no good. I am not flesh or bone, nor do I feel pain."

"What can I give you in return for helping me open the conduit between worlds?"

"You have a child."

"My baby isn't here."

"And yet he is close."

"You can't have him."

There was a heavy silence before the voice said, "And if I cannot have him, you cannot open the border."

"Why would you want a baby? What are you?"

"The child is a magical being who can help me escape. As to what I am…in human terms I am an essence, a force that can manipulate space and time. Your Fae child would be a great boon to me."

Kat got the distinct impression that whatever this was, it was lonely. "But I love my baby. I could never part with him."

"His life would not be so bad. Once I escape, he would be free to do whatever he wants."

"I will discuss this with his father. But I doubt he will agree."

The door creaked open. "Kat?" Bran called.

Kat ran for the voice, her arms finding him in the darkness. "The creature wants Arwen," she whispered. "Where is he?"

"I sent him away. He's gone."

"Gone where?"

"A door opened and I put him through."

Kat let out a sharp cry, her legs buckling under her. She went down on the stone, tears silently coursing down her cheeks.

"A god deigns to visit?"

"Bran—I'm Bran, the blessed."

"Son of Llyr. I knew your father."

"He came here?"

"Back then the gods came often to the Pinnacle. But you...you are not like the gods who inhabit Otherworld now. You love this woman who petitions me for help. You have given up your god powers for her."

"I do love Kat. Without her I'm empty, lost."

"You do not belong here among these selfish gods. If you help me, I will return your powers."

Kat felt Bran's hands searching for hers. She took hold of his fingers and let him haul her to her feet. "You don't have powers?" she whispered.

"Only the ability to become Raven," he admitted.

"Why didn't you tell me?"

"I was embarrassed to tell you. Your father knows."

Kat pressed her face against his chest. "It's all my fault."

"That I love you? No, Kat. That is the best thing that has ever happened to me."

"What will it be?" the creature bellowed. "The child, or helping me escape this prison? Either way you will get what you want."

"Bran? He said he'll return your powers if we release him."

"I don't give a shit about powers. I never have. Maybe that's why your father hates me so much."

"All we ask for is magic to come back to our world," Kat told the entity. "Neither one of us knows how to release you."

There was a heavy sound like a sigh. "I am bound by my promise to the gods. Breaking that would destroy me. But if one of you, or the child frees me, I will do what you ask."

"And what would that entail?" Bran asked.

"It requires taking this prison down."

"It's solid stone!"

The door opened and the specter arrived. "Time is up," he intoned.

A second later Bran and Kat were alone outside, the heavy doors shut. "Who is the dude in the hood?"

"He brought me up here, took away the pain in my ankle. I think he might be the creature's jailor."

Bran didn't answer as he pulled her with him away from the Pinnacle, his breath coming in gasps as they ran through the dark night. When they finally stopped to rest, she sagged against him. "How will I find Arwen?"

"He's with his father."

"What? How do you know?"

"When the door opened there was a man standing there with pointed ears and eyes like blue sapphires."

Kat sucked in breath. "That's Val. And without Arwen to open the door I have no way of reaching them." She began to cry.

"I wish you could have gone with him," Bran muttered.

"You don't want me here with you?"

Bran let out a muffled sob. "I want you to be safe, Kat,

and with your baby, not stuck here without him and no way to get from here to anywhere."

It took them hours to maneuver down the hill, both of them so tired they could barely put one foot in front of the other. They stumbled often, holding on to each other to keep from falling. "I can't stay in Otherworld, but I have no way out of here. And after all that, what I thought was my destiny came to nothing. The border is still closed."

Bran looped an arm around her shoulders, helping her navigate the uneven ground in the dark. "We'll figure something out. But let's find a place to sleep before we attempt it." The wind came up shortly after that, all thought whipped from their minds as they fought to stay upright. A full-blown hurricane was in the making, the sky darkening even further, wind shrieking around them like beasts of prey. Bran grabbed her hand and took off toward the mountain of rock, trying to find shelter.

Kat couldn't stop crying, her hiccupping sobs carried away by the wind. "If that specter, or whatever he is, hadn't come back, I'm sure we could have worked something out."

Bran stopped and watched her with the bewildered look he always had when her emotions got the best of her. "We can try again," he finally said, pulling her with him toward a shallow fissure in the canyon wall.

But how could they try again when her baby was gone and neither she nor Bran had any powers?

The cave was so small the two of them could barely fit inside. It smelled of animal droppings and dust, but it got them out of the wind. "My baby," Kat kept muttering over and over.

"You'll get him back," Bran reassured her, but she could tell he was only saying it to make her feel better.

She finally fell into an uneasy sleep, her dreams filled with visions of running down one path and up another searching for Arwen. In the morning her breasts were swollen and sore, the pain bringing tears to her eyes. Bran helped her express the milk, both of them bleary-eyed and depressed.

"What do I do now?" she muttered, shivering as she pulled her clothes back into place. "Airmid will find us if we go back to where we were, and I have no way out of here."

"Maybe if you try and contact Val, he'll open a door for you."

Kat shook her head. "Arwen was my only connection to Val."

Bran's gaze met hers, his expression bleak. "We have to get off this mountain," was all he said as he hauled her to her feet.

Kat now knew why Bran never used his god powers. She'd been surprised when he got tired and never tapped into what he had to keep them out of harm's way. It was why he'd been so worried about her before this trip. She would give anything to have her powers back, and yet it seemed that Bran had willingly given his up.

19

Storms tore through the forest, fires flaring as lightning struck the trees. Dagda, Siobhan and Mior huddled inside the shack trying to stay warm and dry as the hurricane raged outside. "Kat was right—this has to be Ragnarok," Dagda muttered. "I should have known it was coming."

"Where is Kat? I thought she was stopping this."

Dagda shook his head, his eyes going dark. "This is what happens when evil is allowed to flourish. I saw it when I was here, the greed and the lack of empathy brewing in the businesses I encountered. I am ashamed of what I was. But I am not the cause of it. One god cannot bring down an entire country."

"When I found out what you were doing, I was horrified. You lived and breathed corruption, Dag. But you changed—I witnessed it."

Dagda shook his head, tears welling. "I'm sorry, Siobhan. If this has anything to do with me, I regret every single day I encouraged the baser natures of human beings. I didn't condemn it, but I didn't start it. This evil was here long before I arrived. And without powers I am unable to stop it or even slow it down."

"And our daughter? Where is she? Why hasn't she returned—it's been weeks now!"

"Perhaps Val collected her. I hope that's the case. As much as I dislike the Elven race, I know that their magic can save Kat. If she's found Bran, I hold little hope for her. That god is ineffectual and weak."

"Why do you feel that way? I liked him."

"You might like him, but he can't keep her safe. Believe me, she's better off with Val."

"She's in love with Bran. Doesn't that count for anything?"

"God damn it, woman! In a situation like this love means nothing! We will soon be fighting for our fucking lives!" Dagda shouted.

Siobhan shushed him and placed a restraining hand on his arm. "You're scaring Mior."

Dagda glared at the boy cowering in the corner. "You'd best buck up, Mior," he growled. "You're the only one here who has any power."

When a limb hit the window with a crack, breaking the glass, Mior began to sob. Rain poured in, puddles forming on the floor. He ran for his mother and buried his face in her skirts.

Siobhan was comforting him when Dagda ripped him out of her arms. "You are not a sniveling baby, Mior. You are half god. Now try some of it out on this fucking storm!"

"I don't know how!"

"Wave your arms, say 'stop!' and mean it!" Dagda instructed.

Mior waved his arms and whispered stop before hurling

himself at his mother again. "I can't!" he cried out, sobbing even louder.

Dagda grabbed his arm and whirled him around to face him. "God damn it, boy! You're my son! Use what I gave you! Say it again and mean it with all your soul!"

"Stop!" Mior yelled. He glanced at his father who waved his hand.

"Again, Mior! Louder this time!"

"Stop!" Mior shouted at the top of his lungs, his little face turning red. There was a sudden cessation of wind, everything going quiet.

Dagda beamed. "I told you, you could do it!" He picked the boy up and whirled him around.

"Dagda, please!" Siobhan pleaded, watching Mior's terrified expression. "He's only four years old."

"And look what he's able to do," Dagda praised, placing the boy on the floor.

A second later the wind came up again, fiercer than before. And this time the roof lifted off the shack and blew away. Icy rain poured in, soaking them.

Dagda grabbed Mior's hand and reached for Siobhan, tugging them out of the shack and running toward the small woods at the back of the property. Once they found a hollow under a group of sycamores they hunkered down like animals, waiting for the storm to move through. When Dagda stared at Mior with narrowed eyes, Mior looked away, hiding his head against his mother and whimpering.

But the storm didn't stop. When the temperatures dropped into the single digits, Dagda ran for the shack to retrieve blankets from a chest, his hair and clothes soaked by the time he got back. Siobhan's teeth were chattering, her arms tight around Mior trying to keep him warm.

The hissing sound of fire could be heard in the distance, downed power poles sending sparks flying. Animals hurtled by, terrified. Birds dropped dead from the dark sky. Sirens raged as background noise, the world outside of where they huddled, filled with screaming and shouting. Mostly it was wind they heard, the high-pitched wail like an animal being slaughtered. Mior tried once again, yelling stop, but it did nothing. After that he was quiet, his eyes shut tight, his arms around his mother.

When Dagda took off, Siobhan was too tired to even ask where he was going. Soon after that the trees over them began to burn. Siobhan wrapped a blanket over the two of them, took Mior's hand and ran.

Dagda waded through knee deep water, searching for Daniel. When he entered his favorite bar, the place was deserted, bottles floating amongst the watery debris that had leaked inside. The windows had all blown out, bits of glass glittering on tables and window sills. It was raining still, gusts sending limbs toppling, the storm turning more and more vicious as the minutes went by. Outside was chaos, people running with blank looks on their faces, many floating face down in the churning water. A gray pall lay across everything, color completely leached away. The sirens had stopped now, any hope of rescuing anyone gone as the hurricane turned into tornados and the fires swept through the town.

Dagda spied the driver sloshing though the water and called out to him. "Can you help us?" Dagda shouted. "My wife, my son—we're stuck up on the hill!"

Daniel eyed him, his face as pale as ash. "Is this your doing?"

Dagda shook his head. "I have no powers now, you know that. How could I manage this, and why would I?"

"Your wife, you say? Siobhan is with you?"

Dagda nodded, pushing the wet hair out of his eyes. "The shack is wrecked and we hid in the woods in back, but..." Dagda stopped when Daniel's gaze went beyond him, over his shoulder. He turned to see Siobhan and Mior sloshing toward them, their clothing soaked, hair plastered to their heads. The blankets had been abandoned along the way, only impeding their progress.

Dagda stumbled toward them. "I left to get Daniel!" he shouted.

Siobhan threw herself into his arms sobbing. "The woods are on fire and the shack is nearly ash." She turned her tear-streaked face to Daniel. "What is going on?"

The man didn't answer, his expression closed. When Daniel took hold of her arm and began a slow slog down the hill, Dagda picked up Mior and followed him.

20

Bran and Kat had been walking for nearly a full day when a door appeared in front of them. When it opened Val was standing on the other side holding Arwen. The baby's face was bright red from crying. "He needs his mother," Val said.

Kat rushed through the opening before she could think, suddenly aware that Bran was still on the other side. She turned to look at him, meeting his troubled gaze.

Val nodded to the Celtic god. "Come through."

Bran raised his eyebrows and looked around him before he stepped over the threshold. A second later the door was gone. Kat had already loosened her clothes and was feeding the crying baby, tears tracking down her cheeks as she gazed down.

They were inside Val's garden, the aroma of roses and the sound of birds startling after the mountains of obsidian and the ice-filled winds. When the baby had his fill and fell asleep, Kat turned to Val. "Thank you," she murmured.

Val smiled. "He's just as I pictured him."

Kat turned to Bran worriedly. "Bran, this is Val."

Bran nodded, a look of uncertainty on his face. "I gathered that. I appreciate being allowed in."

"You are Kat's love. I couldn't leave you behind—it would have destroyed her."

Kat watched the two very different men in her life, one so pale and ethereal, the other ruddy and wide-shouldered. She felt pulled by both of them, confusion entering her like a throng of sparrows.

"You are in need of rest and food," Val said, leading the way toward the house. "Later we will talk."

Inside Isabel appeared to show Bran and Kat to a room Kat had never seen before. The baby slept on as she took off her clothes and climbed into bed. Bran was hesitant, his expression confused as he joined her. He still wore his trousers and his shirt, as though worried that Val might burst in and be angry that they were together.

"It's okay, Bran. He knows we love each other. You can relax."

Bran shook his head. "That man loves you. I could see it in his eyes. I could never relax in his house knowing how he feels about you."

But Kat was too tired to listen, her eyes closing as she drifted into sleep.

It was dark when Kat woke, the house quiet. She slipped from bed leaving Bran and the baby asleep as she headed down the stairs to the kitchen. In the dining room she came upon Val sitting in a slice of moonlight, his pale features drawn. A tankard sat on the table in front of him.

He looked up when he heard her bare feet on the floor, his crystalline eyes shimmering when he turned them to her. "You are in need of sustenance," he said.

Kat was naked, her body shivering as she wrapped her arms around herself. "Yes. I think that's why I woke up."

He rose and went into the kitchen, coming back with a loaf of freshly baked bread and some cheese. "Eat, Kat. You have grown thin since the last time I saw you."

"How is that possible?" she joked. "I still carry the baby fat."

He shook his head. "The trauma you've been through since then has been extreme. I've been keeping an eye on you."

Kat abruptly recalled the birth. "Val, did you really deliver Arwen?" she asked, picking up a piece of cheese.

He nodded. "And I've been able to watch over you because of the connection between us."

She added a slice of bread to her snack, chewing hungrily. "I felt you a few times. Bran took what happened between us well, but I know he worries."

"He knows how I feel about you. I'm a threat."

"He's not like that. He understands."

"No man understands when they are face to face with it. He can see my hunger for you."

Kat met his translucent eyes, her cheeks growing hot. She had feelings for him too, her memories of their time together rising up in her mind as they stared at one another. She moved to where he sat and leaned down to kiss him lightly on the lips, but instead she was pulled into his arms and the kiss became passionate. Her ability to resist him drifted away as he rose from the chair, picked her up in his arms and carried her to his bedroom. She was on his bed with him hovering over her when he paused, his swirling eyes meeting hers. "Is this what you want?"

She wanted to say no, to run from him, but her body had other ideas. Kat couldn't speak at all as her arms went wide to welcome him in. When he entered her, she cried out, molten with desire. When it was over, she slept beside him, Bran all but forgotten in the magical dreamworld where she found herself.

Kat woke alone, realization of where she was sending adrenaline coursing through her. She jumped from the bed. Her milk had come in. Horror washed over her as she searched for her clothes and found nothing there. When the door opened, she turned to hide her nakedness, afraid of who it might be.

"I have the baby," Val said, placing him in her arms. "I'll get your clothes."

"But where is...?" The door shut behind him. She was in bed feeding Arwen when he arrived again, carrying a dress and her underthings.

"Bran?"

"He's in the garden."

"Does he know?"

"He came down with the baby this morning, said Arwen was hungry and you weren't there. I told him I'd find you."

"My gods," Kat murmured. "What will I say?"

"Tell him I bewitched you. You did know I have this power."

Kat stared at him. "Are you serious? He'll never believe that, and neither do I... what happened last night was..."

"Sudden, unexpected, impossible to resist? It was unfair of me and I regret it."

"You regret what we did?"

151

"Yes, I do. You are in love with another man and I used my magic to lure you into my bed."

"You didn't give me another baby, did you?"

Val smiled and shook his head. "That would be very unkind and would certainly signal the end of you and Bran."

"I think it might anyway, even without a baby."

"He doesn't have to know. I can make it so he doesn't suspect at all."

Kat put the sleeping baby down on the bed and rose to dress. "I cannot believe what I did. It's not like me at all."

"You *are* attracted to me. If it wasn't for that I'd never have managed it."

"You're not kidding, are you? You really put a love spell on me?"

Val nodded, chagrined. "I couldn't help myself. There you were, standing naked in the moonlight. Didn't you realize what that might do to me?"

Kat frowned. "I didn't expect to see you in the middle of the night, and besides that, I had no nightclothes."

"Get dressed and come down to breakfast. I'll go down now and put a forgetting spell on Bran. Just act natural, Kat, and he'll never suspect. We have many important things to discuss today."

Kat watched him leave and then pulled on the dress he'd left her. It was similar to the brown dress with its shimmering fabric. But how would she explain the clothes? She picked up the baby and left his room, her mind whirling with confusion.

As it happened explaining the dress was the least of her worries, Bran already distraught when she arrived in the dining room. "Val says earth is under siege," he told her, wide-eyed. "It's burning out of control."

Kat sat in a chair cradling the baby against her. She glanced at the Fae man sitting at the head of the table. "What's happened?"

"Ragnarok has begun," he intoned, his crystalline gaze meeting hers.

Kat quickly looked away, the knowledge of how he worked his spells all too clear.

"Earth will come to an end if the borders aren't opened."

"We tried, didn't we?" she said, staring at Bran. "That creature refused to help."

"What creature is that?" Val asked, leaning forward.

"Bran and I went to the Pinnacle and talked to the guardian there. He wanted Arwen."

Val's eyes narrowed. "Why would he want Arwen?"

"He said the baby's magic could release him from his vow and then the

magic could flow between the worlds again."

Val frowned. "The Pinnacle is outside of any known realm. It houses the most

powerful being in our section of the cosmos. You are lucky you came out of there alive."

"He didn't seem dangerous—what I got from him was sadness and frustration at what the gods had done."

Val laughed. "Do not feel sorrow for him. Compared to him you are nothing, Kat."

"That's certainly true." While earth was burning, she'd been in Val's bed, the shame of it turning her cheeks scarlet. "Did you know about all this when we got here yesterday?"

"Yes. It began before you arrived."

"Why didn't you tell us?" Kat cried out. When the baby woke up and let out a thin wail, she rocked him against her.

"Kat, calm down," Bran said, placing his hand on her arm. "Val knew how exhausted we were. He was trying to let us rest for a moment."

Kat looked from Bran to Val, fury burning like a hot ember in her chest. She jumped up from the table and hurried outside, the baby held tight in her arms.

She was sitting on a bench crying when Bran joined her sometime later. "Val says there are things we can do to stop this."

"Val says? That Fae bastard led us on, Bran, he should have told us right away."

"Kat, listen to yourself. He's Arwen's father. He's only trying to help. He told me there's a way to open the borders between the Norse world and Earth."

"And what will that do? If we open the Norse borders it could make things worse!"

Bran took Arwen out of her arms to soothe him. "Why are so angry? And where were you this morning?"

"I...I took a walk," she lied, looking away. "In order to stop Ragnarok I have to bring the magic back. That means a direct line between Otherworld and Earth—the gods have to help if Earth is to survive."

"There are gods here, as well as the Fae. Why not them?"

"I...I don't know," Kat said, dissolving into tears once again. "I don't know how to do anything anymore."

When Bran put his arm around her, she shrugged it off, too ashamed to let him comfort her.

"You're probably right about the borders between here

and earth. Val told me that Alfheim is the only Norse realm unaffected."

Kat gazed up at him, wiping at her tears. "It's the end of the world if we can't stop it, Bran. And I have no powers— none at all." But as Kat lamented this, her hysterical voice rising, rain poured down from a cloudless sky and her waving fingers left trails of rainbow colors.

"You have the baby's magic," Bran said, watching her.

But Kat knew that this didn't come from Arwen; this was Val's essence left inside her. "Did you do this on purpose?" she shouted when she saw Val heading toward them.

A look of bewilderment crossed his face. "Do what? The baby is half yours."

"You know what I mean," she continued, glaring at him.

"Kat, what is wrong with you?" Bran asked.

"Send us back to Earth, now!" she screamed, her anger causing a lightning strike that narrowly missed them.

"Your wish is my command," Val said bowing. A second later a door appeared.

But when it opened Bran grabbed Kat, holding her back. Slanted rain poured down, the sounds of screaming and crying accompanying the raging fires sweeping across the forests. Buildings burned unimpeded; the streets were flooded.

A second later the door closed and disappeared, a shimmer all that remained.

Kat bent at the waist, her sobs causing storm clouds to mass above them. Wind came up, scattering leaves and sending birds careening out of control. "You must stop," Val said, taking hold of her. "Your power is causing problems."

Kat glanced up at him, her anger replaced with exhaustion and sadness. "It's so much worse than I imagined. What can I do?"

Val pulled her into his arms, nodding to Bran over Kat's head as she pressed against him. He stroked her hair and muttered an incantation. When he released her a moment later her tears had dried.

"Are these my powers or yours?" she asked him.

Val glanced quickly at Bran before turning back to her. "Why would they be my powers, Kat?"

"You know why," she whispered.

Bran moved close, his eyes narrowing. "What happened between you two?"

"Nothing happened," Val said. "Kat is referring to Arwen. She doesn't trust that what's going on here is hers and hers alone."

"How can it be, when a day ago I had nothing?"

"You are in a magical realm now and your powers have been restored."

Kat thought about her anger, her distrust of Val, and how unimportant it all was in the face of what was happening to her home. She reached for the baby in Bran's arms. "I've been such a fool."

The garden shimmered, as though a mystical light had been turned on, birds of every color flitting around Kat's head and landing on her arms. Bran took her free hand in his and twined his fingers through hers as they followed Val back to the house.

"I almost had her," the far dorocha muttered.

"Why didn't you kill her?" Carmun shrieked. Her hair was wild, her face ugly and contorted into an expression of hate.

The shadow creature stared at her. "Things happened too quickly. The creature…"

"Do not blame your ineptitude on the creature! I trusted you to do as I asked and you have failed me. If you are not successful the next time, I will…"

The specter grabbed her wrist. "You will *what?*"

She twisted out of his grasp. "I will destroy you," she muttered.

He laughed then, the terrible sound lifting into the air and echoing. "Oh, I will be successful, but not because of your threats, my Queen." He grabbed her from behind and held her against him as she struggled. And when she finally stopped, he turned her to face him. "We are alike, you and I. There is nothing you can do to hurt me. I am the power of the Pinnacle and it is my magic that has kept the creature trapped through millennia. Do not sell me short."

"Oh, I *can* hurt you," she murmured, her fingers moving through his hair. "It is our connection that has allowed you to do this. Without my sorcery you are nothing."

Taking her cue, he pressed against her. "You will never hurt me, because if you did you would not have this."

The goddess let out a little cry, the realization of the truth of what he'd said, drilling into her as she submitted to his advances. He *would* kill her nemesis because he always obeyed her wishes. But he was also powerful in his own right, a force to be reckoned with. This was no different than the many other times they'd worked together. And if it meant enjoying what he had to give, then, so be it. There weren't many who had the nerve or even the fortitude to approach her in this way. Her looks put them off, as did her manner. "I expect it to be done soon," she murmured.

"It will be."

22

Val led the way to the dining room and sat at the head of the table, gesturing to the benches on either side of him. "Plans need to be discussed."
Isabelle bustled in a moment later with tea and savory cakes, placing them in the middle of the table.

"And quickly if you want to contain the destruction," Val continued.

"Or reverse it," Bran added.

"An entry must be opened from Alfheim to Earth to allow the magic to flow. How do these doors work? Would it take more than one?" Kat asked, picking up the teapot.

Val picked up a biscuit and bit into it, chewing for a moment before he said, "They are normally used to walk from one realm to another and are only open for a few seconds. But since my realm is untouched by Ragnarok, perhaps we can find a way to open one for a bit longer."

Kat nodded. "If magic flows from here would it stop the devastation?"

"Fae magic is the strongest magic I know. And with the baby you should be able to curtail the storms. I have never tried such a thing, so I cannot guarantee its success."

Kat poured tea into three cups and passed them around. She sipped and thought, barely aware of the baby cooing in the sling against her chest. At the moment her tears had dried, but she felt them in her throat and behind her eyes. She was overwhelmed and exhausted from the sleepless night, ashamed of what she'd done and feeling the weight of the world sitting on her shoulders. When she glanced at Bran the tears welled, her ability to hold them back disappearing as she fought to gain the upper hand.

Val placed his hand on hers. "You do understand that it is the hormones that are causing your anger and tears?"

Kat pulled her hand out from under his. "I haven't felt myself, it that's what you mean. I can't seem to stop crying."

Val nodded, glancing at Bran. "As time goes on the hormones will settle. But until then I have an herbal remedy for you to take." He rose and hurried toward the map room, arriving a few minutes later with a small muslin pouch. "Take a pinch of this every morning and every evening."

Kat took the pouch from him, opening it to sniff the aromatic herbs. Was this some love potion that would bring her running to his bed when she least expected it? "What's in it?"

"Vitex to balance your hormones, motherwort for anxiety, and skullcap for your nerves." He smiled. "And I laced it with a bit of Fae magic." His gaze met hers. "Nothing untoward."

Kat took a pinch in her finger and downed it with the tea left in her cup. "I hope it helps."

"It will. Now that that issue is cleared up, how about we discuss the way forward?"

In the end things did not go as planned. They never do.

Ragnarok reached Alfheim early the next morning. Warriors appeared on the horizon, riding giant horses. Val alerted Bran and Kat who were still in bed. "You will ride out and meet them," Val told them.

"This was my vision way back when I was searching for you," Kat whispered to Bran as she rose to dress. "You and I were together on horseback."

Bran nodded, glancing at the Fae man who was watching Kat pull on her clothes. "I had the same vision."

Val left them and headed back downstairs to watch from the window in the main room. When they joined him a few minutes later Val was still standing there. "My horses are strong and in good shape, my hounds as well. I suggest that you leave Arwen with me and follow your vision to its conclusion."

Kat frowned. "I don't how to ride."

"You'll remember soon enough." He waved his hand. "Go! I have magic to put in place to keep the Berserkers away."

"Why would Odin's soldiers attack you?"

"This is Ragnarok. There is no logic to any of it."

Bran grabbed her hand and tugged her toward the stables. He quickly saddled two enormous black horses, and gave her a leg up. The hounds circled them, waiting. "Shall we lock the dogs in the stable or let them come along?"

Kat glanced down at the square muzzles, the strength and power they exuded. She'd never seen dogs this large. "I say take them along."

Bran nodded and vaulted onto his horse and led the way out through the gates. When they looked back Val was watching them, the baby in his arms. He nodded and headed inside.

"He could have set up the magic, left the baby with Isabelle and come with us. He knows more about what to do than we do."

"Speak for yourself," Bran muttered, kicking his horse into a gallop. "This was our vision, not his. And if I were you, I'd feel safer knowing my baby was in Val's hands!" he shouted over his shoulder. When Kat's horse took off after him, she squeezed her legs tight around his sides and clung to his mane. It was at that moment that she noticed the sword hilt shining by Bran's side, the scabbard bumping against his leg.

Kat was disoriented, her mind refusing to believe what she was seeing. It was as though she'd entered another reality where she'd lived as another person altogether. She settled into the horse's rhythm, feeling like she'd done this a million times. And she was somehow now dressed in chain mail, a sword at her side. When had that happened? But Alfheim was filled with magic, magic they needed on planet Earth.

When they came to the ridge Bran pulled his horse up, stopping to take a look at what lay in the valley. The hounds bayed, rushing around them in a frenzy. "Looks like we'll be in the thick of it soon," Bran muttered. When he glanced at Kat his eyes went wide. "What the hell?"

"What?"

"Have you seen yourself?"

"How can I see myself, Bran. Have you seen *yourself?*" she asked, marveling at the look of him on the horse and the chainmail he wore.

Bran let out a low chuckle. "You look like a Valkyrie. Not sure how this is happening, but whatever it is, seems like it will stand us in good stead."

"Am I expected to kill with this sword?" Kat asked, glancing down at the scabbard.

"If it comes to that, I would say yes." He scanned into the valley, his hand at his brow to shade his eyes. "Not sure which side we need to dispatch."

"Perhaps neither. Maybe our job is to deflect and turn them away from each other."

Bran turned to her. "That's an interesting take on it."

"If this is Ragnarok, it's my job to stop it, not add to it."

"Lead on, milady!" Bran called out, waiting for her to head down the hill. The hounds took off ahead of them, the baying sending chills down Kat's spine. This was the most exciting thing she'd ever done, she thought to herself as she kicked her horse into a canter.

In the valley the fighting stopped as the warriors eyed the two strangers approaching at a gallop. Already the dogs were wild around them, viciously biting at their horse's heels and snapping at any man who happened to be on foot. Kat noticed she had a horn around her neck and picked it up to blow a resounding deep tone. A second later it began to rain, a heavy mist blanketing the entire valley. Shouts rose up out of the fog as Kat circled them, the maelstrom growing stronger each time she blew. By the time she was finished, the horses had gone wild, many riders bucked off as the winds whirled around them.

"Let's go!" Bran shouted.

Kat watched him gallop off just as lightning struck. Her horse shied, nearly unseating her as the grasses caught fire. She whistled to the hounds and took off after Bran. When she looked behind her it was utter chaos, loose horses and men and women rushing around to put out the fires amid the worsening storms. Friend and foe worked side by side.

When she reached Bran, a door was standing open in front of him. She couldn't see what was on the other side. But when Bran headed in, she followed after him.

The horses turned into mist and disappeared on the way through, Bran and Kat landing in a heap on the other side. "Where are we?" Kat asked, glancing around at the green meadows, the hills rising away from them to turn into blue mountains in the distance. Everything was glassy and bright.

Bran shook his head. "I don't recognize it."

Kat pushed herself up and dusted herself off, surprised to see that she was wearing the wool dress Val had supplied her with. Bran was now in loose trousers and his blue tunic, swords and chainmail gone. "Were you thinking something when the door opened?"

"Of course, I was thinking *something*. But I can't remember what."

"Come on, Bran. You were galloping along and then a door appears? It had to be you who conjured it."

Bran frowned. "All I remember is thinking how smart you

were to do what you did down there. I guess I might have been imagining us making love. But I think about that all the time. It just seemed right that we should go through."

"Where did you think it led?"

Bran gazed around at the mountains, the wide blue dome above them. "Either Earth or Otherworld, but it doesn't seem to be either place."

"Maybe it's a part of Otherworld where you've never been."

"I've explored every inch of my homeland, Kat."

"But not the Pinnacle."

"The Pinnacle isn't part of Otherworld."

Kat gazed at the grass shimmering under a cloudless sky. Birds were singing. "It's beautiful, wherever it is. Shall we explore?"

"Aren't you worried about Arwen and saving the earth?"

Kat stared at him. "I…I hate to say this but I feel happy here. It feels like everything is fine."

"And yet it isn't. You have a dreamy look on your face I've never seen before, and that assessment of our predicament is not at all like you. How do you propose we get back to your baby, or do you even care?"

Kat stared into the distance. "We were just warriors riding horses. Maybe it will take me a moment to regroup."

"No, Kat. Something is off here. This isn't real."

Kat leaned down to pick a blade of grass. "It feels real enough."

Bran shook his head, gazing around. "We've stepped into an alternate reality."

"So what? I like it here," Kat said stubbornly.

Bran let out a heavy sigh. "We have to get out of here,"

he muttered. "Say the words or do whatever you do to find another door."

"You want to leave?"

Bran took hold of her shoulders and shook her, hard. "Wake up! This is a fake place and the longer we stay the harder it will be to leave!"

Kat pulled away from him. "Where shall we go?"

Bran pressed his lips together. "Try Val's place, Kat. You need to feed Arwen."

Kat glanced down at the wet spots on the bodice of her dress. "Oh," she said absently.

It took a full five minutes before a door appeared and even longer for Bran to coax Kat to come with him once the door opened. He finally picked her up and carried her through. They ended up in the dining room inside Val's house. The sky outside had turned to dusk, night quickly coming on. A meal had been left untouched on the table, the sound of singing coming from the kitchen.

Footsteps echoed from the direction of the stairs as Val appeared carrying Arwen. "Where have you been?" he demanded harshly.

Kat didn't answer, only pulling the dress down to expose one breast and reaching for the baby.

Val handed her Arwen and turned to Bran. "What's going on?"

"We walked through a door into some alternate world and Kat ended up like this." He gestured to the vacant look on her face, the absence of any feeling regarding the nursing baby.

"I can *hear* you," she said in a sing-song voice. She began to hum.

Val blanched. "How long were you there?"

"Twenty minutes—a half hour?"

"You were gone for five hours, Bran. If you were where I think you were, that world will take your life. You're lucky you escaped at all."

"It was beautiful," Kat said dreamily, handing the baby back to him and pulling up her dress.

"It might be beautiful, but it's also dangerous," Val told her, trying to get her attention. When she continued to stare into the distance, he handed the baby to Bran and grabbed her chin. "Look at me, Kat!" he demanded.

His eyes bored into hers, an incantation muttered under his breath as he held her head steady. Her eyes glazed over as she sank into his arms. "Will you make love to me, Val?"

Val looked horrified for a moment before he let go of her and clapped his hands.

Kat's eyes flew open, her gaze going to Bran and Arwen before landing on Val. "What happened?"

Val let out a sigh. "You were lost to yourself. Any longer in that realm and you wouldn't have returned."

Kat's mouth dropped open as she took in the expression on Bran's face. "What did I do?" she whispered.

Bran handed her the baby and turned away, his measured pace taking him up the stairs toward the bedroom.

Kat stared after him in shock. "He knows about us."

"It seems he does."

"What should I do?"

"Let him process."

Kat sat heavily at the table, her head in her hands. "Why? Why would I tell him?"

"You didn't have to tell him. It was how you reacted to me that made him aware. He's not stupid." Val sat with her for ten minutes before he rose from the table. "Go to him, Kat."

Once she heard Val's bedroom door shut, Kat left the dining room and headed up the stairs. When she arrived at the bedroom she and Bran shared, the door was locked. "Bran? Please let me in. We need to talk." There was no answer and after a while she gave up and went away. She spent the night sleeping in a chair in the dining room, the baby in his sling against her chest. She cried quietly until she finally fell into an uneasy sleep.

In the morning she headed up the stairs again. This time the door was unlocked, but when she went inside Bran was gone. The window was wide open, two shiny black feathers left behind on the sill.

Kat picked up the feathers, smoothing them between her fingers. She pressed them to her nose before letting them float away on the breeze. A sinking sensation went through her, her eyes filling with tears.

When Val arrived for breakfast Kat was already there, a heavy cape around her shoulders. "Bran's gone and I'm leaving to find him."

Val nodded. "I saw the raven fly away."

"You hate me too, don't you? Can't say that I blame you. I've been horrible to both of you."

Val covered her hand with his own. "You know how I feel about you. As far as Bran, this happened because of that alternate world you were in. He's proud. This new revelation has to be hard on him."

"He was so good about the baby, Val."

"He loves you."

"Not so sure that will be enough. Do you think he's still in Alfheim?"

"As Raven I would imagine he flew to Otherworld."

Kat remembered her trip here as hummingbird, the bird's ability to skirt areas and find ways in and out. She could no longer count on that. "That means I'll have to open a door. Can I do that?"

Val glanced at the baby sleeping in her arms. "As long as you have Arwen, yes."

"If it's Arwen who opens the doors, how did that other one open? Arwen wasn't with us at the time."

The Fae man looked away, his expression closing down. "I cannot answer for sure, but I have an inkling of who it was."

"Who?"

"The same creature you encountered at Odin's castle. This dark witch and her minions are after you."

"But why leave me there?"

"Because it renders you impotent, that's why. There are powers at work that would like nothing better than to see the entire universe destroyed."

Kat frowned and glanced at the baby in her arms. "You mean the same one who took my memories."

"Correct. Now hurry before Raven is completely out of reach." He pulled her to her feet and walked out with her. "The best place to open a door is at the edge of the woods at the top of the hill. It's a highly charged area and the energies there will help."

"That's how I got here the first time."

Val took her in his arms and kissed the top of her head. "Please bring Arwen to see me from time to time."

"Or you'll track me down?" Kat asked, attempting humor.

"If I have to, yes. I want Arwen to know his father."

She nodded, holding back the tears that had been threatening all morning. Their eyes met once more before she turned and went through the gate and headed toward the hill. The memory of fake Freya intruded in her mind, the possibility of the witch and her cohorts trying to destroy the world sending terror coursing through her body. She had no power, other than the baby in her arms. How could she combat such evil?

23

Siobhan climbed into the car beside Daniel, pulling Mior onto her lap. Dagda was in the back leaning forward. "Where is this bunker? I hope it isn't flooded."

Daniel had stolen a car, taking them up and over the mountain into a different town. "It isn't flooded, man. I told you I've been staying there since this shit began. Now sit back and quit whining."

Dagda wanted to shout at him, to demand respect, but in the circumstances he felt powerless. If they didn't find shelter, they'd all die.

His land was under two feet of water, the town of Pasadena washed away. How the fires continued during the rain he had no idea, only that the forests he'd come to love were gone. Rats swam in the water that cascaded downhill, human bodies floating. There had been so much death it was hard to imagine anyone living through the wreckage.

The bunker was set into a mountain, the heavy steel doors shutting on them once they were all inside. Daniel lit an oil lamp and carried it high to show the way. "Watch out, there are steps here and they're steep."

Dag carried Mior and let Siobhan go ahead of him, his anger at his own weakness growing with every step he took. Why was Daniel in charge? He should be the one leading this party. When they arrived at another door he waited in the dark as Daniel unlocked it.

"It's fitted out with everything we'll need for several months," Daniel said, swinging the door open. He lit another lamp that was set into the wall and headed toward a makeshift kitchen. "Food and drink here, bedrooms over there." He pointed past the chairs and couches toward a couple of doors on the other side of the room. "Make yourselves at home," he said, pulling a couple of beers from the gas-powered refrigerator. A generator hummed from somewhere in the background. He handed a bottle to Dagda before making his way to a couch and flopping down.

"Bathroom?" Siobhan asked, watching Mior's agitation.

Daniel pointed and Siobhan hurried across the room with Mior in tow.

"How long have you had this?" Dagda asked, lowering into a chair.

"Since before you left, old man. I knew you'd set some shit in motion and I was damned if I was going to go down with the rest of them because of your crazy crap."

"I thought you respected me and what I was doing."

Daniel scoffed and took a swig from the bottle. "I did for a while, but when I saw how you treated your wife, I changed my mind."

Dagda drank from the bottle, trying control his anger. The man was a grifter. He should never have hired him back then. "I paid you well, Daniel."

"That's true enough. But no amount of money can buy loyalty to a man who cares nothing for anyone except himself."

"I love my wife—I always have."

"That's not what I saw. You're damned lucky she's here with you now."

When Siobhan and Mior reappeared, Dagda rose to give them his seat. "I want to look around," he said, moving toward the closed doors. Once he was in another room, he gave way to his anger, his hands turning into fists. His feebleness repulsed him, his weakness making him feel sick to his stomach. He wanted to punch Daniel, to make him pay for what he'd said. But this body wasn't up to it.

When he returned, Daniel and Siobhan were sitting on the couch talking. When they heard him, they both turned to look at him. Was that a guilty expression on his wife's face?

"Daniel has been telling me how he built this place. Isn't it remarkable? What a feat of engineering." Her eyes went dark. "So many people dying out there. I wish we could bring them here. There's a lot of room from what I've seen."

"It's too late," Daniel said, placing his empty bottle on the coffee table. "If I tried to find them now, I'd get swept away with the rest of them. I'm sorry too, but we left it too long."

"Some others must have taken precautions as you did," Siobhan said hopefully.

"I'm sure so," Daniel assured her. "Are you hungry? I have lots of frozen food and tons of cans of this and that."

"Mior?"

"Yes, I'm hungry," the boy said, casting a nervous look at his father.

Dagda narrowed his eyes, wondering how long he could stand being in the same vicinity as Daniel. As a god he would have killed him by now.

When Daniel went into the kitchen to heat up food, Siobhan asked," Where is our daughter, Dag? And her baby?"

"Arwen," Mior supplied. "Where is Arwen?"

"I wish I knew. But she's a goddess, she can manage."

Siobhan's eyes filled with tears. "Not anymore."

"Arwen will help!" Mior crowed, racing around the room. "He's a wizard!"

But Dagda barely heard him, his attention on the anger coursing through him about being a broken-down old man. How did humans stand this? He was no longer immortal, maybe it was time to end it.

"Dag?" Did you hear what I said?"

Dagda turned to his wife, unable to focus on her because of the splitting headache that had just arrived in his skull. He grabbed his head with both hands. *What the fuck is this now?*

Siobhan hurried toward him. "Dag? What's wrong?"

"I have a motherfucker of a headache," he managed to mutter.

Siobhan put cool hands on his forehead and massaged his temples. "Lie down on the couch and let me work on you."

He did as she asked, unable to think past the pain. She sat next to him and rubbed his skull, her fingers working magic as she massaged. He let out a groan, his eyes closing on the room, the presence of Daniel, and the disgusting smell of whatever Daniel was cooking.

"Is it better?"

Dagda opened his eyes, taking in her worried expression. Daniel was right—he was lucky to have her. He nodded.

"I worried that maybe you were having a stroke," she confided. "A bad headache can be a symptom."

"What in hell is a stroke?"

"Never mind. Whatever you had is gone now. It was more than likely due to stress."

Dagda took her hands in his. "Do you know how much I love you?"

Siobhan smiled. "I love you too. Having you with me again is...I don't have words to describe it."

Dagda pulled her down and kissed her.

"Get a room, you two."

Siobhan pulled away from Dagda, her cheeks turning scarlet as Dagda pushed himself up. "She was helping me with my headache."

Daniel laughed. "Is that what that was? Soups on, folks. Come and get it."

As the days went by Dagda grew more and more agitated, his anger breaking through on more than one occasion. He and Siobhan had been forced to share a room with Mior, a situation that made it impossible for him to approach his wife. He was positive Daniel had arranged this on purpose.

There were many rooms available.

Siobhan was restless too, her legs twitching with nerves when she crossed them. "I think if I can't get out of here soon, I will lose my mind," she muttered.

"I'll check things out today and see what's happening," Daniel told her. "I'm only trying to keep you safe."

When Siobhan smiled up at him Dagda nearly lost it. "Safe is one thing, prisoners is another," he growled.

But that was only the beginning. In the days to follow their lives would be tested in ways they couldn't even imagine.

First it was Daniel's attentions to his wife, and then it was Mior treating Daniel like a long-lost uncle. Daniel lapped it up, his gaze going to Dagda as Siobhan asked him questions and the boy hovered around his legs. Daniel was young and virile, his body strong. Dagda watched them, his sense of who he was disappearing in a cloud of dusty smoke. He was nothing, nobody. She would be better off with a man who could satisfy her and raise her son properly. Dagda realized now that he was no match for the man, his need for Siobhan lost in his inability to perform. So far, he hadn't tried, but whenever he was alone and attempted to test it, nothing happened.

And when his anger burst out, as it did with more and more regularity, Siobhan would chide him and then try and make up to him in a way that he found condescending. When she did that, he pushed her away, making things worse. His son yelled at him often, and when he tried to discipline the boy, either Daniel or his wife would tell him to stop.

There was a razor in the bathroom that tempted him, its blade sharp. Every morning he looked at it and ran his thumb across the edge, drawing a thin line of blood. It wouldn't take much to finish himself off.

24

K at reached the spot Val had told her about, the energies making themselves known at the same moment the baby began to fuss. "Really, Arwen? Now?" She sat cross-legged to feed him, her eyes closing as he nursed. It was a pleasurable experience that always soothed her moods, no matter what was going on. While he fed, she allowed her mind to open to what was around her. Fae energies swirled with colors behind her closed eyelids, a hum in her ears. "This is definitely the place," she murmured. But something disturbed her, the idea of opening a door and leaving Alfheim bringing a frisson of fear. What if the door led back to that horrible place? If Val knew who had opened that door, it could happen again. And then she wondered if he'd been lying, that Val had opened it. Maybe he'd hoped that Bran would walk through without her and be lost forever. She shook her head, dismissing the idea.

Val was devoted to her happiness and he'd been nothing but kind to Bran. But a tendril of doubt remained. Val had bewitched her again, and what she'd done with him as a result, had threatened her future life. Val was a magical being who wanted what he wanted. Even though he said he did, Kat doubted that he cared much about Bran. The Fae man would be happy if she spent the rest of her life in a bewitched haze, as long as it was in his bed.

She let those thoughts go and concentrated on Bran, hoping the Fae magic would help her discover where he'd gone. When she had a vision of Raven, forlorn and on a branch in a forest of dead trees, her eyes flew open. He wasn't here and he wasn't in Otherworld. He was on Earth. And from the look of it, he was in the forest above Dagda's shack.

She hurried to rearrange the baby in his sling before visualizing the woods she knew so well. "Open sesame," she muttered. A second later a door was there, standing open. She hurried through.

Raven was still on the branch when she sloshed through the mud and debris to reach him. "Bran," she said softly, reaching out her hand.

He flew to her and landed on her shoulder, his talons clutching her cape. He pressed his downy head against hers. She smoothed his feathers, the tears she'd been keeping at bay finally bursting forth. "I would never want to hurt you," she murmured. "Please come back to me." But instead of heeding her wishes, the bird lifted on wide wings and disappeared into the thick fog.

Kat watched him go, a pain in her heart so strong it felt like it might break apart. He'd just said good-bye. When the baby let out a sharp cry, she glanced down at him. He was clutching a raven feather in his fist and the tip had pierced his skin. She had not seen the raven do anything to Arwen, but the blood was there. And the sight of the red in contrast to the gray world was startling. She carefully dabbed the blood away and gently removed the feather from Arwen's hand, placing it in the pocket of the cape. After that she took another pinch of the herbal concoction.

When Kat attempted to get down the hill, she discovered that all roads were blocked. They had either flooded or there was so much floating trash that they were impossible to navigate.

Her father's property was now gray, her father's shack, a pile of ash. The sycamores behind his house had burned, leaving smoldering charcoal stumps. When tears came again, she brushed them away. Anger at herself and the situation suffused her with a raw energy. At the very least she had to find her family.

Winds had stopped for the moment, the sirens silent in the gray mist of morning. She saw no one and heard nothing, other than the wind whistling through the crackling limbs of trees that had burned. Anxiety entered her like a coiled snake, making its way from her solar plexus to her heart, destroying confidence as it traveled. She held the baby close, wishing she'd left him with his father. But when he suddenly waved his baby fingers and created a spiral of rainbow colors around them, she re-evaluated that thought. The colors moved off in all directions, latching onto the dull trees and sending tendrils into the branches. The area around them was soon full of green and brown. "Arwen," she gasped. When she looked down, his eyes swirled with light. It was the first time he'd smiled.

Kat took the baby out of the sling, hoping he would

continue with coloring the world, but instead he fell asleep. "Can I do it?" she asked herself, waving her fingers. Sure enough, colors flowed from the tips of her fingers, landing on the gray mud and turning it brown, swirling around the wildflowers and turning them yellow and blue. It felt as though she was painting a picture with her fingers. "I can't do this for the entire world," she muttered as her arm grew tired. As her hope vanished so did the color, the trees returning to gray. The baby slept on.

Kat wandered for miles, skirting around flooded areas and searching for the living. She was drenched and shivering, her dress and legs covered with mud and slime. Her boots had leaked, her feet cold and wet.

The water had receded some, leaving great swaths of sludge and debris, including bodies of the drowned. When she ran into a man with hollow eyes she stopped. "Do you have shelter?" she asked him.

He stared at her as though she wasn't really there and then turned away, walking slowly along the edge of a flooded area. She watched him go, afraid of what would become of him. He was one of the ones who had blanked out.

The only other people she saw alive were a group of thug-like individuals carrying rifles. They were talking in loud voices and waving their rifles around, hunting for something to shoot, no doubt. She hid from them and headed in another direction.

By now she'd given up the expectation that her parents were close by, expecting to see them on the ground along with the others. Her dread grew the further she went. Every building she entered was either flooded, fire damaged, or destroyed by the quakes that came at regular intervals. Her legs felt like lead, her brain short circuiting as she grasped the extent of what had happened and was still happening. Any powers she might have had could never undo what had been done here. As far as knowing the extent of this, there seemed no way to find out. Any newspapers she came upon were soggy and unreadable. Cell phones were on the ground, abandoned and useless, powerlines down and live wires hissing and twisting.

Houses were empty, doors hanging askew, clothing, electronics and keepsakes strewn across the mud. When she searched inside for food everything had spoiled, the stink of bad meat making her feel sick. The cans left behind were impossible to open, she realized, as she searched uselessly for can openers. Pipes had broken, raw sewage adding to the chaos and the stench. Storms raged in the distance, the sound of thunder rumbling. When the quakes came, buildings rattled. Many had collapsed.

She huddled in an abandoned building for more than a week, her hearing attuned to the roving gangs. She fed the baby, her own hunger impossible to ignore. She'd found water at least, the bottles keeping her from dying of thirst. How long would her milk last? There had been no more sign of the raven, her heart heavy with the loss of the man she loved. It was all her fault, from losing Bran to the destruction of Earth. If she stayed here much longer, she would likely die, the baby with her.

During her weeks of searching, the baby grew. Now he squirmed in his sling and was nearly too heavy to carry. She finally pulled him out and put him on the ground, surprised to see him take a few unsteady steps before landing on his bottom. He was barely over five months old and already looked like a two-year-old.

Luckily during the past week she'd found a bag of nuts, some moldy cheese and some apples, devouring them so quickly she was very nearly sick. The day after that meal was the last day Arwen nursed, his attention going to the world around him. When she tried to coax him, he turned away and made a face. But Kat's body was not ready for this, and she also had nothing to feed him but her own milk. She suffered in silence, trying not to force him to nurse. But he had to eat something. She took the herbal formula three times a day now.

A few days into Arwen's milk fast she saw her mother sitting on a park bench in the distance. She shouted and ran, but when she reached the spot, there was no bench and no sign of her mother. "Am I going mad?" she asked herself after the fourth time of this. It finally occurred to her that it was Arwen's doing. "Arwen, seeing your grandmother is disturbing for me. Please stop conjuring her."

Arwen looked up at her, a frightening expression in his crystalline eyes. Kat wondered later if she had imagined the contempt she saw there. Now he walked beside her, his hand in hers for balance.

And then came the day that he wouldn't even do that. He was as big as a three-year-old, his legs sturdy and strong. He ran ahead of her, searching in rubble piles and entering abandoned houses, despite her shouting at him to wait. He found food in the most unlikely places—stale bread, nuts and meat that had rotted. But when she tried to take the meat away, he bit her and ate it anyway.

He'd begun to babble nonsense, but occasionally she heard real words come out of his mouth. His precociousness scared her, his magic coming out in various weird ways that upset her further. He lured fish in a small stream that ran in town, bringing them to the surface and grabbing them to gnaw on while they were still alive. Birds met their demise the same way. He ate like a savage, gnawing the bones, his little teeth shining in the low light. She watched him warily, hoping not to get on his bad side, but one day when he killed a bird and laughed about it, she grabbed his arm. "That is not okay, Arwen," she scolded. "We do not kill unless we are hungry. Do you understand?"

His eyes narrowed, and when his hand waved in the air, she was flung from him, landing on her backside on some sharp rocks. Instead of getting up she stared at him, a sudden fear of who he was making its way into her consciousness. He needed his father to teach him right from wrong. From that day forward she kept her distance. He sensed her fear, using it to his advantage and doing things he knew would upset her.

The day he threw rocks at her was the day she decided she'd had enough. Her head ached from the one that hit her, her fingertips coming away covered in blood. She imagined Val in her mind, picturing his garden and his pale ethereal face. A second later a door opened and she scooped Arwen up and hurtled through.

But instead of the beautiful gardens she remembered,

there was a gray pall, the manor house burned to the ground. Arwen let out a howl and turned on her, attacking with such speed she fell backward. She screamed but it didn't stop him, his sharp teeth sinking deeply into her neck. A moment later a voice boomed out from the shadows. "Arwen, stop!" The child froze, giving Kat a chance to scrabble backward. She pressed her fingers to her bloody neck.

Val strode into view and grabbed Arwen, his worried gaze on Kat.

"Another minute and he would have killed me," she whispered.

"I'm sorry, Kat. I should have warned you. Fae children need a guiding hand in their formative years."

Kat let out a shaky laugh. "He's a monster."

"It is only because you are not Fae."

Kat rose to her feet, taking in Val's haggard face. "What happened here?"

His shoulders slumped. "Ragnarok happened. Alfheim is in ruin." He reached for her hand. "Come with me. I've set up a temporary place to live in the stable."

Kat eyed the child he held with his other arm.

"If you don't mind, I think I'll be on my way."

Val seemed to notice the blood for the first time, his fingers moving lightly across her skin. "It's deep," he muttered. He glanced up at her. "Are you still breast-feeding?"

Kat shook her head. "He stopped that quite a while ago. It's taking my body a long time to adjust to it."

"Keep taking the formula I gave you. It will help with this and also with the sudden loss of your child." He waved his hand and muttered some words under his breath. "As far as Arwen goes, you're better off leaving him here. He needs strict rules and discipline to undo what he's become."

Kat gazed at Val, unable to speak for a moment. "I don't want to leave him, Val, but I'm scared of him."

Val glanced down at the child held tightly in his arms. "As well you should be. I didn't expect a baby between us to behave this way, but as I've said, it does happen from time to time." He glanced at her. "Where have you been? What has happened while you've been gone? Did you reconnect with Bran?"

Kat looked away. "Not yet. And I haven't found Siobhan and my brother, or Dagda."

Val seemed to shrink into himself, his crystalline eyes lackluster. "And where will you go now?"

"This thing with Arwen has been a shock. I haven't thought past today, really. And I hate to leave you here alone."

"I'm not alone. Many Fae are living here—we've banded together to fight off Ragnarok. We still have our magic. You have a mission to accomplish. I suggest you get on with it."

Kat winced as though she'd been slapped. "Earth is destroyed. There is nothing I can do."

Val smiled sadly. "Belief in yourself will bring it all back. Your powers will return and then you will accomplish what you set out to do."

She shook her head. "It's too late. It's already lost." When he moved toward her, she backed away, afraid that if he touched her, she would never leave. Everything seemed impossible now. "Why haven't you left this place?"

she asked him, glancing at the destroyed house, the gardens that lay fallow and black from fire.

"This is my home."

She nodded, her eyes filling. "I have no home and no one now," she whispered.

He stared at her for a long moment. "You have yourself, Kat, and I'm sure you and Bran will find each other. If there is a chance of restoring what has been destroyed, it is you who will accomplish it."

She was about to protest when a door appeared. She stared at him, uncertain. "Val, I…"

He waved and the closed door opened. "I will watch out for you always."

Kat hesitated, the idea of leaving him and Arwen crowding out anything else. "I don't want to go," she whispered. But by that time, she was walking through.

Kat had no idea where she was, wishing fervently that she'd asked Val where in hell he was sending her. It became clear when she heard a familiar voice and the murmur of another voice she recognized. She made her way carefully to the edge of the woods and peered out. Airmid's spring had two people in it, and from what she could determine, one was Airmid and the other was Bran. And they were both naked. Her nerves seemed to collapse in on themselves, a scream rising in her throat. She pushed it back and swallowed. Val had sent her directly to Bran.

"So, where is she now?" Airmid asked, raking her fingers through her thick hair and pulling it up off her swan-like neck.

Bran shook his head. "I have no idea, but I wish we could get the 'powers that be' to open the borders to Earth. The place is in shambles."

"And you care, why?"

"Goddamn it, Airmid. You know why. I wouldn't have come here for your help if I'd known this attitude of yours hadn't changed in the past few months. And do not try to lure me into something I will regret," he added, watching her move closer.

"What would it hurt, Bran? You told me she betrayed you. I know it doesn't mean anything, but it's pleasurable, isn't it? You certainly seemed to enjoy it the last time."

When Bran shook his head and stood, Airmid grabbed him from behind and pulled him into the water. The splashing kept Kat from seeing what was happening. She finally heard Bran yell, *Stop!* his voice ringing out angrily as he climbed from the pool.

Before Kat could think what to do, Bran had turned into Raven and flown away.

"What a spoilsport," Airmid muttered, sinking back. She hummed a little tune.

Kat backed away and ran.

Tears trickled from the corners of her eyes as she hurtled through the forest, her ability to control her emotions fading with the memory of the hellish months she'd been struggling through. She'd just had to leave her child in a world she could never reach again, and the man she loved had given up on her. Just seeing him had sent her heart racing, anguish taking over as she realized he was lost to her.

She stopped to rest in a meadow, startled to see the beauty of the place. Ragnarok had not penetrated here. And then she remembered the Pinnacle. Could she open a door without Arwen? She tried to conjure one for the next half hour, finally giving up. It was Fae magic, not hers. And besides that, the creature hadn't been willing to help the last time, so why would he do it now? *No, it's impossible,* she thought to herself.

After seeing Bran and Airmid together, and hearing Airmid's comment that he'd 'enjoyed it the last time', she felt defeated and exhausted. The loss of her baby weighed heavily on her, the probability that she might never see him again, insinuating itself around her heart. When she waved her hands around, hoping for the colors, nothing happened. She was a demi-goddess, but without resolve, her abilities had retreated.

She lowered herself to the ground under a tree, tuning in. It took a while before she felt the tree energies, the awareness of her connection to the forest giving her back a bit of what she'd lost. "What do I do?" she whispered, trying not to feel sorry for herself. "Have I lost all ability to function?"

The message was slow in coming and ponderous as the trees bent toward her. She heard the limbs creaking before leaves came loose and fell all around her. They were unconcerned about time or about urgency. They were ancient, and their message was primal and difficult to decipher. The world would survive and it seemed she would have a chance sometime in the future to make things right. They said nothing about the Pinnacle.

"But what should I do now?" The silence was deafening and she had the sense that they refused to answer stupid questions. Humans were inferior beings, on the earth for a millisecond in comparison with their lengthy lives. She would have to decide for herself.

She let out a sigh and rose to her feet. When she came out of the woods the Pinnacle was in full sight, as though waiting for her to approach. Her run away from the spring had brought her here, and she took it for a sign. There was no one to ask whether this was right or wrong, only her inner voice that urged her on. This was her path.

The Pinnacle had seemed close when she first observed it, but in truth it was very far. She lost weight as she traveled, her diet of seed heads, small plants and lichen not enough to sustain her. A few nuts found in the woods afforded her some protein, mushrooms supplying her with vitamins, but her stomach ached every day, the dress hanging off her, the tattered hem loose and trailing. Val's herbs had to be infused with something that kept her going, otherwise she'd be dead by now; she noticed that the bag never got empty. She slept on the ground huddled into hollows, the cape she wore the only thing that saved her from the bitter wind blowing: the material was ragged and stiff with mud.

Seeing herself in her mind's eye made her laugh, the crazy sound of it scaring her. She was turning into a mad woman. Thinking about the hero's journey was the only thing that kept her going, the words her mother had said to her reminding her of who she'd once been. *No more tears*, she told herself several times a day when her throat closed and her chest tightened.

Once she left the woods behind the weather turned sharply colder, wind whistling by her ears and making them ache. The day it began to snow was the day she began to lose her forward momentum. She was so tired, so hungry, and with the snow she shivered and could not get warm. A blizzard developed, snow drifting across the barren landscape to turn everything white. Kat tried to continue, but finally it was too much for her. She shook with cold, her teeth chattering as she lowered to the ground and curled into a ball. Knowing that her almost irresistible desire for sleep would probably kill her, she struggled to stay awake. But in the end, she gave up, her eyes closing on the snow, her life and everything she'd fought so hard to achieve. And as she drifted in a pleasant place that seemed comforting and warm, she no longer cared what happened to her, any hope of making a difference disappearing with the tiny flakes that swirled around her.

Kat was dreaming when she heard the caw of the raven, her heart swelling with the memory of Bran and what he meant to her. She smiled in her sleep induced coma, wondering if he would come to her now and join her within her dream. Crystals had formed on her eyelashes, her numb fingers frostbitten and blue. In her dream the bird landed and shifted into Bran, arms wrapping around her. *I love you,* she murmured, as warmth spread through her body.

It was hours before she was able to open her eyes again, her vision distorted and hazy as she took in her surroundings. Bran held her close, and when she looked up, his mossy eyes met hers.

"I thought I'd lost you," he whispered.

"How are you here?" she asked, attempting to shift her stiff and aching body. The snow had stopped, but great drifts of it lay around the cave where he'd taken her.

Bran's mouth tightened. "My pendant. It got so hot I had to take it off. I could see you in it, Kat. It showed me where you were. Where's Arwen?"

Kat's eyes welled. "Arwen turned into a monster and tried to kill me."

Bran's eyes widened. "What?"

Kat tried to laugh and ended up choking. "Apparently, Fae children need a Fae parent."

Bran frowned, staring at her. "My gods, Kat. What did you do?"

"I took him back to Val and left him there." She wiped at her eyes which had decided to let go of all the tears she'd been holding back.

"And how did you end up here?"

"Val opened a door into Otherworld and I stepped through. I saw you and Airmid in the spring together."

"Jesus. That was months ago. Have you been out here since then?"

Kat nodded. "I'm so sorry," she murmured, more tears tracking down her chapped cheeks.

Bran shook his head, staring at her. "Don't worry about that now. We'll talk once you're well."

Kat recovered slowly, Bran's steady diet of cooked rabbit and greens bringing her back from the brink. He'd taken her to the woods and built a small shelter, tending to her until she regained her strength. She reveled in the attention, leaving the past behind as she rested and recovered. But the day arrived, as she knew it would, when Bran brought up the subject both of them had been avoiding.

It was morning and a light rain had begun to fall, Kat waking to see Bran propped on his elbow staring down at her. Shadows played across his unshaven face, his mossy eyes deep with distress.

"I guess it's time to talk, Kat. To be honest I'd given up on us."

"I thought so when you came to me as Raven. It felt like you were saying goodbye."

Bran nodded. "I was." He gazed at her, troubled. "What the hell was that all about—that thing with Val?"

"Val put a spell on me."

"What are you saying—a spell? Did you sleep with him again?"

"I…I thought that's why you were upset, why you flew away."

"I was upset because the first thing out of your mouth was asking Val to make love to you. Meanwhile I was standing right there. It hurt, Kat, like I meant nothing to you."

Kat could hardly look at him, shame stealing over her.

"When did it happen?"

"The first night we got to Alfheim," she admitted in a small voice. "I woke up in the night and went downstairs and he…"

"He was there."

Kat nodded.

Bran shook his head. "I should have known. In the morning he was acting kind of weird and muttering shit."

"He admitted that he'd bewitched me."

"That's a poor excuse for betraying me and lying about it. I did wonder why you were so angry with him."

"I was furious, but mostly with myself."

Bran grimaced. "Now that I've met him, I can visualize

the two of you together. That's the worst part."

Kat looked away, the realization of the pain she'd caused filling her with regret. "I can imagine it would. When I think of you with Airmid it makes me feel sick."

"That was nothing compared to this. You have a baby with this guy."

"I don't love him."

"Don't you? I'm not so sure about that."

"I'm attracted to him, but it isn't even close to what I feel for you." She lifted his pendant. "We're bonded, Bran."

Bran seemed to soften, the muscles in his face relaxing. "I can't go through this shit again."

Kat gazed at him, her heart beating erratically. "I'm yours. I always have been."

Bran frowned. "How long were you with Val this last time?"

"Not long. I told you I had to take Arwen back."

"And what happened? Will you have another Fae baby?"

Kat looked down. "No, Bran. But without you, I felt like my life was over."

Bran sighed, letting a minute tick by. "If you see Val again this same shit will happen. I'm sure of it. He's in love with you and he'll do whatever's necessary to get you into his bed."

Kat breathed in deeply and let the breath out slowly. "I don't know what to say to that. I can assure you that it will be a long time before I see him again. I can't get there on my own, and I have no desire to be around my monster child. If and when I do go, I want you with me."

"I was with you the last time and look what happened."

He gazed into the distance frowning before he turned to her again. "What in hell were you doing out here, Kat? Jesus, you were very nearly frozen through."

"I was on my way to the Pinnacle to talk to the creature again."

"You never would have made it. I told you, the Pinnacle is impossible to reach without someone from Otherworld along."

"You never told me that. I didn't even know where Val sent me until I saw

you and Airmid together."

Bran sighed and stared into the distance. "I don't trust you anymore."

Kat went on, trying to ignore how his words made her feel. "Val still seems to think I can fix things. That's why I was heading to the Pinnacle. But when the snow began, I gave up. Without you in my life everything seems empty and useless."

Bran reached for her, his head against hers. "I hate feeling this way. It fucking hurts." He moved away and glanced into the distance again. "I talked with the gods, but they refuse to do anything to help. They seem to think that humans deserve everything they get."

"Because we forgot about our them in our headlong rush for progress."

"That and other things. Last I saw, the planet was destroyed. Did you find your mother?"

"No, and I spent months down there searching."

Bran's face fell. "I'm sorry, Kat. It doesn't mean they're not alive."

"I know. Dad's with her and I'm sure he's found a way to keep her and Mior safe."

"I can help you search if you want."

Kat gazed at him. So much had happened she had no idea what direction to take. "Can we talk about it later? Right now, I only want to sleep for a while."

"Like a hundred years or so?" Bran joked.

"Something like that. I feel shattered, like nothing matters. Earth is ruined, I can't stay in Otherworld, and Alfheim has been taken over by Ragnarok. My baby has turned into a monster and you don't trust me."

"Alfheim too," Bran muttered before meeting her gaze. "Take a rest and we'll revisit it all later. I have to go forage for dinner."

When he rose, she grabbed his pant leg. "How long?"

He crouched next to her. "You're afraid," he said, surprised. "I've never seen you like this."

Kat's eyes filled. "So much has happened—it's like my entire world has shifted. I could have died out there because of my stupidity. You said you don't trust me? Well, I don't trust myself."

Bran put his arms around her but was unable to find any words of comfort.

As the days passed by Kat began to feel more like her old self. At least physically. Bran was remote in a way that was hard to bear, his moodiness keeping him away for longer than was necessary. She longed for the wall between them to fall away, but knew that time was the only thing that would heal the rift between them. But after a month when nothing changed, she had to rethink things. An urgency had taken over her dreams as well as her waking life. She saw her parents running, heard Mior screaming as the world disintegrated. She couldn't wait for him anymore. She had to act, despite feeling inadequate to the task. Words of encouragement came back to her as she fought against her insecurities: *Listen to your own heart.* Cerridwen's words. And Val's encouragement before she left the baby with him. *Belief in yourself will bring it all back.* Val was Fae and what he said was not only designed to make her feel better—it was the truth he'd seen.

The day she made the decision was a day like any other. It had been over a month, but she and Bran had yet to make love. They slept tangled together, her head on his chest, but he'd never once kissed her, nor had he said he loved her. When she tried to talk about it, he either changed the subject or told her he had to go hunt for food. His expression was always closed now, no smile on his features as he did what was necessary to keep them both alive.

Bran left early that morning, telling her he was planning to search for mushrooms in the forest to the east. As soon as he was out of sight, she threw on her warm cloak and laced up her boots. She took the trail that led toward the Pinnacle, determined to reach it this time.

26

Dagda followed Daniel out the heavy metal door. "Jesus Christ. It looks like a bomb went off," Dagda said, gazing around at the downed trees, the wash of mud and the chasms that had opened up.

Daniel frowned, his hand going up to shade his eyes. "It's a good thing Siobhan isn't with us. I would hate for her to witness what's happening down in that valley."

"My daughter should have fixed this," Dagda muttered. "Why didn't she?"

"You expect one young girl to stop whatever this is? What do you think she is, a goddess? The gods have turned on us, Dagda. There's no coming back."

"I thought you didn't believe in the gods."

"You mean that crazy story you spewed every time you got a little frustrated? You're right about that. I was speaking metaphorically."

"Oddly enough your assessment is right. The gods *have* turned on us. If they hadn't closed the borders this devastation would never have happened."

"Give it a rest, old man. This is global warming, pure and simple."

"If my daughter were here, she'd tell you that earth's feminine energy is rising up to shake off this male-dominated world."

Daniel gave a hollow laugh. "You're nuts, you know that?"

"I always thought you believed me, Daniel. You certainly acted like it. Was that only to placate me?"

"I knew where my bread was buttered. Too bad you got old and lost your way."

Dagda was sure Daniel had known what he was. There were too many instances where Dagda worked magic to get his way. Why the man was acting like he didn't, was mystifying, to say the least. Maybe it was due to how old Dagda was now, how decrepit and inept he'd become. He turned to see his wife and Mior emerging from the dark opening. "No, Siobhan. Go back."

"I will not go back. I'm sick of breathing stale air and living in a metal box. It isn't storming or windy or anything else."

Dagda glanced at Daniel who was frowning. "Siobhan, you do not want to see the death down there."

"Don't tell me what I want or don't want, Daniel. I'm a grown woman."

Dagda was proud of her, his heart swelling with love. He nodded to her and took her arm. "Let's go forage for some alcohol."

Siobhan laughed. "Is that what you're missing? I want green vegetables."

"I want alcohol too, Papa," Mior piped up, grabbing his sleeve.

Dagda took the boy's hand and moved past Daniel.

"Where is our daughter," he muttered.

"Something terrible has happened. I know it," Siobhan said worriedly.

Dagda let out a humorless laugh, scanning the broken asphalt, the holes that lay in wait. "She obviously did not fulfill her part of the bargain."

"What bargain is that?"

"It was her fate to stop this mess from happening—you knew that, didn't you?"

"With a small baby in tow? How in the world could she manage that?"

Dagda frowned, navigating around a deep crevasse and making sure his son didn't fall in. "She's *my* daughter, Siobhan. I was once very powerful."

The scene down the hill came into view, the floodwaters still raging. Death was everywhere, animals and humans scattered like flotsam. Siobhan screamed and tried to shield her son, but he pulled away from her. "Why don't they move?" Mior asked, kneeling next to a deer.

"It's dead, Mior."

"What is *dead*?"

"It means the creature no longer breathes," Dagda said, grabbing hold of him before he took off.

"I can make it breathe."

Dagda kneeled next to him. "No, Mior. Even if you can, it isn't a good idea."

"But why?"

"Because this animal has been dead for many days. You can't restore what happened to it. It would be a broken thing. If it had died recently, maybe, but not after this much time has passed."

When Mior ran off, Siobhan took hold of Dagda's hand to help him up. "Do you think he could really bring it back to life?" she whispered.

"Possibly."

Siobhan turned pale, her eyes widening as she stared toward her son.

27

The mountain rose up in the distance, black against the storm filled sky. Despite Bran's insistence that Kat could never get there on her own, she had to try again. If she'd learned anything as she flailed from one thing to another, it was that in order to do anything of worth, she had to trust herself. Val had said it. Cerridwen had said it.

When she looked back at the past months, every turning had led her somewhere, none of it wasted, even if it felt that way at the time. The Underworld, Val and the baby, Mimir's well, all of it had happened for a reason. What she couldn't abide was this thing between herself and Bran, the lack of trust that left her feeling so alone. There was no denying that her behavior had been despicable, but was it unforgiveable? If he was unable to let it go there was no point in being together anymore.

Was this her test, to be forced to leave everything she loved behind? She'd been through more tests than she could count, all of them leading to this moment. The last time she'd been here, it had seemed that the mountain never got any closer. But this time she decided to ask for help, at least for the first phase.

"Val, if there is any connection left between us, please show me a door that will get me where I need to go," she murmured.

When a door immediately opened in front of her, she hesitated, peering through. An impenetrable blackness was all she could see. A voice came to her, *do you not trust me?* She stepped through.

There was not a sound or a breath of wind. She could see nothing. She tapped into what she knew as a blind person, listening for tiny sounds, sniffing the air. Water dripped somewhere, and the air smelled of something she couldn't quite place until she remembered being here before. It was the aroma of ages past, the scent of time itself. The air shifted and changed; a breeze touched her cheek. Something had entered the space. She held herself as still as possible, barely breathing. She waited.

"You have returned," the creature said. "What do you hope to accomplish *this* time?"

Kat felt a surge of annoyance. "I expect to open the borders between here and the earth."

There was a huff-like laugh. "You tried that once before."

"But this time I'm certain we can do it together."

"What has changed?"

"I…I believe in myself now."

"Did you bring the child in trade?'

"The child is with his father, but I have other things to trade."

"You have nothing I am interested in."

"Would you like to be free of this place?"

There was a long pause. "I am bound here for all eternity."

"What if I told you, you could leave?"

"It is a falsehood."

"If you open the border you can walk through a door into another world. I will make it happen."

Kat could hear breathing and felt the creature's uncertainty. Yes, he was all powerful, but Kat had tapped into his Achilles heel. He was lonely. Now that her eyes had adjusted, she could see him, an amorphous cloud of dark mist that moved and changed within the deeper darkness. He wasn't solid.

"You cannot fathom what living in this dark and dank prison is like. I long for light."

"Can you exist in the light?"

"I once had a body, and I was once a god, and my memories of that time still plague me. Perhaps I could be solid again."

"I know of a world that would consume a normal human being, but maybe you could survive there. It's light-filled—beautiful. If I free you will the border open automatically?"

"If I am gone and the jailor is no longer in charge, the border will open. It is him and the darkness that surrounds him that has sewn chaos and confusion, both in Otherworld and on Earth. Yes, it is storms and wind and earthquakes that are destroying your planet, but dark energy opened the gates to allow it in."

Kat shivered, pulling her cloak close around her body. "Who is he?"

"The far dorocha is a sorcerer who is servant to the dark

queen of evil, the one who calls herself Carmun."

"Where is he now?" Kat whispered.

"His first concern is Carmun, so he comes and goes. If you have the ability to release me, it must happen when he is away from here."

"But then he'll come back and the border will still be closed!"

There was a long silence. "Well then, we have no choice. You must kill the jailor."

Kat felt a distinct sense of dread. "I have no power to kill him, nor do I think I'd want to."

"If you want the light to come back to Earth, you must."

Kat shifted her weight, trying to stop the ache in her knees from standing on the hard stone. "I want to call you something—what is your name?"

A moment passed before he answered. "Long ago I was known as the 'shadow who wakes'."

"I'll call you Shad."

"Shad," he echoed. A few seconds went by before he asked, "How can I find this world you speak of?"

"I have an Elven friend who can open a door into this parallel world."

The sound of grinding stone interrupted their conversation and then a voice penetrated the darkness. "What is this?"

Kat immediately recognized the specter's voice. "I am here to discuss business with the creature imprisoned here," she said firmly.

"Whatever business you have must go through me."

"Who are you to demand that?"

"You know what I am."

"You're a jailor, an evil being who keeps the light out.

What do you get out of this?"

"It is my duty as instructed by the queen who commands me."

"What queen would want this creature imprisoned forever? He's been ignored for millennia. The gods no longer care what happens to him, or to you, for that matter. What will it take for you to release him?"

There was a weighty silence before he spoke again. "There is nothing you can bestow on me to release him. He is part of this mountain."

Kat thought for a minute, remembering that the specter was once a living being. She'd seen his ravaged skull, the scars. "What if I told you that you could both go to a light-filled world where your queen would never find you."

"I would say you are ill-informed."

"I've been there, and although it was not a good place for an earth being, I think it would suit you and this creature you guard."

There was a sound of a hoarse laugh. "My queen will not allow it," the jailor said, his body turning into shadow. "She has commanded me to dispatch you," he continued.

Kat backed up when she saw the shadowy blackness coming toward her. When he closed around her, she felt a cold and crushing agony. She screamed as it pressed inward. She couldn't breathe.

"No!" she heard the creature bellow. "You have kept me here long enough. You will not keep me from freedom."

A sound like wind whistling across empty space, a sharp cry and then nothing. Kat was afraid to look, afraid of who might be left behind. When she peered through the darkness the jailor had turned to mist and was breaking into small tendrils to drift upward.

"He is gone," the creature said. There was sadness in his voice.

"If you could kill him so easily why haven't you done it before now?"

A moment went by before he answered. "He has been my only companion for as long as I can remember."

"I'm sorry for that. But this world where I plan to send you will certainly have other beings on it." Kat called on Val in her mind, reminding him of the world she and Bran had returned from after their warrior ride across the valley floor. "I'll owe you," she whispered, knowing that the Fae loved holding debts to be collected at some future time. She felt him contemplating, could almost see his fingers raking through his hair. When the door opened, bright light filled the space. She shaded her eyes and pointed. "Go!"

The creature moved toward it, his nebulous shape flowing and changing as he drifted through the door. Before she could say goodbye and wish him well, the door shut with a sharp snap, leaving her alone in the cave. "Now, how do I get out?" But that problem was answered when the rock behind her slid open. She hurried through.

As she rushed down the hill, she could hear the rocks cracking and breaking behind her, a tumble of jagged pieces rolling by. A resounding rumble moved the ground beneath her feet. She ran.

Kat was halfway down the mountain before she realized she had no idea if the creature was telling the truth about the conduit now being open. If it was, would the earth begin to regenerate now that the specter was gone? But the witch was still alive.

Even that disturbing thought wasn't enough to stop the happy laugh that came from her when she imagined the creature floating nebulous in a cobalt blue sky. She'd saved him, and that's what counted. Perhaps without the power exerted on him from Otherworld and the specter, he would even regain his god shape. When she stopped to look back, the dark peaks of stone were no longer there. An undulating slope covered in heather stood in its place. A thought drifted by that maybe saving this creature had been an important element of the twisting path she seemed to be on.

The raven soared, his harsh caw disturbing in the silence. When he suddenly dive-bombed her, Kat crouched down with her hands over her head. A second later Bran was standing there, his features distorted with fury.

"I guess I don't need to ask where you've been!" he yelled. "I can't believe you took off without telling me. I was sure you'd walked through a door into Alfheim. I've been searching for hours!"

"I did walk through a door, but not into Alfheim. I asked Val for help. I released the creature, Bran. He's in that world we went to, the parallel reality. He…"

Bran grabbed her shoulders. "Are you *trying* to tear us apart?"

Kat pulled out of his grasp. "How can we be torn apart if we aren't together? You've made it abundantly clear that you can't forgive me, Bran. Doing what I did today has helped me regain confidence in myself. I can't go on like this. I understand how you feel, but I can't live this way."

Bran glared at her. "And what exactly did you accomplish by taking off without saying a word?"

Kat gazed at the mountain in the distance. "See for yourself."

Bran shook his head. "Even if the conduit is open, Earth is already destroyed. I saw it with my own eyes."

Kat wrapped her arms around her body. "I set the creature free, Bran. Shad...that's what I call him...said that his jailor was in league with a dark witch. They're the ones who've been working against me all this time. They created chaos on Earth and that's why the storms got in. Shad killed the jailor. He turned into wisps and disappeared right in front of my eyes. Shad said that..."

Bran made a sound in the back of his throat. "*Shad* was pulling your leg, Kat. What about Ragnarok?"

"I'm sure this was always part of my mission. It wasn't only about opening the border, it was about setting that creature free. Magic can flow now between Otherworld and Earth. Now all I have to do is find the witch and stop her."

"You have no idea what you're talking about. Do you know where the witch is?"

"She was the one who took my memories when I was at Odin's castle. She's around, Bran. Val said she was after me. And now that her stand-in is dead, I'm sure I can find her."

"And how do you propose to get anywhere?"

Kat stared at the ground. "Maybe Val will open another door?"

"Jesus, Kat. For someone who wants to go it alone, you

certainly rely on him. I'm sorry losing my powers has inconvenienced you so much."

"That isn't fair. It's only the doors."

Bran let out a sigh and ran his fingers through his hair. He gazed at the Pinnacle, his eyes widening in surprise. "You really did it."

Kat smiled, watching his look of utter wonder as he perused the beautiful sloping mountain range in the distance. "I *told* you."

When she started away, he grabbed her. "Where are you going now?"

"I don't really know. We aren't together anymore so I've got to go it alone. I'll figure something out." She turned back to the trail.

He grabbed her roughly and pulled her close. "You are seriously driving me crazy, Kat. I can't take the stress anymore. I've been cold, I admit it. But I keep seeing you with Val and I can't stand it. Please tell me you haven't given up on us."

Kat stopped and faced him. "It wasn't me who gave up, Bran. I made a terrible mistake, but I also apologized and told you how I feel. I never loved Val. You're the one I love. But love isn't enough if there isn't trust between us."

Bran's eyes welled. "I want to trust you."

"But?"

He shook his head and wiped angrily at the tears. "Can we start again? I promise I won't shut you out. Please don't head off on your own like this. I worry about you and I…"

"If I need to head off on my own, I will. And if you can't tell me you trust me, I don't want to be together. How long does it take to forgive?"

"I love you, Kat. The idea of not being together makes me cold all over. Can you trust that I'll try?"

She gazed into his mossy tear-filled eyes. "I'll give it a few days, but if things don't change, I'm out of here."

Bran nodded and took hold of her hand. Together they skirted around rocky outcroppings to find the path that led back to the shelter. Behind them sunlight shimmered across the mountain range, animating the bright yellow gorse and purple heather.

I t began with fireflies. It wasn't even summer, and yet there they were. Kat was nodding off, drowsing in the shelter when one landed on her hand. It was turning dusk, the flash of brightness shaking her out of her stupor. "Bran, since when have there been fireflies in Otherworld?"

Bran turned from where he was replacing branches in one corner of the hive- shaped house. Some had rotted in the last rain. "Fireflies? Never."

Kat held up her hand where one had landed. "Well, they're here now." The radiance blinked on and off, the tiny wings heaving with each change.

Bran moved close to examine the bug. "Why is it here?" he muttered, mostly to himself.

"It's a message from earth. It's telling me that magic does indeed flow between our worlds."

"And that it's time for you to check out what's happening?"

Kat sat up, staring at him. "You think I haven't been trying? You refused to allow me to call on Val again, and without magic it's impossible."

"Kat, you've had nightmares every night for the past week, and I'm certain they're about your family and your home."

"How do you know? I can't remember any dreams."

"Maybe because you yell *Mom* almost every night, as though you're trying to find her?"

Kat looked down at the same moment the firefly lifted into the air. It hovered there for several seconds before it buzzed away. "Mior sent that firefly," Kat whispered, watching it illuminate the darkening woods. There were many of them there, lights blinking on and off like a village of tiny people carrying lanterns.

Bran nodded. "That's my guess too. Your brother is growing up."

Kat let out a sigh, settling back against the pallet Bran had fashioned out of her damaged cape and pine needles. "But how do we get there?"

"Too bad you can't fly anymore. Have you tried?"

"Bran...I gave that up to Mimir. Remember?"

"Yeah, but who knows? Weirder things have happened."

Kat shook her head and put her mind on other things.

It was late afternoon when they heard voices. Bran moved to the edge of the woods to look out. When he turned there was worry in his eyes. "It's Forseti and Airmid. Looks like they're searching for us," he whispered.

Their voices drifted on the wind. "They must be here somewhere," Airmid muttered. "That stupid half goddess has no powers, and neither does Bran. What a waste of a god he is. I have no idea why I was so enamored of him. Can't we just kick him out of here?"

"The Pinnacle's gone!" Forseti shouted. "How did *that* happen?"

Airmid tripped over an upright stone and let out an expletive, her hand going to shade her eyes as she followed his gaze. "How do *I* know how the damn thing changed?" She glanced away and continued where she'd left off. "Bran was mooning about and acting like a love-sick puppy. I figured Kat must have come back, otherwise he would have returned to my pool, and we could have resumed…"

Forseti grabbed her arm. "Airmid, listen to me. The mountain is no longer black. I don't know what this means, but it does not bode well for our borders. Something's happened."

Bran turned to Kat and put a finger to his lips. He pulled her with him into the deeper shadows and found a wide tree to hide behind. "Pay no attention to that bitch," he hissed in her ear.

"I'm over it," she whispered back. "She can say whatever she wants."

He moved to peek out. "They're heading toward the Pinnacle. Once they really see what's happened, they'll organize a meeting with all the gods. I suspect there will be a reckoning. We need to be gone before that happens."

"Where will we go? If you don't want me to contact Val then we're stuck here, or at least I am."

"Shush," Bran whispered. "They're coming this way."

Airmid and Forseti were on the narrow animal trail that led to their shelter.

"So, they *are* here," Airmid mumbled, gazing at the few pieces of clothing and foodstuffs. She kicked at the bedding, a frown on her face.

"Looks that way. I suggest we concentrate on the Pinnacle and organize a search party later. They'll be caught and punished if that fucking border's been opened." Forseti turned to glare at her. "Do you have any idea what it means if that's happened? The plague that is Earth will infiltrate Otherworld. It will be the end of us!"

Airmid sniffed the air, her eyes narrowing. Her face seemed to change shape for a moment, her eyes turning dark. She seemed reluctant to leave, but she followed Forseti out of the woods, their voices fading as they walked away.

Bran kept watch, finally breathing a sigh of relief. "They're gone."

"Airmid—she looked weird for a second, Bran. Her face…"

But Bran was already striding away.

It was early the next morning when Bran insisted that Kat at least attempt to turn into a hummingbird. "I don't see how you could have given it up. It's a part of you, like your ear, or…"

"Odin gave up an eye, Bran."

"What I'm trying to say is, you *are* hummingbird. It would be like giving up part of your psyche. And besides, this is a sacred place, Kat. It's where the gods chose to build a circle." He pointed into the shadows where the worn upright stones leaned precariously. "This is where the veil between worlds is the thinnest. I've felt it and I'm sure you have too. The magic is dense here."

Kat shook her head, her lips pursed. She'd felt the energy of the place, heard the whispers, but she didn't think any magic would restore what she'd given up. "If you need proof then here it is," she said, focusing her mind on how she'd always managed the shift. She let out a gasp as it began to happen, Bran's grin the last thing she saw before she was hovering in the air.

When she shifted back, her eyes went wide. "I...I can't believe it! What did I leave in Mimir's well?"

"You left hummingbird's shadow, but you kept the spirit."

Kat let out a frustrated sigh. "And all this time I could have turned into hummingbird? Do you realize what I've had to do to get from one place to another?"

Bran's mossy eyes met hers. "You've had to call on Val for help. I bet you anything he knew this all along. I don't trust him."

Kat ignored his outburst, trying to think the best of Val and not have her mind turn to the child she'd left behind. Her heart ached for her child. "When shall we leave for earth?"

Kat watched Bran scan the green glade where they'd been living for the past month. It was secluded enough to keep the gods away, the energy from the stones allowing them to feel safe. She knew what he was thinking. But now, despite the stones, they'd been discovered. "I'm fine with going alone."

His eyes narrowed. "I'd never let you go alone."

Kat thought about the past weeks. She'd been keeping her distance until she was sure he trusted her again. And so far, he had not said the words, nor had he indicated a change of heart. Even the way they slept at night was different, their bodies barely touching. She knew he missed their physical connection, she did too, but until he let go of his doubt it would have to be this way. Something in her had shifted after releasing the creature. It was as though that one success had restored her faith in herself. She still loved him as much as she ever had, but she no longer needed him. At least not in the same way.

Bran shifted first, and waited for her. Once she was hummingbird, he spread dark wings and lifted into the sky. The hummingbird flew beside him.

They were still on the Otherworld side of the border with Otherworld and Earth when Raven let out a cry. In her hummingbird mind she felt his pain, her bird eyes watching him plummet downward. She'd seen the arrow, witnessed how it pierced him, dark feathers floating all around as he fell. She tried to follow, tried to change direction, but fireflies had found her, her ability to move stymied as they swarmed close, taking her with them. Carried along, she lost all sense of what was happening, the memory of what she'd seen disappearing as she struggled against the force that drove her forward.

29

"Mama, the little lights are here! I sent one to Kat."

Siobhan glanced down at her son who was growing like a weed. His hair was long now, dark curls hanging to his shoulders. He'd grown tall during the months they'd lived inside the bunker. "What little lights are you talking about, Mior? And how could you send one to your sister—we don't know where she is."

"The light bugs," he cried, pointing. The sun was nearly gone, and fireflies danced in the long shadows cast across the muddy yard. "It doesn't matter where Kat is—it will reach her." He hurried away, attempting to capture the bugs in a glass jar he'd discovered in the rubble.

Dagda arrived, a rake in his hand. "Mior is quite something," he murmured, glancing at his wife. "We may see fireworks very soon."

"Fireworks—what do you mean?"

He let out a snort. "I mean something surprising and god-like." He went back to raking the ash, cleaning out the spot where the little shack had been.

The woods behind the house were gone, burned to the ground in the last fire that swept through. Now he could see the abandoned houses on the other side, the mansions that had lost roofs and windows. The neighborhood was decimated, so many of the people still missing or dead. Mass burials had taken place in the last week, giant holes dug in hillsides with machines that still contained fuel, the bloated bodies tossed in and covered over. Disease was rampant, water contaminated and the air filled with toxins from the asbestos and gods knew what else that had been unleashed by the destruction.

Bedraggled people had returned with the retreat of the storms, their eyes hollow, their faces ravaged by loss. Businesses were getting their lights back on, men and women gathered together in groups exchanging horror stories. The town at the bottom of Dagda's hill was coming back to life.

Daniel appeared, his eyes roving across Siobhan's body before he headed to Dagda. "So, this is what you had to do today? I thought you might be cleaning out that bar downtown, serving drinks to the survivors. God knows, they all need it."

Dagda leaned on the rake. "Have *you* done anything useful today? Seems to me your laziness could cost us our lives, Daniel."

"And how is that, old man? I provided a roof over your head for months, not to mention food. So far, I haven't heard a thank you or anything resembling payback. From what I can see the storms are over. Time to take advantage of what the people want. There's money to be made," he said rubbing his thumb and fingers together.

"Maybe, maybe not," Dagda replied, gazing up at the

darkening sky. "This could be the calm before the real storm. Ragnarok is no small thing—but you wouldn't know anything about that, would you?"

"I've read mythology. But that's all it is. Why do you insist on believing that what we experienced was Ragnarok?"

"Because I was once a god, you moron. And I still retain the knowledge of a god, despite the human body I occupy."

"You, a god?" Daniel scoffed. "I do recall what an arrogant asshole you were, but I never really believed that bullshit you spouted."

"How did you explain my ability to wield so much power?"

"There are many men who consider themselves gods, Dagda. You were just another one of my clients who thought too highly of himself."

"I suggest you get off my property before I throw you off. And if I catch you leering at my wife again, I'll tear you limb from limb," he hissed.

Daniel let out a laugh. "You don't deserve her."

"Probably not, but she loves me and we have two children together. Now get off my property."

"I suggest you treat me with respect, *Dag*. You never know when you might require my services. The only reason you're still alive is because of me."

"Fuck you."

"What are you two talking about?" Siobhan asked, hurrying over to loop her arm through Dagda's.

The two men glared at each other. "Your husband wants me to quit staring at you," Daniel told her with an innocent smile. "But it's hard to take my eyes off a woman as good-looking as you are."

Siobhan blushed deep scarlet, turning her attention to Mior playing in the mud.

"If things don't go well, you know where to find a hot meal and a shower and a soft bed," Daniel told Siobhan, before he turned toward the gate.

Once he was out of earshot Dagda frowned. "That man is a…"

"Daniel put us up for several months, Dag. He's a good man."

"Not from where I'm standing," he muttered, watching Daniel climb into the black town car. It was the same car Dagda had bought for him when Daniel worked for him. Now the man did whatever he wanted, his blatant disrespect for Dagda driving the former god crazy. The months spent in the bunker had nearly driven him mad, with Daniel flirting with Siobhan every chance he got. Daniel had also managed to appear every time Dagda had a moment alone with his wife, surprising them in the kitchen and even in the bathroom. He and Siobhan had not yet been intimate and it was weighing heavily on him. Did she want him? Because if she did, she hid it well.

The sun disappeared, and without streetlights the stars began to appear, twinkling to life as though switched on by the gods. Dagda had a moment of reverence

as he stared at the sky. Gratitude for his life washed over him unexpectedly, tears welling. He walked to where Siobhan played with Mior, and when he reached her,

he pulled her into his arms and kissed her firmly on the mouth.

"My goodness, Dag, what's got into you?" she asked, breathless after he released her.

Dagda stared into the darkness, wishing he was someone else. "Got to get a shelter built before it's time for bed," he muttered, working his way back to the charred planks and leftover roof panels. Luckily the night was mild, their need for heavy blankets mitigated. As long as they had a mud free area and a roof over their heads, it could all wait until tomorrow.

That night Dagda lay awake, his arms around his wife. Siobhan slept lightly, her skin pale blue in the darkness of the teepee type shelter he'd managed to erect. A heavy wind would send it toppling, but for tonight it would have to do. Mior lay on her other side, the boy deeply asleep and snoring.

During the early morning hours clouds had moved in, the threat of storms arriving, a strange wind as harbinger. Without his powers he wasn't sure if he was imagining things or not, but he felt the stirrings of something much more powerful than the storms and earthquakes they'd already endured. What would he do if he was right? Going back to the bunker was out of the question now, and he wasn't capable of building a shelter strong enough to withstand what might be on the way.

He missed the days when he could conjure things by visualizing them. He missed being strong and handsome and desired. He shifted his position, turning on his side to draw Siobhan closer. His need made itself known then, rising up to taunt him. She stirred against him, moaning as a dream claimed her. He wanted her with every fiber of his being, and yet he couldn't have her, not now with his son so close.

"Dag?"

"Go back to sleep, Siobhan. I didn't mean to wake you."

She turned toward him and kissed him, her lips warm and soft. He moaned, his ability to stop what had started, painfully difficult. "Siobhan, I…"

"I know," she whispered. "We'll find a way soon."

Dagda worked hard for the next week, rebuilding what had been destroyed. When Daniel came around, he ordered him off the property, his anger like a fire he couldn't put out. Siobhan was not happy with Dagda's temper, but she tried to understand, her continued support buoying Dagda's blacker moods and assuaging his impatience with himself about his weakness as a mortal. He still couldn't get used to the idea that he would age and die, and could not turn Daniel into a toad when the guy pissed him off. And the aches and pains his body was plagued with had him fuming.

"Why does my back hurt?" he asked Siobhan one morning as he was attempting to carry planks.

Siobhan laughed. "You have to bend your knees, Dag, not bend over from the waist."

"Why?"

"Because it strains your back muscles when you pick things up that way."

"Fuck," he muttered, trying to follow what she showed him. "I have to get this shelter up and strong before the next storm arrives."

"What storm?"

Dagda glanced up at the sky that was now clear. "Something's coming. I can feel it in my bones."

Siobhan chuckled and looped her arm through his. "Arthritis does tend to ache when the pressure drops."

"God damn it, woman! I'm talking more than arthritis here."

Siobhan balked and moved away. "I didn't mean to offend you." She glanced at the horizon where darkness gathered. "Perhaps you're right."

Dagda frowned, his eyes narrowing as he followed her gaze. "Yes. That's exactly what I'm talking about. It will arrive either late tonight or early tomorrow."

Voices could be heard in the distance, angry shouting. Siobhan's eyes widened and she went to gather Mior, rushing back to Dagda. "There's a mob coming up the road," she muttered, pointing.

Dagda moved to the edge of the property and glanced down the road at the group of men carrying rifles and sticks, his heart pounding. He was only a man now, not a god. How would he protect his wife and son? He fetched the pistol he'd managed to scavenge, loading it with bullets he'd discovered a few days before in the deserted bar. "I want you and Mior to hide in what's left of the woods behind the house. "I'll deal with this."

Siobhan glanced up at him, her eyes welling with fear. "There have to be twenty of them, Dag. Come with us."

"And let them destroy what I've started here? Hell, no."

"I can help," Mior whispered. "I've been practicing."

Dagda glanced down at the boy. "Practicing what?"

Mior grinned.

When the men drew close and came through the iron

gate, Dagda shot his pistol in the air. "Do not take one step closer!" he shouted.

The men looked at him. A chuckle went through the group. "And what do you plan to do about it?" one of them yelled.

Dagda watched his son climb onto the pillar.

30

The witch let out a shriek that reverberated across the sky. Her black dress billowed as she flew upward, her hands turning into claws as her anger and frustration built. "He is dead!" she cried out. Her body somersaulted as she let the sadness take her, her dress ripping as the wind began to rage and howl. By the time she was finished with her dance of grief, the dress was in tatters, her hair tangled and knotted.

"This was her doing," she muttered, returning to the ground. "She killed my far dorocha, my servant, my lover and my partner." Tears flowed down her ravaged face, her dark eyes filled with pain and anger. But as she stood in the quiet aftermath of what she now knew, another expression crossed her features. She had other means to kill the one who thwarted her at every turn. There were many dark entities she could call on. The demi-goddess would not get away with this, and would never, ever succeed in saving her home planet. She had the ability to inhabit other bodies. She'd done it before and she would do it again. It was an easy way to gain trust, and when the time was right, she would rid the world of her nemesis.

The dark goddess took off then, heading to a place of refuge to call on those who she knew would help. The half-goddess bitch would not get away with this, and the witch knew many who would happily assist in wiping her off the face of the earth. It was winter and the gates of the Underworld stood open. For the first time her lips curled up in a near smile.

31

The hummingbird tumbled toward the ground, the only thing saving her from instant death, the swarm of bugs that closed around her. As soon as she touched the ground she shifted, her human body aching from the impact. She lay still for a few minutes, trying to get her bearings and recall who she was. A second later she remembered the arrow and the raven's downward plunge. Bran was hurt and she wasn't there to help him.

The lightning bugs surrounded her, little lights blinking on and off as they attempted to tell her where to go. She was in a forest she didn't recognize and when she stood, she was dizzy and disoriented. "Bran," she whispered, her heart hammering against her chest. But when she tried to shift to go back, the bugs closed in.

"Okay, I'll follow you," she finally muttered, wiping away tears. "Lead on, small ones."

The fireflies formed an arrow and flew ahead and Kat followed.

When Kat came out of the woods, she thought she knew

where she was, but the landscape had changed so much it was difficult to recognize. Instead of the mass of firs and cedars, there were charred stumps and areas of the ground that had cracked and split, as though from an earthquake. She skirted around them, glad when she reached the road. But as soon as she came out onto the asphalt, she realized it was more precarious than the forest. The road surface had buckled, with deep gaps and uneven ground that she tripped over in her haste to catch up with the fireflies. And that's when she heard the voices.

Kat stopped to peer down the road, squinting to see what was happening. A crowd of men had gathered around the entrance to her father's property. The fireflies who had been leading her took off in a swarm, joining many others that formed a thick cloud in the air above the men who were carrying weapons and screaming at the top of their lungs. Dagda stood back from the gates and Mior was standing on top of one of the pillars next to the obsidian raven. He waved his arms and yelled, his high-pitched voice wrapping around Kat and sending shivers down her arms. There was power there, too much power for a small boy. He was speaking words Kat couldn't understand and apparently affecting the fireflies, who seemed to be attacking the crowd of men. They fired their guns randomly, chaos ensuing as the new fireflies joined the others. Kat scuttled across the street and moved closer, trying to see what was going on.

"Begone!" she heard her brother shout. Some men had fallen in their haste to escape the fireflies, others were lying still. Dagda and Siobhan watched from a safe distance as Mior directed, his arms waving like a conductor. By the time Kat reached the gates the only men remaining seemed to be dead.

"I didn't kill them!" Mior yelled. "They shot each other!"

Dagda hurried toward the gate and grabbed Mior off the pillar, hugging the boy close. When he looked up and saw Kat, he let out a roar and hurried toward her. "Where in hell have you been?"

But before Kat could answer, Siobhan was there, pulling her into her arms. "Kat, oh my gosh. We thought you were gone for good!" Once Siobhan released her, her mother's expression changed to one of worry. "Where is Arwen?"

Kat shook her head, her eyes filling.

It took quite a while to fill her mother and father in on what had happened since she'd last seen them. She didn't tell them what she'd learned about the dark witch, afraid of scaring her mother, who was already traumatized.

"Will you go back to Alfheim and reclaim your son?" Siobhan asked querulously.

"I don't know, Mom. Until I know for sure that he's changed, I don't want to be responsible for him. And also, to get there Val would have to help me. I've had no more interaction with him since the last door he opened."

"And Bran?"

"He was shot with an arrow when we were leaving Otherworld. He might be dead," she whispered, the word reverberating in her mind like a lock clicking into place.

"Maybe it's better this way," Dagda muttered, staring into the distance.

"No, Dad, it isn't better. We love each other. He told me why you don't like him, and frankly, you should know better."

Dagda stared at her, his eyes narrowing. "He told you he gave up his powers over a woman?"

"He told me that when he fell in love with me, he lost his powers. It didn't happen all at once, you know. But I think you've hated him for longer than that. What started it?"

Dagda's mouth turned into a thin line. "He...his father was a thorn in my side. I quarreled with Llyr."

"Why do you hang on to this? The creature at the Pinnacle knew Llyr and he had nothing bad to say about him."

"We..." Dagda glanced at Siobhan. "Llyr and I were in love with the same woman many, many years ago."

Kat shook her head. "Seriously? Hundreds, or possibly thousands of years ago? Don't you think it's time to leave it in the past?"

Siobhan moved close, slipping her arm through his. "Especially since you are no longer part of that world."

Kat was happy to see her father's expression lighten. "I have to get back to Otherworld and find Bran. I can go as a hummingbird but I may not get back in. Are the borders open?"

"Judging by what I think is coming, I doubt it," Dagda muttered. "Didn't you say you reached the Pinnacle?"

"I did. It's beautiful now."

Dagda chuckled. "I'm sure the gods aren't happy about that. Good for you, daughter. But knowing how things work there, they've probably installed emergency means to keep it closed. Who did you say shot Bran?"

Kat shook her head. "I have no idea, but I think they were trying to kill me. Someone who's a good shot with a bow." She glanced at Dagda. "How do I get back in? I would hate to end up at the barrier and beat myself to death trying to get through."

Mior grabbed her hand. "The fireflies will take you through, just like they brought you here!"

"They can get through the barrier?"

Mior grinned and danced around her. "They're magic."

Kat stared at him in shock. "I thought maybe you sent that one, but...you control all those lightning bugs?"

He nodded, looking very pleased with himself. "I can call them back if you want to go, but you just got here."

Kat knelt down next to him. "I have to help Bran. You understand that, don't you?"

Mior nodded. "Will you come back after you help him?"

"Yes."

"Do you promise?"

"I promise, Mior." Kat pulled him close and kissed the top of his head before turning to her parents. "Looks like life is returning," she said, glancing at the lights in the distance.

"For the time being," Dagda said. "But I have a sense that this won't last."

Kat noticed the worry on her father's face. He was no longer a god, but he did seem to have an intuition about these things. "I'll be back as soon as I can and hopefully Bran will be with me."

Siobhan pulled her into a hug. "Good luck, and please be careful," she whispered.

Mior muttered some words and waved his hands and a second later the swarm of fireflies arrived in a cloud, hovering above his head. At the last moment Dagda grabbed her and pulled her close. When he released her, she noticed that his eyes had filled with tears. A second later she was a bird, her senses taken over by the twinkling fireflies and the hum of tiny wings.

When Kat returned to human form she was by their shelter, moonlight glancing off the small stone circle that stood by the woods. There was no sign of Raven or Bran, only a few dark feathers amongst the leaves. Dried blood clung to them. Her chest felt tight, her breathing shallow as she searched, expecting to find him lying dead around each turning. When night fell, she hurried back to the rough shelter of twigs he'd fashioned, and curled into the bed he'd made for them. But instead of sleep her tears flowed, her sobs muffled by the increasing wind that blew through the tree branches. Her fingers wound around the silver pendant. She'd been keeping him at arm's-length for weeks, and now he was gone without knowing how much she loved him. "Please help me find Bran." The pendant warmed in her fingers, a vibration moving through it. Kat fell asleep with the silver necklace held tight in her fist, dreams taking her on a voyage to mystical lands.

Kat woke with a gasp, her heart pounding. It felt as though she'd walked through a veil and entered another life in another place. Bran had looked basically the same, aside from his rustic clothing and the beard. The pendant hung around his neck, and in the dream, when her fingers went to her own neck, she found her matching one. A child played in the dirt in front of her, his eyes the same shade of green as Bran's. They were linked forever, their love as deep as it was now, if not deeper. The community where they lived lay nestled into a beautiful valley surrounded with rugged mountains. They raised goats and grew vegetables. She was contented and happy, her belly swollen with their second child. There was no stress of saving the world, no dark forces, no evil witch. It was a normal life. She burst into tears.

It was close to dusk before she finally discovered the trail of blood. It led across a wide expanse of blowing grasses and into a canyon. She clambered down the rocky cliffs to the bottom, but once she reached the canyon floor, the dark spots disappeared. And that's when she looked up to see Raven huddled into a crevasse. The bird was nearly unconscious, his head lolling sideways, his wing held at an odd angle. "Raven," she whispered, gathering him gently into her arms. He was cold, his feathered body shivering from shock. She held him against her to warm him, her tears landing on the downy head that rested against her chest. "Bran," she whispered, "please live. I'm sorry...so sorry."

Kat was dozing when she felt the bird move, snuggling closer. She shifted her body to accommodate him and fell asleep again, exhausted from searching and the relief of finding him. As far as whether he would live or not, she didn't want to think about it until she had a chance to examine his wound in the light. The dream from the night before continued, taking her away from Otherworld, away from Ragnarok, away from her parents and the daunting task of saving the world. She walked through long grass next to a lake, her child's hand clutching hers and Bran right beside her.

"Kat?"

Kat woke with a start, surprised to see Bran peering at her. Half asleep and still in the dream, she reached for him, her mouth searching for his. She was by the lake lying in the long grass, caught up in a haze of desire. But when she moved against him, he let out a yelp.

Kat came fully awake, her eyes widening when she realized where she was. Bran grimaced as her fingers went to his upper arm. "The arrow's still there."

"Kind of hard for a bird to remove it, but I did try."

There were scratches and splinters on the shaft. "Why didn't you shift?"

"I couldn't—too stressed. It's only because of you that I was able to manage it."

Kat ran her hands over his arm, trying to figure out how to remove the arrow. "If I pull it out…"

"I'll bleed like a motherfucker."

"What can I do?"

"I hate to say it, but I think I may require the aid of Airmid and her healing spring."

Kat grimaced. "The last time we saw her, she…"

"I know," he said, wincing in pain. "It's the only way, Kat."

"And after she helps you, she'll drag us both off to Forseti and we'll be imprisoned."

Bran shook his head. "She was jealous. She has to be over it by now."

"Hell hath no fury like a woman scorned," Kat intoned.

"Yeah, don't I know it."

"At least the bleeding stopped. That's a good thing, right?"

Bran glanced at his upper arm. "The arrowhead went into the bone."

"What if it was Airmid who shot you?"

Bran shook his head. "She wouldn't do that."

Kat let out a sigh. "If not her, who?"

Bran shrugged. "Someone who didn't want me to go down to earth with you."

"Maybe they were trying to hit me, but since I was so small, it hit you."

"If that's true I'm glad. You'd be dead now." Bran stood unsteadily. "We should go before I lose any more blood."

Kat took hold of his good arm. "Put your arm around my shoulder."

Bran did as she asked, stumbling against her. "You must have made it to earth considering how long you were gone. How is it?"

"Things were calm—if they hadn't been, I wouldn't have come back so quickly."

"And I would have died," he muttered.

Kat felt a pang of guilt, sorry for the distance there'd been between them.

They set off with Bran leaning heavily on Kat as they walked. He was pale as ash, his forehead covered in sweat despite the chill wind that blew. Kat grew more and more worried as the day progressed; her earlier calm was replaced with a vision of him collapsing before they reached the spring. She filled the air with stories about her short trip to earth, regaling him with Mior's abilities with the fireflies, and what was happening with Dagda and her mother. "The damage from the storms was terrible, but the weather has improved. Maybe Ragnarok is over."

Bran glanced at her. "Don't count on it."

"Why do you say that? I'm trying to be positive."

"When I'm Raven, I get messages from the wind. Ragnarok is just beginning. I don't know what's coming, but it will be far worse than what's already happened."

Kat shivered, trying not to see the vision that flashed across her mind. "I had this incredible dream," she said, turning her mind to something more pleasant. "We were married and I was pregnant and we already had a son around four years old. We lived in this valley between two mountains, and we were so happy. We weren't gods, Bran, we were normal people with a normal life."

"I hope that dream comes true."

When Kat glanced at him there was sadness in his eyes. She wrapped her arm around his waist and struggled forward.

By the time they reached Airmid's spring Bran was nearly dead on his feet. Several times he shifted into Raven so that she could carry him, his wing hanging useless over her arm. But when they drew closer, he stayed in human form, unsure whether he could guide her properly. "It's right at the top of the ridge in that copse of rowans and hawthorn bushes. There's another stone circle up there."

"I recognize it," Kat replied. "But I didn't know about the circle."

"Yeah, it's the reason for the spring. Airmid's usually here this time of night," he muttered, lurching against her.

Kat grabbed him to steady him. "Can you make it? The hill's steep."

Bran nodded. His breath was shallow when he placed his hand on her shoulder and let her pull him upward. When the spring came into view Bran slumped against her and stumbled. "Airmid," he called out weakly, struggling to stay upright.

"Airmid, are you here?" Kat shouted.

Airmid appeared from behind the pool wearing a gossamer night dress. She stared at the two of them before her eyes went wide. "Help me get him into the spring," she ordered, slipping off her nightdress.

Kat took his other arm and between the two of them they were able to slide him into the water. Airmid glanced at Kat. "Take off your clothes and climb in. I will need your assistance. "

Kat didn't question her, only doing as she asked. Once Kat was in the pool Airmid slid in beside Bran, her hand going to the back of his head to keep him from going under. "He's close to death," she whispered, examining him in the moonlight spilling across the water. "Who did this?"

Kat shook her head. "I have no idea."

Airmid examined the wound, her fingers pressing and releasing until Bran let out a groan of protest. "When did it happen?" the goddess asked.

Kat shook her head again. "We were on our way to Earth as birds when he was shot. I went down there without him. I was gone maybe half a day. I couldn't just leave without finding out what was happening," she said defensively. "My parents and my brother…"

Airmid's worried gaze met hers. "I understand, but a half day down there could be a week in Otherworld. You shouldn't have left him this long."

"I had no choice. The fireflies took me."

Airmid stopped what she was doing to gaze at her. "Fireflies?"

"My brother conjured them."

"Dagda's son did this? How old is he?"

"Four."

Airmid shook her head and turned away to deal with Bran. "Fireflies are magical beings. They no longer exist here." She reached for the arrow and glanced at Kat. "Hold his arm steady and do not be disturbed by what you see."

Kat moved close and took hold of Bran's arm, holding it firmly with both hands. A moment later there was a terrible rending sound and then a rush of dark blood. Bran let out a strangled cry and fell back, his head disappearing under the surface.

"Get behind him and hold his head above the water!" Airmid yelled.

Kat did as Airmid said, her hands shaking as she pulled him to the surface.

Airmid placed her fingers on his chest. "Bran is dead," she whispered.

Kat felt numb inside as she watched the blood continue to pour from Bran's arm. She let out a sob. "What should I do?"

"Nothing more than what you're doing. When I say the words, you must keep very quiet and reach out to Danu. She is the mother of the Tuatha de Danaan, and the mother of all the gods. Danu nurtures those who are hurt and protects those who are alone. Hear me Danu!" she shouted, her head flung back. "Help us heal this god who has been shot with poison!"

"Poison?"

Airmid shook her head, placing a finger on her lips. "Blood to blood, bone to bone, sinew to sinew…"

The healing prayer went on and on. Kat's hands grew tired, her arms weak. She watched the man she loved, hoping for some sign of life, but he never moved, and his eyes remained closed. Her tears fell endlessly, landing on his face, his hair and in the water. Kat was no longer here, she was in a place of no sound, no life, only death and the end of everything. *Please, Danu—please save him…*

"Kat…Kat!"

Kat opened her eyes to see Airmid frowning at her. "We need to move him now. Help me pull his body from the water."

"Is he…?"

"He will live," Airmid said tersely, dragging him from the pool. "Wrap him in the blanket there and keep watch over him until moonset. If he hasn't opened his eyes by then, it is a sign that he is lost in another realm. If that happens…" Her eyes bored into Kat's. "If that happens it will be up to him to find his way back to us. There is no more healing I can do." Airmid pulled her shift on and disappeared behind the spring.

Pale mist rose from the water, wafting about her as Kat tugged at Bran's body to wrap him up. It took all her strength, her chest filled with dread as she took in his pale skin, and shuttered eyes. She spent the rest of the night holding him close, her arms tight around him. She prayed for hours, finally falling into a stupor-like sleep just before moonset.

'Katel', the muffled underwater voice called. Kat opened her eyes to see a beautiful dark-haired woman staring at her. She was dressed in a gray-blue gown, her eyes close to the same color. Mahogany hair cascaded over her shoulders in waves that shimmered in the light from the moon. A stone circle surrounded her, the stones looking newly chiseled with rough tools, no moss marring their surfaces.

"I am Danu. You are my protégée and as such you must heed my warning. There is a darkness around you, a force that is poised to do you harm. You must go deep into the forest and ask the trees for help—you are connected to the trees and it is there that you will find me. Do not delay. You are not who you think you are. The divine feminine is upon us, Kat. The earth is crying out and it is up to those who care to stop the destruction."

Kat woke with a start, every fiber of her being on high alert. The most ancient and esteemed goddess had just sent her a message, but what did *protégée* mean? Bran lay as still as a stone, but some color had returned to his cheeks. She leaned over to kiss his forehead, tears of gratitude welling and spilling over. *Thank you,* she whispered.

32

I t came like a vengeance, the strength of it shaking the
earth. It was more than an earthquake, more than a
tornado, more than a volcano, the sheer size of it
obliterating any chance of denying what it was. The sky
darkened and grew black, despite it being the middle of the
day. Dark horses, their riders covered from head to toe in
black, the hooves pounding without sound across the sky
like a plague. A roar began, filling every molecule of air with
sound, and causing those who still lived to hold their hands
over their ears. And when the roar ended a screeching
began.

Siobhan ran, Mior in her arms. When Dagda caught up
with her, her face was white with terror. "What is this,
Dag?"

"It's what I warned you about. This is the true
Ragnarok, Siobhan. There is no place to hide from it."

"What do we do?" she cried, looking up. Her expression
registered the horror of seeing horses and riders galloping
across a sky gone dark.

"I know where to hide," Mior murmured.

"But do you know how to combat this evil?" Dagda asked his half-god son.

Mior's face fell. "No, Papa. Why are there horses up there?"

"Because someone has opened the door between our earth and the Norse world."

"Where is this hiding place, Mior?" Siobhan asked frantically.

"Follow me," the boy said, hurrying off.

Mior led them down the road and into an abandoned building that had once been a bar. Behind the bar he pulled uselessly at a trap door until Dagda helped him open it. Mior summoned fireflies to light their way down the steep stairs into a wine cellar. Oddly no water had leaked in, a musty smell all that remained from the recent storms. Dagda grabbed a dusty bottle off a shelf and pulled the cork, sniffing the contents. "Cognac," he muttered, taking a hefty swig.

"Dag, do you think that's a good idea?"

He turned. "You should have some, Siobhan. It's good for the nerves."

She sniffed and wrinkled her nose. "Is there a bottle of wine down here?"

The fireflies lit up the interior for Dagda as he searched. "Here's one and it's a decent red and a screw top. You're in luck." He unscrewed it and handed it to her.

Siobhan tasted it before drinking some down. She let out a sigh and placed it upright on the floor. "Now if we only had some food. What will happen up there? What will those riders do?"

"You don't want to know," Dagda muttered, lifting the cognac bottle to his mouth.

"Yes, yes I do," she said, gazing at him.

"They will destroy everything in their wake, Siobhan. If we live through this there will be nothing left of this town."

"No people or animals?" Mior asked.

"No people, no animals, no buildings, nothing," Dagda muttered, upending the bottle.

Dagda didn't sleep, worry etched into the skin around his eyes. They'd heard the
terrible sounds of war, the screams, the cry of horses in pain, the shouts and the rat-at-at of guns. He wished now he'd taken his wife and son to Daniel's bunker. This place was not safe. They would be discovered—it was only a matter of time. They'd had nothing to eat for two days, only the alcohol which he'd even allowed his son to drink. Since there was no water it was all he could offer. It was time for them to get out of here, time to find out the truth of what was happening. If they didn't, they would die here. *Six to one, half dozen to the other,* he thought morosely. *Some fucking protector I am.*

"Time to go," he muttered, shaking Siobhan awake. She glanced up at him, her beautiful eyes full of tears. He let out a sob. "I'm sorry, Siobhan. But if we don't get out of here, this building and everything in it is going to come down on top of us."

Siobhan turned to Mior curled up sleeping beside her. "Wake up, sweet boy," she murmured.

Dagda grabbed Mior and rushed toward the trapdoor. When he pushed it up, he heard a roar as the roof lifted off the building and something heavy lumbered by. When he tried to see what it was, a funnel cloud whirled out of nowhere, sucking them into the spinning winds, along with the rest of the building and everything in the immediate vicinity. Siobhan's scream was the last thing he heard.

33

Kat was still thinking about Danu when Airmid arrived. Dawn was just chasing away the shadows, birds beginning to wake, their sweet songs heralding the new day.

Airmid placed a hand on Bran's heart and closed her eyes. "Bran is in the place where I feared he might go."

Kat felt a jolt. "Is this because of the poison you mentioned?"

Airmid nodded, her eyes darkening. "I will make a drink from the herbs I have, but the only real way to bring him back is to send love."

"I can do that—I've been doing it all night."

Airmid smiled sadly. "I know you have." She gazed into the distance. "There is something I must tell you." She let out a sigh as though wishing she didn't have to say whatever it was. "When I came after you that day and threatened you, I was taken over by something…something evil had hold of me. Yes, I have always loved Bran, but not in the way you do. He's like a brother to me."

"But he said you had sex, and I've seen you with him in the pool."

Airmid nodded. "This thing, whatever it is, has taken over my spirit on more than one occasion. I never meant to hurt you. You were and are my friend. As far as trying to keep you two apart, it was only because of the laws of gods. I didn't know then that you were a demi-goddess. Bran has given up his powers for you. Did you know that?"

"But what about that day you said I didn't belong here? You were nearly hysterical."

Airmid's hazel eyes welled. "I was under the same influence, although what I remember saying about the Elven baby is true. The Fae are not welcome here."

Kat nodded, wondering if she should believe what the goddess was telling her. "But what is it that takes you over? Could it be the same entity that shot Bran with a poisoned arrow?"

"It's very likely. You may or not believe me, but I would never hurt him nor would I hurt you. I only came to earth to help you. I taught you herbal lore and assisted your understanding of the powers you inherited."

"What about that day you were with Forseti—when you two went to the Pinnacle?"

Airmid nodded. "I was not myself that day. When it happens, it feels as though I'm split in two, but the real me is unable to take control. Bran has seen me like this several times, but I was too ashamed to explain it for fear he would think I was making excuses for my nasty behavior."

"You must know who or what this is, Airmid. You can't tell me an entity took you over and as a goddess you have no clue."

"And yet it's the truth. I must seek out Danu. She's the only goddess powerful enough to undo what has been done. It could happen again. If I act strangely you must leave immediately. I fear that this entity wants to use me for something truly evil."

"Like killing me," Kat muttered. "Danu came to me in a dream—she said I'm her protégée. What does that mean?"

Airmid seemed surprised, a look of wonder crossing her face. "It means the ancient mother goddess is looking out for you. You've received the greatest gift you could—Danu has taken you under her wing."

Kat took that in, a feeling of warmth settling around her heart. "She told me that I have darkness around me. She said she'd help, but I wasn't to delay."

"Darkness," Airmid repeated her eyes glazing over. "Do you know where to go to speak with Danu?"

"The forest, but I don't know which one."

"Danu can be found in any forest. I suggest the one at the top of the hill there," she said, pointing. "The standing stones weaken the veil between the worlds, giving her the ability to appear to you."

Kat glanced down. "I can't leave Bran."

"I'll stay here and watch over him. And when you return, you will know what to do to bring him back."

"She didn't mention him at all—it was more about me and the darkness and the divine feminine."

Airmid smiled. "The earth is the embodiment of the divine feminine." She waved her hand. "Now go to Danu."

As Kat climbed the hill, she wondered at the power of whatever had taken over Airmid's spirit, causing her to do unspeakable things. It was hard to believe, and yet it had the ring of truth. The person she'd known had disappeared in those moments, even her face changing as she screamed at Kat. The woman she'd witnessed in the spring that day, was heartless and self-centered. Was this the same darkness Danu mentioned? And if so, could it take her over as well?

When she reached the line of trees, she followed the dawn light, letting it lead her deep into the forest. When she came upon the standing stones she stopped, gazing into the mists that hung paper-thin between worlds. The moss-covered stones seemed lit from within, waves of energy pulsing from them where they formed an irregular circle in front of an enormous oak tree. "The druid tree," she murmured.

"Yes, exactly so. But it is also the goddess tree."

Kat turned to see the woman from her dream. But in this reality, she was even more beautiful. Mists sparkled around her body, as though she was encased in crystals. Her hair was thick and reddish brown, a silver torc encircling her head to hold the tangle back from her pale face. "Danu."

"Yes, my child," she answered, moving forward to clasp Kat's hands. "I can see that you have a deep concern about your god who lies by Airmid's spring. Airmid was correct in the way to heal him, but I think you know that already. Love is a powerful force, Katel. And you have much to give."

Kat stared into the blue-green eyes, a deep sense of peace flowing over her. "And what of this darkness?"

"You will be confronted very soon. I cannot impart more than that. It is shadowy still, an unknown. I can only tell you that it is this darkness that you've been seeking."

"Seeking? I wouldn't seek darkness."

"Your destiny lies with this darkness. It is the future you have already grasped. It is the counterpoint to your light, Katel."

Danu let go of her hands and began to fade away.

"But, what should I do? How do I deal with this darkness? Is it the witch?"

The forest glade still shimmered with magic, but the goddess was no longer there.

Danu's cryptic messages made little sense to her, only that she would have some horrible fight with an unnamable force. She let out a heavy sigh and hurried down the hill. When she reached Bran, he lay as before. "No change?" she asked Airmid sitting next to him.

"He is still in the twilight place," she answered, rising. "What did you learn from Danu?"

Kat was reluctant to talk about it, worried that this darkness Danu had spoken of might be lurking about. "She said love is a powerful force."

Airmid smiled. "I'm sure there was more to it than that." She pulled one of the leather bags off her belt and held it out. "Take a pinch of this. It will relax you and allow you to sleep." The brown-haired goddess turned and disappeared behind the spring.

When the herbs began to work, Kat's head nodded. She hadn't slept a wink all night and with the excitement of Danu she was even more drained. She curled up next to Bran, rested her head on his chest and fell asleep.

The words were garbled, the place she was in, hazy. Bran was there, his eyes glazed and expressionless. "Bran," she whispered, "where are we?"

Bran turned his vacant gaze to hers. "I don't know," he said, the words distorted as if they were both underwater.

The place was as empty as his words, a thick fog filling in the spaces where there should have been something, anything to suggest a landscape or a certain locality. Fog swirled, encircling the two of them, and wrapping around them both. "Stop," she muttered, attempting to move away from the suffocating sameness, the feeling that she was underwater in some lightless box. Bran sat on the ground, his head lolling. And when she touched his shoulder, he didn't look up or acknowledge her in any way. The wound on his arm had healed, a thin red mark the only thing remaining. And yet…he was lost here, unable to extricate himself from this seeming purgatory.

"Bran, we have to get out of here. Bran!" Kat shook him, trying to get him to look at her, but when he did, his eyes were unfocused and dull. She heard a cackle to her right, but when she glanced in that direction there was nothing there but shadow.

Kat heard a harsh whisper from beyond the fog. "It won't be long now." A laugh followed, filled with loathing. It had to be what Danu had warned her about. She had to get Bran out of here—whatever this was, would kill him. She took hold of his arm and forced him to his feet. "We have to go!" she shouted, but he was still unresponsive, like a rag doll, his wobbly legs buckling a second later. When he fell, she knew she didn't have the strength to lift him.

"Kat!" She heard the familiar voice from afar, her senses pulled. When she glanced at Bran, he was lying on the ground with his eyes closed. "Kat!" The voice was more insistent this time, harder to ignore. She struggled against it, but when she felt fingers close around her upper arm, she opened her eyes.

Airmid bent over her. "Where were you? I've been trying to wake you for over ten minutes!"

"I was…" she rubbed her eyes. "I was with Bran in

some horrible place. He could barely talk. And there was something in there with us."

Airmid's eyes widened. "You went to the in-between? It's a dangerous place and those who enter rarely come out. No wonder I couldn't rouse you."

Kat glanced down at Bran, her eyes welling. "He's barely alive."

"He won't die, but if we can't get him out, he will remain there in the state you saw him in."

Kat stared into the distance, her recent faith in herself draining away. "I'm supposed to save earth and yet I'm here, hoping to save the man I love. I have nothing to offer anyone."

Airmid cocked her head. "Are you sure of that?"

Kat thought of what Danu had told her about love. Despite the months in which she'd kept her distance, waiting for him to trust her again, she loved Bran with all her heart. Her fingers went unconsciously to her pendant. She let out a cry and pulled them away. "The silver...it's so hot!"

Airmid moved to examine the necklace. "Bran has one just like this. There's ancient magic here. I suggest you tune into what it wants to tell you."

Kat was alone with Bran when she examined her pendant more closely. The silver was still hot to the touch but it no longer burned her. She pulled it from her neck and stared at it, marveling at the intricacy of the Celtic knot and the dragon entwined within it. She traced the dragon with her finger. They were guardians of wisdom and knowledge and they possessed the power of prophecy. "What are you trying to tell me?" she whispered. Kat shrank back when the dragon uncoiled, one eye staring up at her. *'The link will break. Do not despair. The prophecy will come to pass.'*

Kat wasn't sure if she'd heard the rumbling words inside her mind or if they'd been spoken out loud. When she looked again, the dragon was back the way he'd been, coiled and silent. What prophecy? She removed Bran's pendant from around his neck. His was the same as hers, except for the Gaelic words engraved along the knot. He'd told her what they meant: *'may our hands be ever clasped; may our hearts be joined in love'.* Was that the prophecy? She placed both pendants on the ground and reached to take his limp hand, twining her fingers through his as she opened her heart. "I love you," she whispered.

When she glanced down the pendants had begun to glow, an inner fire licking around the edges of the hand wrought silver. A second later they were in flames, the acrid smell of burning metal assaulting her nostrils. She flung dirt on them to put it out, but all it did was fan the flames. Smoke rose, hiding the pendants within a gray haze. Her love for Bran burned inside her, reflecting what was happening with the two pendants. And as she watched, a mystic light lifted from the two pendants, cascading over Bran in rainbow colors and disappearing into his body. "Please," she murmured. "I pledge myself to you forever, through this life and the next one and the one after that."

And as she prayed, a vision came to her of the two of them in some far-off distant land of sand. They rode side by side on small ponies, their hands clasped as they fought the grit-filled winds. Scarves were tied around their heads and over their mouths, colorful cotton robes trailing. She felt his presence next to her like a balm on her soul. When the scene faded, another one came, and then another after that: Kat giving birth in a small hut somewhere deep in the woods, the baby's cry as it emerged from her womb. Bran gazing at her with such love she thought she might die of it. Another life where they both wore dark robes and moved together along forest trails in woods so deep and dark it seemed they would never end. The trees were ancient, enormous, from a bygone time. Her vision blurred, salt tears flowing over him like water from a stream.

Kat was asleep when she heard Bran stir next to her. Her eyes flew open to see him on his knees staring down at her. "You saved me," he murmured just before his lips touched hers.

It wasn't until sometime later that Kat realized that both pendants had disappeared.

34

Earth was on fire, flames so hot that entire trees were consumed within minutes. Fenrir, the wolf son of Loki, flew over the lands, devouring everything in his path. Jormungand, the giant serpent, was coiled in the sky, ready to consume what was left.

Communities, cities, farmlands, rivers, were all gone now. All that remained was the smoldering ruins of what had been.

Dagda carried Siobhan, tears flowing down his face as he searched for a place of refuge. All he could see in every direction was a wasteland, devoid of color with no life. There was no place to rest. Mior hurried beside him, his sobs filling the utter silence. "Is Mama all right?"

"She will be if I can tend to her. She's hurt, Mior. She breathed in a lot of smoke, and when we were taken by the tornado, she was hit by flying debris."

"I can fix her," the boy murmured.

Dagda stopped his endless slog to look down on his son. "What can *you* do?"

"I know how to help, Papa. It's part of me now." A

second later a swarm of fireflies appeared, hovering around the boy.

Dagda let out a sigh, his gaze roaming across the landscape. "Where do we go?"

The fireflies flew off and Mior pointed after them. "Follow the little lights."

Dagda thought back to their flight from the cellar, the smoke that had filled the place, the tornado's wrath and Siobhan's cry of terror and pain. It had been his decision to leave the cellar at that moment. If he'd waited, perhaps…but then he remembered that not only had they been sucked into the whirlwind, but also the entire building had been in there with them. It was a wonder any of them had survived.

He watched Mior running ahead, the fireflies in the distance. His son did have magic, that was undisputed, but he doubted whether Mior could get them out of this one. Earth was too far gone, his wife in a near coma in his arms, no food, no water, and no place safe to shelter.

They'd been traveling non-stop for days now, his body weak from hunger and thirst. Somehow, he was still upright, but he knew that his legs would fail him soon. This human body was frail and fragile. The world he'd known was a distant memory, everything beautiful gone. No birds flew, no trees stood, the rivers had been diverted and had mostly dried up. Not a sign of life remained in the desolation he took in through the haze of tears.

When he glanced at Siobhan, he let out a moan of worry. She was deathly white, her eyelids fluttering. Maybe they would die here together. The sky was dark again, storm clouds riding the thermals. It would soon rain and then they would all be wet and cold, as well as starving. He had no cloak to keep them warm, no rain-proof boots or warm socks. He let out a roar of frustration, raising his fist to the heavens. "Why?" he shouted. "Why did you do this to me?" There was no answer.

They came to a slight hollow by a rocky outcropping. The fireflies hovered above it, waiting. Mior danced around Dagda. "Let me fix Mama."

Dagda placed his wife gently on the ground, watching his son. Mior bent over her and muttered some words and then placed his hands on the deep cuts and heavy bruising on her legs and arms. Dagda watched his son's face change, the babyish features turning into someone he didn't recognize. It scared him for a moment until Siobhan opened her eyes. "Where are we?" she asked, sitting up.

He reached for her, his heart swelling with gratitude. The cuts were gone, and the purple bruises were hardly noticeable now. He was overwhelmed and shocked by Mior's abilities. The boy was *his* son, he thought proudly. He reached out to tousle his dark curls. "Thank you, Mior," he murmured.

"Mama!" the boy shouted. "We have the entire world to fix! Isn't it fun? But we need Kat." He frowned, looking around. "Where is she?"

"I don't know," Dagda replied, kneeling next to Siobhan. "Maybe you can find her."

Mior gazed into the distance. "Maybe I can," he murmured.

With Dagda's help, Siobhan stood, her shocked gaze on the bleak landscape stretching in every direction. "What has happened?" she whispered.

Dagda's eyes darkened. "Ragnarok."

35

Kat had a feeling of impending doom, as though something terrible had happened or was about to happen. "Are you well enough to travel?"

Bran looked up from where he was soaking in the healing spring. His eyes had lost their dullness. "I'm getting there. Where's Airmid?"

"She...I don't know. The last thing she said was something about Danu."

Bran disappeared under the water, rising to shake silver droplets in every direction. "Get in here," he ordered, reaching for her.

"I..."

"I need you, Kat. It's part of my healing."

Kat laughed. She shed her clothes and climbed in. She needed him too.

He kissed her and pulled her under with him, both of them rising a minute later laughing. His eyes turned liquid and soft as he pulled her close.

"What about Airmid? Don't you think that...?"

"Thinking is not what I had in mind," he muttered,

pressing against her.

His arousal moved against her, his hands on her breasts. She took a quick look around before surrendering to the desire that swirled between them. When they came together her heart opened and lifted, visions of their soul lives whirling through her mind as he moved deep inside her.

They were still at it when Airmid arrived, both unaware of her presence until she cleared her throat. Kat pulled away and dunked under the water, attempting to compose herself.

Airmid smiled. "You seem better."

Bran laughed. "Kat saved me from that hell."

Airmid frowned. "You saw the witch?"

Bran shrugged, reaching for Kat when she rose from under the water. "All I know is she would have kept me forever in that limbo place."

Kat avoided him and climbed out of the pool, reaching for her clothes. "Have you learned anything? I had the strangest premonition."

Airmid let out a sigh, her eyes clouding. "The earth that you remember is no more."

Kat let out a cry, her hand going to her mouth. "Dagda, my mother, Mior?"

"They live, at least for now."

"How do you know?"

"I saw it all in the forest pool that lies close to the stone circle. It's where I do my meditations."

Kat felt something shift inside her. "This was my destiny," she whispered.

Airmid stared at her. "You do not understand how things work. Ragnarok is unstoppable. It was meant to be."

Kat shook her head. "Meant to be? I was supposed to stop it, it's why I freed the creature. I don't understand."

By now Bran had climbed out of the pool and was pulling on his trousers. "Kat, what Airmid is saying is true. It's written in the annals. No one could have stopped this."

Kat covered her face with her hands. "My family is down there, my baby brother…" she dissolved into tears.

Airmid placed a gentle hand on her shoulder. "I have only witnessed the vision in the water. These visions are not always accurate."

Kat wiped her eyes. "I thought that opening the borders would save it—things seemed so much better the last time I was there. Every time I do anything, something happens to stop me from taking the next step. If Bran hadn't been shot, I would have been down there to help. I feel like some force has been working against me."

Airmid raised her eyebrows. "If anyone's working against you, it's the dark witch. She wanted Ragnarok."

"Well, she got her wish," Kat muttered. Her mind went to her baby, and how he'd turned on her, her two useless trips to the Pinnacle, Bran stuck in the twilight world. All the time she'd wasted. "Who *is* she?"

Airmid let out a heavy sigh. "Her name is Carmun. She's the goddess of evil, a sorceress who wants only destruction."

Kat nodded. "The creature told me her name. The jailor he killed was working with her or for her. Danu told me my destiny is entwined with this darkness, but she didn't name it. How can that be?"

"It is not my place to question Danu. If she intimated that your fate is connected with Carmun, then it must be true. But do not forget what you know inside yourself."

Kat stared at the goddess. "You mean about saving earth? What is there to save?"

"Did you think you were to save earth *before* it was destroyed? The word you want is restore, not save. I told you that your family lives. Isn't that a start?"

Kat glanced at Bran. "What do *you* think?"

"I think it's time to check it out for yourself."

Kat had pulled on her ragged Fae dress and the heavy boots when the fireflies arrived. "Bran, look!" she cried out. "Mior must have sent them!"

Bran grabbed her hand. "Let's go."

Hummingbird and Raven landed in a featureless wasteland. There was nothing there, not the forest, or the town, not even a hint that anything had ever been. The sky was black with cloud, the air bitter cold. There wasn't a tree, a bush, a flower. The ground had been leveled as though a giant bulldozer had rolled across the land and taken everything in its wake. Kat willed away her tears and took in a deep breath. "We know my parents and Mior are here somewhere. But where? And how can we get our bearings in a place that has no landmarks?"

"Easy. We fly."

Kat nodded, trying not to be dismayed by the lack of vegetation, houses or people. "Everyone's gone," she whispered.

"Not everyone," Bran replied, giving her a hard look.

"And if they're alive, others are too."

She'd never considered that stopping Ragnarok before it started wasn't her destiny. Maybe it had been, and she'd failed. If she'd confronted the dark witch maybe this wouldn't have happened. Now she was faced with the awful truth. Ragnarok had come and gone, and if Airmid was correct, she was responsible for bringing life back to a planet devoid of anything. She gazed at the bleak landscape, the darkening sky. It was very difficult to keep the tears at bay, to not let despair take her over.

She shifted, waiting until Raven was beside her before they flew together across the broken terrain. When it began to snow, the hummingbird ignored it and kept going.

Hummingbird's wings were coated, ice on her beak. She shivered under her layer of feathers. There was nothing she could do to stop the fall. When her eyes closed and her wings stilled, Raven moved beneath her to catch her. She lay frozen on his spread wings as he drifted downward, finally landing. He folded his wings around her. When she finally came back to human form, Bran was staring at her worriedly.

"It's freezing," she muttered, clasping her arms around her body.

He pulled her close to hold her against the heat from his body. "Hummingbirds don't do well in the cold." He squinted into the falling snow. "When I was Raven, I saw some color over that way." He pointed into the flat sameness, the falling snow obliterating any view. "The fireflies were heading in that direction, but then it began to snow. Can you walk?"

Kat stood shakily and followed him across the colorless

landscape. Soon she was following Bran blindly, unable to think or talk or do anything but place her feet in his footprints. The wind came up, sending snow into her eyes and coating her eyelashes.

"There!" Bran shouted. He grabbed Kat's hand and pulled her forward through the blizzard.

"What if it isn't them?" she shouted, but Bran either didn't hear her, or he ignored her. Kat could barely see, but when she heard Mior yell, she slipped out of Bran's grasp and ran. A second later Mior, wearing an enormous bright red sweatshirt, hurtled straight into her, his arms going tight around her waist. "I knew you'd find us!" he crowed.

Her brother led them to a small hollow beneath a rocky outcropping. It was nothing more than an animal den, but it kept the wind and snow out, and afforded a place to curl up and sleep. Once they were inside, she was able to see how much Mior had grown. "You're so tall!"

He laughed, glancing at his mother and Dagda huddled into the shadows. When they saw Kat and Bran, they both rose, her father more slowly than her mother. Siobhan looked pale, but the smile on her face when she held out her arms was full of warmth. She gathered Kat into her arms, a sob coming from her chapped lips as she pulled her daughter close. "I feared we'd never see you again," she murmured.

"How many times have you said that?" Kat whispered. "Maybe this time I can stick around for a while."

Dagda stood behind her, his twilight eyes on his daughter. "Where have you been all this time?"

"Everywhere, Dad. So much has happened the past few months."

"Months? It's been a year since we've seen you!"

Dagda's gaze went to Bran, who stood awkwardly in the mouth of the cave. "Didn't you explain to her the way time works in Otherworld?"

"I sort of forgot about it with everything going on."

Kat glanced at her mother who was wearing a loose-fitting tattered wool dress. She moved away from the opening, her arms protectively around her belly. "Mom? Are you pregnant?" she asked, her gaze on the obvious bulge.

Siobhan smiled. "I am." She glanced at Dagda. "And this one won't scare me so much," she added in a whisper, inclining her head toward Mior who was forming snowballs and tossing them into the air to turn into birds and fly away.

Kat stood open-mouthed, her ability to speak temporarily suspended. "How can that much time have gone by?" she finally stammered. "And how have you survived? Being pregnant can't be easy when you have no real shelter and no food. This place…it's dead."

"We have Mior," Dagda said, glancing proudly at his son. "He has a knack for finding things. You'd be surprised how many animals survived the devastation. With this snow, water will collect and the plants will germinate. And with your help maybe we can begin rebuilding."

Kat thought about that, wondering what powers, if any, she had. Before she could respond, Mior turned from his game. "You do," he said, reading her mind. "You have tons of magic!"

Kat turned to see Bran, his hair wet with snow. She reached for his hand and tugged him inside. When their eyes met, she saw something in his that frightened her. He didn't want to be here. "Bran?"

He shook his head and turned away.

36

"It is done," the witch said, her empty eyes on the specters circling her. "I have opened the gates and let Ragnarok do its worst. Now we must rid the world of the girl. She is all that stands in the way of complete annihilation of Earth. She will come after me. I have seen it when I scry. But what the future holds is still in darkness."

She moved to light the candles, flame coming from her gnarled fingers. She placed them in a circle and bade the others to come closer. They ranged from the newly dead to those who had expired a thousand years before, their partially fleshed bodies hidden beneath their dark hooded capes. Their eyes were empty holes in their skulls, but they were alive—brought back by the necromancy with which Carmun was so adept.

"Come and say the words with me. We must build our power, send it into the night. Let it be the shadow that sees, the darkness that watches and brings the message back. We will know soon what our next move shall be." She led them in a chant, the words growing louder as they repeated them over and over.

Let the darkness be all, let the light disappear, let the world turn dark, let the sun burn out and turn to dust. Let evil rule from now until eternity.

Once silence returned, the smoke from the candles lifted into the air. It formed a shadow and drifted out the cave mouth, disappearing into the dark night.

Day moved into night. Not that there was much change. The snow continued to fall, blanketing everything. It was sometime later, when the conversation slowed down, that everyone settled in to sleep. Kat huddled on one side with Bran, watching her parents and Mior gather together as though they'd done this a thousand times, each one taking a certain position to maximize the warmth of the others. Kat felt a pain in the region of her heart as she watched them, intuition of what they'd been through settling into her like a lead weight. Tears welled and trickled down her cheeks.

Bran pulled her close. "It's okay, Kat. They're alive, we're alive. Tomorrow we can think about it all and make a plan."

"I know you don't want to be here," she whispered.

"It doesn't matter what I want. I won't leave you."

The morning came too soon, Kat's sleepless night leaving her groggy and out of sorts. The idea of facing this empty world depressed her and made her ashamed of what she hadn't done. It was her fault this had happened. She thought of the things Dagda had told them the night before, the rush for shelter when the first of it began, the death they'd witnessed, the deprivation. And always waiting for her to return; their belief that she would follow up on her promise. Mior was the one who led them on and on, his fireflies helping them find cover out of the wind, out of the rain. He'd found the cans left behind, the food buried under sand and stone. While she was walking to the Pinnacle, Mior was saving her parents.

"Kat," he whispered. "This isn't your fault."

When she turned, he caught her tear-streaked face in his hands. "You've done so much, had so many crises to get through. You gave birth, you saved me twice, you gave up your child, you opened up the borders between the Pinnacle and Earth and nearly died because of it."

She shook her head. "And all that time I should have been here. Have you seen this place? The Earth I knew no longer exists."

"And your parents and brother are alive, your mother will soon have a baby. Remember what Airmid told you— saving earth couldn't be done *before* it was destroyed, now could it?"

"I was supposed to keep it from *being* destroyed, Bran."

He took hold of her hands, holding them in his. "No. That was never your mission."

"I see that you two are awake," Siobhan said, pushing herself up from the nest of threadbare blankets. "Kat, why don't you help me prepare breakfast."

Bran kissed her before she rose to join her mother.

"We have two can of beans and one of corn. That makes a complete protein. There is no way to make a fire, so cold food will have to do. I have a few bowls and a couple of forks we found a while back. Can you open the cans?" She handed Kat a much- battered metal can-opener. "I'll gather some snow and bring it inside to melt to quench our thirst."

Kat grabbed her arm as she turned. "How have you managed, Mom?"

Siobhan pulled on a tattered shawl and tugged her outside. "What a beautiful day," she said, staring up at the crystalline sky. She glanced back to make sure Dagda and Mior were still asleep before she said, "It hasn't been easy. And when I realized I was pregnant, I panicked. Your father's been wonderful. Despite his arthritis he forages with your brother every day. He's so excited about this baby I carry," she continued, her hands cupping her girth. "I'm happy, as strange as that sounds. God knows what will happen in the future, but right now being with Dag like this, having your brother to love, and another baby on the way, is almost more than I can take in." Her eyes welled with tears. "And now you're here. My heart is so full."

Kat hugged her Mom, ashamed of herself. "I can't believe any of this. I was sure I'd never find you."

It was a few moments later that her father appeared shirtless and wearing a pair of torn trousers, his thick hair standing on end. He'd cut it short since she'd seen him last.

His worried gaze went to Siobhan. "Are you feeling all right?"

Siobhan smiled. "Yes, Dag. I'm fine. And I'm so happy that Kat is here."

Dagda turned to his daughter. "I'm glad too." He

reached for Kat and pulled her close. "Now maybe we can do something of real worth," he whispered just for her.

The words washed over her, the pressure of being able to 'do something of worth', sending adrenaline coursing through her. She had no idea what she was capable of anymore, and looking around at the emptiness was enough to send positive thoughts scuttling.

The cans were open, the beans and corn divided up, by the time Bran emerged from the cave. His eyes were red-rimmed as he sought out Kat where she sat on a tattered piece of rug. Kat moved over to give him room. "Have some beans," she said, holding out the bowl.

"This is the first time I've seen the sun in months," Siobhan said, watching the brilliant orange ball rise in the east. "You brought the light, Kat—you and Bran."

But after the initial welcome a pall came over the small group, the seriousness of what they faced etched into their expressions. It was Dagda who spoke first, his voice ringing out in the white silence that stretched as far as the eye could see.

"There are others alive—we've seen their footprints. But we've been reluctant to search them out after what happened a few months back."

"Gangs attacked us," Siobhan said, continuing where Dagda left off. "They had guns and they took all our food. This was before the worst of the fires and whatever it was that came through after that. We never saw it, never knew it was coming until it was here. I've never been so scared in my life. If I didn't know better, I'd said it was a gigantic wild animal, something I've only seen in nightmares."

"Fenrir," Bran muttered. "Loki's wolf spawn."

Dagda nodded, studiously avoiding looking at Siobhan. "The serpent, Jormungand, still lies coiled in the sky."

"What serpent?" Siobhan asked, her cold-tinged cheeks turning ashen. "What does that mean?"

"Jormungand is another son of Loki's. He was destined to be a part of Ragnarok," Bran answered. "He normally lives in the sea around Midgard." He turned to Dagda. "Have you actually seen him?"

Dagda's eyes went dark. He nodded.

"Daddy saw him before I did!" Mior shrilled. "He had to point him out to me. I bet I can tame him."

Siobhan's eyes went wild. "Mior, no!"

Dagda placed a gentle hand on her shoulder. "Let the boy use what he's been given. Perhaps he can."

Siobhan settled under his touch, letting out a sigh. "Battling mythological beasts is not my strong suit," she murmured.

Kat stared up at the pale colors in the sky, the crystalline white that sparkled in the early morning rays. The snow had covered all the ills, leaving behind a pristine landscape that stretched on and on. For a moment her mind settled. "Food gathering first, or should we find a bigger cave?"

Dagda chortled. "Practical is new for you, isn't it? I say we do some exploring and I'll relate what we've gleaned since the end of the world." He glanced at Bran. "You too," he muttered, a glaze of annoyance replacing his earlier lightness.

"I don't like this anymore than you do," Bran said, looking him straight in the eyes. "But I love your daughter and she loves me. I suppose we'll both have to get used to it."

Dagda gave a short nod and stood. "I have some warm clothes in the back—you'll need them."

Dagda led, Mior right on his heels. Bran and Kat followed. They'd left Siobhan alone, despite Kat's insistence that she join them.

"She's too pregnant to walk that far," Dagda had told her when Kat protested. "As far as I can tell there are no people close by. We've been here a week now and I have yet to see another human being."

"I'll be fine," Siobhan had agreed, waving them off. "Just come back soon."

Before they left Dagda had stood staring at her for more than a minute, as though reconsidering his decision. "We won't be longer than an hour, maybe two. Are you okay with that?"

Siobhan let out a chuckle. "Yes, Mr. Protective. You've left me alone before. Now go!"

The sun was fully up by the time they reached a sharp ridge of rocks. There were bricks mixed in with the jagged and rounded stones, a few splinters of wooden planks stuck her and there. There were many prints in the snow, human and animal. Bran, Mior and Dagda, were searching through the debris when Kat let out a shout. "What do you think happened here?" she asked, pointing to bloody tracks in the snow. There were boot tracks and others that looked like dog prints. The dog prints headed away across a small hill, blood droplets alongside them. And that's when she found the bullet casing. She held it up. "The animal's injured."

Dagda took a look. "I never heard a gunshot. With the

273

silence you can hear for miles."

Mior had stopped behind them and was down on his knees examining the blood. "He's hurt. A man did it." He took off despite all of them yelling for him to come back.

"Mior is obsessed with animals," Dagda muttered, hurrying after him.

Bran took off running. He passed Dagda and kept going, disappearing over a hillock in the distance.

"Must be nice to be a god," Dagda muttered.

"And to be young," Kat reminded him. "Now tell me the short version of what's been going on. What is Mior capable of these days?"

Dagda ran his fingers through his shorn hair, making it stand on end. "The boy comes up with new skills every day. He can bring animals back to life, Kat. I suppose he can do the same with people, but we haven't had the chance to test it. The fireflies seem to represent his spirit. They're always around. Your mother has been horrified by his abilities. When she became pregnant, she told me she was relieved I was no longer a god. The pregnancy, well…it's worried me no end. If she makes it to term, I'll be surprised."

Kat tried to ignore his last statement. "Food? Where do you look for it? What have you found?"

"Cans mostly. Everything else was destroyed. Mior seems to think we can dig and discover everything we need. He insists that underneath this flatness there are intact cities. I think telling him about Atlantis was a bad idea." He let out a sigh. "I worry about running into gangs. When they came before I could do nothing to stop them. You cannot imagine what it's like to have been a god and to have it all stripped away. I feel…I feel helpless, unable to protect my family. Your mother is the only thing I have going for me right now. That and Mior, of course."

"Actually, I can, Dad. I've been going through the same thing. Mior seems to think I have magic at my fingertips; I hope he's right." She glanced at Dagda. "Please try to accept Bran. We're together now."

Dagda gazed at her. "It could take a while, Katel."

"Why, Dad? If it's about his father you shouldn't be taking it out on him."

At that moment Bran returned carrying Mior. "We found the dog. It's a coyote and it's hurt. I promised we'd go back so Mior could 'fix' it." Bran rolled his eyes.

"Please Papa! It was scared, but I can tame it."

Dagda smiled indulgently, grabbing the boy and lifting him into the air. "Lead on, but don't get out of my sight," he said, placing him on the ground. Mior took off running.

"The coyote's in bad shape," Bran said, watching Mior. "I doubt he can do much to help."

"Mior's a healer," Dagda muttered, moving past him.

Bran's eyebrows shot up. He glanced at Kat. She nodded and grabbed his hand, following Dagda along the trail of footprints in the snow.

By the time the three of them reached Mior, he was down on his knees next to a skinny dog-like animal with gold-green eyes full of pain. "Don't come any closer," he yelled when he saw them.

Dagda, Bran and Kat watched from a distance as Mior placed his hands on the gunshot wound, muttering foreign words.

"What's he saying?" Kat whispered.

"Hell if I know," her father replied. "That language just

sprung out of nowhere."

"He wants to stay here," Mior said a few moments later. "He doesn't trust humans."

"For good reason," Kat muttered to herself.

"I want him to be my dog, and he said he would."

"So how does that work if he won't come with us?" Bran asked.

"As long as I go with him, he'll follow us."

"Your mother will not be happy with this arrangement, Mior," Dagda said sternly. "And with how hungry we are it doesn't make sense to have another mouth to feed."

"He can help us find food—he said so."

"Oh brother," Bran mumbled. "Seems more logical to kill the thing and eat it."

Dagda wheeled on Bran, his eyes narrowed. "We don't have wood or a way to start a fire. You want to eat it raw? And for your information, Mior's telling the truth. He can communicate with all creatures."

"So can I, but they've never told me they could help me find food. Your wife is too thin, and you…"

"Me, what?" Dagda shouted, his face going red as he stared at Bran.

"You're gaunt, Dad. You look exhausted," Kat supplied, widening her eyes at Bran.

"I've been giving my portions to Siobhan. She needs it more than I do."

"Selflessness? That's a new one," Bran muttered.

"Bran," Kat hissed, "don't bait him."

"Enough of this jibber jabber. We need to get back to your mother," Dagda ordered. "Mior!" he called, "Follow us with the coyote, but if anything happens along the way, your new pet gets left behind. Is that understood?"

"Yes, Papa."

"We got nothing accomplished," Bran muttered, glancing at Kat. "We have no food, no new shelter and no wood to start a fire. What a waste of a day."

"The day is not over," Dagda growled, moving past him to lead the way. "And tell me, *Bran, the blessed*, what have *you* accomplished? Seems you have nothing to offer us aside from screwing my daughter."

When Bran opened his mouth to respond, Kat pinched him. Twenty feet behind them Mior walked beside the limping coyote, his hand resting on the animal's head.

38

The next day they searched from dawn to dusk for a new shelter, with no success. In the end it was Mior and the coyote who found the cave. The narrow opening proved to be somewhat intimidating, but once they'd wriggled inside, the burrow was spacious with some dried grasses left over from the last occupants. "Coyote was raised here," Mior told them as the animal slunk in behind him. It hid in the far shadows, watching the others warily.

Bran pulled a couple of candle stubs out of his pockets. "Can you light these?" he whispered to Kat.

Kat glanced at them. "Good question."

"Can you at least try?" Dagda roared in an irritated voice. "It's dark as a fucking dungeon in here."

Kat focused her attention on the ends of her fingers. She didn't expect anything to happen, and when it did, she let out a gasp, trying to contain the sparks to the wicks and not catch the grass or her clothing on fire.

When the coyote let out a howl and attempted to run out, Mior grabbed him and whispered to him. He calmed and settled back where he'd been.

"See?" Mior said. "I told you you had magic."

"That's what I had before the borders closed, Mior. It's nothing."

Mior grinned. "There's more," he murmured, dancing around the flames that flickered on the cave ceiling.

"Like what?"

He let out a laugh. "You'll see."

"Now for food," Bran muttered, glancing into the back of the cave.

"Coyote can find a rabbit, but who will skin it?" Mior asked, seeming much more adult than a boy of five.

"I will," Bran answered. "But we'll need wood to start a fire. Can't cook it over these candles. I have a few more of these, but we need to conserve them."

"Should the coyote and I go now?"

"No, Mior!" Siobhan yelled. "It's dark. We'll have to fast tonight and find food tomorrow." She frowned at Bran before settling next to Dagda.

"Mom, are you okay?" Kat asked, watching her grimace and grab her belly.

"I…I'm tired, is all. And hungry."

Dagda pulled her close. "You'll have meat tomorrow, Siobhan. I promise."

Kat worried about the baby she carried. Her mom was way too thin and it looked like she was only a month or two from term. "When is the baby due?"

Siobhan shook her head. "I have no idea. I haven't been counting the months and I don't know when it happened. I stopped bleeding a year and a half ago."

"Not enough body fat," Kat murmured."It's amazing you got pregnant."

"Where is Arwen?" Mior asked suddenly.

Kat turned to her brother. "He…he's with his father."

"But why? He should be here with us."

"He hurt me, Mior. He threw a rock at me and he also bit me and drew blood."

Siobhan gasped. "How could a baby do such a thing?"

Bran put his arms around Kat. "You'll see him again," he whispered.

"Will I? I have no way to get there without the doors. What if he hasn't changed?"

"I'm sure Val has disciplined him. He could be nearly full grown now." He smiled. "And don't forget, you have powers."

Kat suddenly wanted nothing to do with her status as a demi-goddess. Her dream of a normal life with Bran shimmered in her mind, the simplicity of it tugging at her. Tomorrow she would be called upon to do something magical to bring this world back. What it would be she didn't know, but the idea was terrifying. What if she failed and let everyone down? She'd already done enough of that. Bran had given his up, and no one expected anything from him other than skinning a rabbit, cleaning it and cooking it. Tears came, tracking silently down her cheeks.

"What's wrong?" Bran whispered.

She shook her head and wiped her tears with the sleeve of her dress. When she glanced down, the material was lit up, colors glittering inside the fabric, sparkles radiating into the darkness. She let out a humorless chuckle. All this time worried about not having powers and now she didn't want them.

When Kat woke early the next morning, Bran was not next to her. And when she glanced at her father and mother, Mior was missing too, as well as the coyote. Out hunting. She made her way carefully to the opening and wriggled through, surprised by the clear sky and absolute silence. She gazed across the smooth white landscape taking in deep breaths of the clean crisp air, trying to get her bearings. The forested areas still rose as they had before, but now there wasn't a single tree. Where Pasadena had been was an enormous hollowed out bowl, the hills behind it rising into rocky cliffs. Nothing remained of what humans had constructed—no roads, no cars, no telephone wires. Nothing. It was eerie and hard to comprehend how this had happened. Where was the debris? It must be somewhere, or had it simply vaporized, like what would happen in a nuclear war?

When she thought about her parents and Mior, her mind reeled. How had they lived through this? She would have to question Mior. That little boy was full of surprises.

She scooped some snow and let it melt in her mouth, wondering about the coming day. Somehow, they had to find a way to cook, even if it meant using extra clothing to start a fire. In the distance two figures and a dog appeared, heading her way.

When Kat turned, Dagda was emerging from the opening. "Hope they have meat. Your mother will lose the baby if she doesn't get some protein."

Kat nodded, worry for her mom rising up and sending acid coursing through her empty stomach.

Mior ran toward them, his face lit from within. "Coyote found a rabbit!" he announced. "He ate part of it, but there's enough left for us." He turned to Bran who carried the carcass. "Bran said Kat can cook it with her fingers."

When Kat saw the bloody rabbit, she nearly gagged. It was gnawed and torn, skin and fur hanging. "I can try, I suppose."

Bran placed the rabbit down on the snow. "Better do it quick before this coyote decides not to share. We had a hell of a time getting the thing away from him."

Kat met the coyote's narrowed yellow eyes. She knew now what he was. "You can have the bones," she told him. He looked up at her before he curled into a ball and closed his eyes.

"He likes you," Mior said.

Kat smiled, thinking about the dog who'd guarded her back when her memories were gone. Coyote was the same creature—a shapeshifter known as a pooka. Danu had sent him to guard Mior. "Someone needs to skin it and clean it," she said, glancing at Bran. "Who has a knife?"

Her father had a razor in his pocket and took out the blade. "Not as sharp as it once was, but it will have to do." He handed it over.

Bran cut himself several times as he worked on the fur, grimacing as he shifted the razor from one hand to the other. "Your turn," he finally said, placing the skinned carcass on the ground before wiping his hands on his filthy trousers.

Kat pointed her fingers at the gelatinous mass, trying not to see it. She thought fire, watching the sparks fly before flames licked around the rabbit's body. She kept them there, watching the fat catch, the smell of roasting meat rising. "I think it's cooked," she finally said, moving back.

Dagda came close and ripped off a hunk of meat, burning his fingers in the process. "I'm taking this to your mother," he announced, heading for the cave.

When Dagda didn't return, the three of them took turns eating, their hunger increasing the more they ingested. When the meat was gone, they gave the entrails and the bones to the coyote.

The pooka proved invaluable, digging for rodents, as well as chasing them and catching them. The steady supply of meat brought the roses back to Siobhan's cheeks, her belly becoming more pronounced as the days went by. The animal was also adept at finding cans, his ability to smell them out, bordering on the uncanny. "See? I told you!" Mior yelled after the animal found two cans of peaches in a hole he dug.

"Where did everything go, Dad?" Kat asked her father. "What happened to the power poles, the cars, the buildings?"

"Ragnarok scoured the land."

"But the buildings, the grid, the cars…everything? How is that possible?"

"And I used to be a powerful god and now I'm human. How is *that* possible in the lens you're looking through? I shouldn't have to tell you about supernatural forces, Katel."

"But this isn't Otherworld, it's Earth."

"And someone opened the borders and let Ragnarok through. Nothing will ever be the same."

Kat felt an adrenaline rush. "Did I do it?"

Dagda frowned, watching her. "I don't know, did you?"

Kat tried to think back to her trips from the Norse realm to Otherworld and then to Earth. "Maybe I did," she muttered. "The specter told me I would be the one."

Dagda looked down at the mud around his booted feet. The weather had warmed and the snow was melting. "What specter are you talking about?"

"The one who worked for the witch—the dark witch named Carmun. He's dead now."

Dagda's dark eyebrows pulled together. "Carmun. Haven't heard that name for centuries. She was responsible for an earlier destruction. I thought she was long dead."

"She took my memories and kept me off balance for all those months I should have been down here helping."

"It this is indeed her work, there will be more to come. I suggest you put on your goddess hat and go after her."

"But, what about Mom? She's going to need me when her time comes."

"I can help her. I actually know how to assist a woman through childbirth."

"Since when?"

He scoffed. "You don't think that during all my centuries in Otherworld I might have had occasion to do this?"

"I thought goddesses brought forth their babies without pain or the need for help."

Dagda let out a chortle. "And how was Arwen's birth, Katel? Pain free?"

"Are you okay with Dad delivering your baby?" Kat asked, turning to her mom who was busy prying open a can.

Siobhan looked startled. "Dag? What's happening here?"

He put an arm loosely around her shoulders. "I'm trying to get my daughter to follow her destiny and kill the witch who unleashed this hell."

Siobhan glanced at Kat. "You would leave us *now?*"

"That's what Dad wants."

"Before darkness descends again," Dagda muttered. "And if Carmun is the perpetrator, it will."

Siobhan's eyes widened. "How much darker can it get? There's nothing here!"

"The witch could take the sun and the moon and leave us in perpetual night."

Kat glanced at her mother who had gone pale. "And how do you propose I get rid of her, Dad? I'm only half-goddess and I've barely begun to reclaim what I lost."

Dagda waved his hand and shook his head. "You're half mine, Katel. Tap into that."

Kat shook her head. She had no intention of leaving her mother when she was so close to term. The idea of her father delivering the baby was laughable.

"Are you leaving?" Bran asked her once her father was out of earshot.

"No, Bran. Mom needs me. Did you see her face when she heard that Dad was planning to help her through the birth?" She let a snort and shook her head.

"That's good because without you here there's no point in me staying."

When Kat really looked at him, she saw the unhappiness etched into the skin around his eyes. "They need you, Bran. Dad's got arthritis and Mom will soon have a baby to take care of. You're a strong man—a protector. I'm going to have to leave sometime, you know."

"And I won't be going with you?"

"I…I hadn't really thought about it. I can see why you wouldn't want to stay here, but…"

"But what?" he asked angrily. "I'm supposed to stay behind and watch over your family while you put yourself in extreme danger somewhere? I thought we were a team!"

Kat reached for her pendant, surprised for a second that it wasn't around her neck. Fear surged through her. The pendants linked them and now they were both gone.

"Yeah, that too," Bran said, watching her. "This is too fucking much, Kat." He turned and stalked off.

Kat was sipping coke from a can the coyote had dug up when her brother burst from inside the cave. She'd awakened early, slipping away from Bran to think. What he'd said a few days before had disturbed her. Her thought processes regarding the witch were unclear and it made sense that he'd be upset about her leaving. They'd gone through so much, their love carrying them through. It made perfect sense that when the time came, he'd expect to accompany her. They had not spoken of it again, but the tension between them lingered. She glanced at her brother who was staring at her with wide eyes.

"Want to help me bring the world back?" he asked, dancing around her.

Kat gazed at him, wondering if he was part of a conspiracy to make her feel bad. "What are you talking about?"

"You and the forests—you can redo them."

"Redo...you mean conjure trees?"

Mior nodded. "And once you conjure the trees, the animals will come back and we'll have nuts and mushrooms and..."

"Mior, I can't do something like that—I'm barely able to light candles."

"Yes, you can! You only have to think you can!"

His enthusiasm was infectious, but Kat was skeptical. When he grabbed her hand, she let him tug her toward the bare hills in the distance. "That's where the trees belong." He looked at her. "I can color them but you have to bring them first."

"And what then? Will we bring back the towns and all the people?"

"They're here, we just can't see them."

"Where, Mior? Where are the people?"

"Under the ground, silly." He frowned at her, like she was an idiot for asking, and then pointed toward the ridgeline. "There's where the trees go." He watched her, willing her to try.

Kat thought of the forest she remembered, the enormous oaks, maples and the conifers, the peace she felt when she walked amongst them. It was there that she'd found the way to Cerridwen. Was the goddess still hidden away in the Underworld or was she gone too?

The trees in her mind whispered to her, their branches bending toward her. She'd loved it there, her heart singing every time she walked under the heavy branches. It was where she and Bran sheltered together—where they made love. Her heart filled. She missed them so much. When she turned, the pooka had joined Mior, both of them staring at her expectantly.

She let out a heavy sigh. "Here goes nothing," she muttered, waving her hands in configurations as though painting a picture of the trees on a blank canvas. Her fingers traced up one trunk, waving in the air to fill in the branches, and traced another one.

"It's working!" Mior shouted, pointing.

Kat shaded her eyes against the rising sun. Sure enough, trees were appearing along the ridge, their shapes filling in the more she waved her hands and fingers. Soon the tall shapes reached along the ridge and began to trace downward as they had before, filling in the lower hillsides. When she glanced at her brother, he was muttering something and had his eyes closed. And when she looked again, the colors of the forest had deepened, the differing greens and the trunks and the understory, awash with vibrant color.

"The deer are there and the squirrels and the birds and the mice and the skunks and all the insects and the mushrooms and the…" Mior went suddenly white and fell, his face buried in a snowdrift. The coyote moved next to him and licked his face, looking up at Kat.

Kat knelt, feeling his pulse as she pulled him up to sitting. It was thready and weak. She shook him gently, trying not to be alarmed. "Mior, wake up."

When he opened his eyes, they were glazed with worry. "Mama," he muttered. "The baby's coming. Something's wrong."

Kat tugged him to his feet, picked him up and ran.

39

B y the time they reached the cave, they could hear Siobhan screaming. Mior's eyes pleaded with Kat's. "Help her."

"What is it, Mior? What's wrong with the baby?"

He shook his head, and began to cry. "It can't breathe," he muttered.

Kat hurried away and squeezed through the narrow opening. A candle lit up the dark interior, her father's face ragged with worry. "Dad, move out of the way," Kat told him, going to her knees to check between her mother's legs. "Mom? Tell me what you're feeling."

"The baby—he's stuck. He..." When she let out a piercing shriek Dagda bent over her, his eyes welling.

"How long has she been in labor?" Kat asked her father.

"Since last night. She suffered in silence because she didn't want to wake you."

Kat glanced at Bran hovering in the shadows before turning to her Dad. "I think you and Bran should get out of here and leave me to it. Not sure I can do it, but I think the baby is breech and needs to be turned."

"I can't leave your mother."

"Do what she says, Dag," Siobhan murmured weakly.

Dagda let out a heavy sigh and signaled to Bran.

Once the two men left, Kat breathed a sigh of relief. Things were difficult enough without having Dagda hovering over her. When she placed a hand on her mother's abdomen the energy in the cave shifted. She saw herself in a long black robe, her hair braided and pulled back. She was a member of the Banduri, a druidic priestess from long ago. She knew what was going on and how to fix it. "He hasn't dropped because he's in the wrong position," she murmured in a voice that didn't sound like her own.

"Can you turn him?"

"Yes, but it will not be pleasant."

"I know, just do it," her mother grunted.

Kat had never delivered a baby, but whatever energy was inhabiting her body knew exactly what to do. She watched her hands work on her mother, her fingers moving gently inside the birth canal. She felt the baby's legs and pushed against them, attempting to get the baby to do the work. When he didn't, she worked to twist him. "Come on," she whispered. She placed one hand on Siobhan's belly, applying gentle pressure as she pushed and twisted carefully with her other hand. Magic curled from her hands and fingers as she worked, sparkling tendrils weaving into her mother. "You have to push now."

But Siobhan lay like a dead fish, her body slick with sweat and her eyes closed. "Wake up!" Kat shouted in a strange deep voice. "You must push!"

Siobhan's eyes opened. "I...Kat?"

"Push. If you do not, both of you will die." Kat sent

energy coursing through Siobhan's weakening body, her fingers emitting sparks and light.

Siobhan grunted and lifted herself up before uttering an anguished cry, her body rigid with effort. When the baby's head emerged, Kat told her to push again, but Siobhan had fallen back, apparently unconscious.

"Okay, little one. It is up to you and me," she muttered. She felt for the shoulders and tugged gently, working to free him without damaging her mother's delicate membranes. Magic sparked and flickered in the darkness as the baby arrived in a whoosh of fluids. "Dagda!" she shouted. "I need the razor!"

Dagda was there in an instant, his worried gaze on his wife. "Is she alive?"

"She's unconscious, but right now I need you to cut the umbilical cord and help me clean her up."

Dagda glanced at her, his eyes widening in surprise before he produced the blade from his trouser pocket. His hands shook and tears coursed down his cheeks as he did what she asked. "It's a girl," he murmured, turning to Kat. He placed the baby at Siobhan's breast and pushed the damp hair back from her face. "Siobhan?" he whispered. "We have a baby girl." He kissed her and bent over her sobbing, as though his heart would break.

Kat felt Siobhan's pulse. "She is only exhausted. She's lost a lot of blood." A moment later the baby let out a lusty cry.

Dagda smiled, his tired gaze going to Kat. "You did it, daughter."

But Kat knew that what she'd accomplished came from another source. She washed her hands in the bowl of water her father brought in, and found a cleanish T-shirt in which to wrap the baby. After that she wriggled through the opening, her gaze going to Mior. "Your sister is here," she told him, shooing him inside before she headed across the empty snow-covered landscape.

Kat walked for a long time, her need for silence overriding everything. A raven flew across the sky above her, wide wings spread to pick up the thermals. He soared, his caw sending shivers down her spine. He was unhappy. Right now, she couldn't think about Bran or his problems, her mind on what had happened back in the cave. Who was this druidic priestess? She didn't know if it was a past life or if this person had entered her body at the precise moment when she needed her. She thought of the robes and the magic, the knowledge she was aware of as she worked. The face had not been hers, but the consciousness had seemed deeply familiar. She let out a sigh, glancing at the ridge for the first time. A deep forest of green had replaced the emptiness, meadows of wildflowers surrounding the trees. Shadows played across the sunlit landscape as the branches moved gently in the breeze.

When Kat entered the forest, she felt the past as though it had moved into the present. When she glanced down, she was dressed in robes, her consciousness that of the priestess. She walked amongst the trees, hearing their whispers of welcome. When she came to a pool, she removed the robe and entered the water, awareness of a life lived long ago presenting itself. Bran had been with her there, a druid who walked beside her. They'd been friends and colleagues and lovers. He was a priest in the same order, and although women were not given credit for what they did, he'd stood up for her, supporting her abilities. It was because of him that she'd thrived within the circle of men. It was as Danu said—she was not who she thought she was.

40

K at returned from the woods feeling strange and not herself. But when she tried to relay what had happened, Bran wasn't interested, his concerns making themselves known as he grabbed her arm and dragged her away from the others.

"Your father just made it clear that he will never approve of us."

"I don't care what he thinks, Bran. Do you?"

"Yes, I do. He used to be the all-father god, Kat. Do you realize how powerful he was? I can't ignore his wishes and act like he has no authority."

Kat stared at him in surprise. "He is no longer a god, and the two of us can do whatever we want. It's not like you have to ask him for permission. I'm not a medieval maiden."

Bran didn't get the humor, his frowning face turning even darker. "Giving up my powers was the wrong move," he muttered. "If I hadn't done that your father would respect me. As it is, I can't live with him."

"Do you want to find another home for the two of us?"

"What about your brother, your Mom and now your baby sister?"

Kat shook her head, and stared into the distance. "Did you see what Mior and I did up there?" she asked, pointing. "We can repopulate the earth with plants and trees and maybe even animals."

Bran glanced where she pointed and turned back to her. "What I'm talking about is the continuation of *us*, and you're going off about plants?"

"This is my home and what I'm doing here is of paramount importance! Do you want to live in a wasteland?"

His eyes narrowed dangerously. "I don't want to live where I'm not wanted," he muttered.

She grabbed his arm. "Bran, what has gotten into you? Of course you're wanted here!"

He pulled out of her grip and shook his head. A second later he was Raven. Kat watched him fly up and away, a black dot disappearing into the distance.

Kat and Mior worked together for the next few months, bringing life back. Kat had no idea how other places on earth were faring, but she was ecstatic about what they'd managed in such a short time. Now there were deer grazing along the edges of the forests, more rabbits than they could eat, and berry bushes where they collected gooseberries, blueberries, raspberries and blackberries. Deer grazed in the meadows, foxes roamed, skunks could be seen.

Nikki Broadwell

When she wasn't doing magic, Kat agonized over Bran's continuing absence. Her father had been too occupied with Siobhan's recovery to question, but as her mother improved, she finally confronted him. "Dad, were you responsible for Bran leaving?"

Dagda frowned and stared into the distance. "I only told him he wasn't worthy of you."

"But I love him!"

"What has he accomplished, Katel? While you and Mior have been restoring the world, he's been sitting on his ass twiddling his thumbs."

"That isn't fair! You haven't helped restore the world either."

"I didn't willingly give up my abilities. They were torn from me. To be a god one must behave like a god—I know that now. He could have helped down here, but instead he spends his days either flying around in raven form, or bringing back what the coyote catches and maybe skinning and cooking it. Powers are not to be taken lightly, and to act like you never had them is shameful. He doesn't deserve you, especially after what we all witnessed during the birth. You are much more than I could ever have imagined. He left because he knows this."

"He left because you shamed him, Dad."

Dagda shook his head and turned away. "You'll thank me one day."

But Kat couldn't accept what her father had said to Bran, or how Dagda felt. Giving up his powers for *her*, was what Bran had done. Was it willingly? She didn't really know. All she knew was that he loved her enough to sacrifice what he'd always been. But now he was gone and she had no idea if he'd come back.

She thought back to the months they'd been here, how there was no privacy. They were both pent up, frustrated about not being able to express their affection. She'd suggested finding a place for the two of them—why hadn't he gone with that plan? He seemed to be behaving as though he'd asked Dagda for her hand in marriage and her father had refused him. Old-fashioned in the extreme, and very out of character for him.

The baby was one month old when they had the naming ceremony up in the woods by the spring-fed pond. Kat presided as her druidic persona, saying the words that came to her to protect the baby. The name Dagda and Siobhan decided on was Tus Nua, Gaelic for new beginnings. Siobhan had regained her health, her eyes sparkling as she shed her clothes and carried the baby into the pond. Mior was next and Kat followed, the festive feelings sending their happy laughter cascading across the landscape. When Dagda finally took off his clothes and joined them, they shouted it to the treetops. His grumpiness made them all laugh as he complained about the cold water and tried to pretend he wasn't having the time of his life.

They had fresh caught rabbit for dinner, along with blackberries and greens they found growing along the newly established streams. Dagda skinned the animal and cooked it in a firepit with the downed wood they'd gathered. The only thing missing was Bran, an emptiness that continued to plague Kat. She'd expected him back, but there'd been no sign of him.

It was barely a week later that they came upon the survivalists, a clan of around twenty-five people who had built a house into the side of a hill. They'd been there before it all started, with food enough to last them at least a year. There were men, women and children in the group, all of them wearing crosses around their necks. They looked at Kat's family with suspicion and distrust.

"Do you worship the devil?" one of the men asked, staring at her waist length braided hair, the tattered Fae dress she wore and her bare feet.

"No," Kat told him. "We worship the goddess and the trees."

"That's the same as devil worship," he informed her. "Stay away from us and we'll leave you alone."

"I used to be Catholic," Siobhan told them. She was holding the baby in her arms, her long skirt trailing in the mud.

"We fixed the forest!" Mior piped up. "And now we have animals again!"

The man was bald, tattoos on his upper arms. He laughed nastily. "God did that, you little pissant. Who in hell do you think you are?"

Siobhan blanched and glanced at Dagda who was frowning.

"We are living in difficult times and there are not many of us left," Dagda began. "I suggest you develop a more forgiving attitude, considering the circumstances."

"We'll do whatever the fuck we want, old man. Now, as I said, stay away from us and we won't give you any trouble." He turned on his heel, signaling to the others. "Be warned," he called over his shoulder.

"Well, that didn't go well," Kat muttered. "Hope we don't have any more run-ins with them."

"He's the one who shot the coyote," Mior whispered.

Six months had gone by since Bran's departure, every day that he was gone hurting Kat in a way she couldn't describe. He'd promised her he wouldn't leave and yet he was gone—and it seemed for good. Twice she'd had run-ins with the survivalists, their belief that God had created the woods and the meadows and the flowers, infuriating. She decided not to push it, knowing that with their violent tendencies they could hurt her and Mior. From then on, she instructed Mior to stay away from them and not play with the children. If they got wind of what he could achieve, they could easily do something crazy.

All of her little family had participated in the building of a house along the edge of the woods, the rustic shack reminiscent of the one her father had built on his property. But this one was fashioned out of the curved limbs they gathered and twisted together. It looked like a fairy house from a book, leaves still sprouting as though the limbs were attached to a living tree. Mior and Kat had added a layer of magic to the roof to keep them dry, and Mior had woven a spell around it to keep them safe. They didn't have electricity or even running water, but it kept out the wind and the rain and it was cozy, with thick grass floors that they replaced often, and seats fashioned out of other downed limbs. Their beds were made of pine needles and grass covered with the blankets left from their cave days, deerskins now keeping them warm. Their clothing was torn and ragged, but still functioned. They bathed in the pool in the forest and got their water from the spring. On warm days they went naked.

For some reason the survivalists did not visit the forest, their days seemingly spent hunting and building walls out of the stones they lugged from other places. They were creating a compound to shut out the world, or what was left of it. "They're afraid of us," Mior exclaimed in surprise one day as he and Kat walked through the meadow gathering herbs. "Why?"

Kat straightened from where she was picking chamomile. "Because we're different."

"What's wrong with being different?"

"Nothing, Mior. But there are those who don't want to take the time to understand others. We aren't doing much to bridge the gap between us either."

"But that's because they don't like us."

Kat nodded. "Exactly right."

The fireflies still followed Mior around and helped him locate beehives, instructing him on how to extract the honey. Since then they'd been able to make beeswax candles that lit up their home on dark nights. Kat pondered her earlier feelings of wanting to have a simple life with Bran that didn't include her powers. Lately she'd been grateful for everything she could do, from bringing the forest back, to welcoming her druidic abilities when they appeared. She'd changed since Bran had gone, embracing what had always lived inside her. But it didn't take away the pain of his absence.

She wondered about the dark witch and Danu's warning. She felt her lurking at the edges of her mind. Biding her time. Recently she'd seen a shadow creature that reminded her of the specter. It was a darkness hovering within the branches of the trees and a phantom that followed her across the meadows. When the pooka saw it, he barked and chased it away. It didn't worry her.

She'd felt Danu when she bathed alone in the forest pool or collected hazelnuts, or discovered the mushrooms that grew at the base of the trees. No message had come, but she knew the goddess was watching over them. Mostly she just lived, enjoying Tus Nua and her brother. There was a newfound peace, joy that had been missing for a very long time. Dagda looked younger, a smile replacing the frown he'd worn. Siobhan laughed and sang while she worked. Life was worth living, every day like a precious jewel.

There were dark clouds on the horizon the day it happened. Kat was walking in the meadow with the coyote, collecting herbs for the teas she'd begun to make, her mind on what she was doing. She heard a whisper, a familiar voice that sounded urgent. "If you want to stop the witch, you have to come now." When she looked up there was a door in front of her. It opened, and on the other side she saw a tall smiling boy around twelve years old who looked very much like Val except for the dark wavy hair. Behind him stood the man Kat had nearly forgotten, the father of her child. When she glanced back at the pooka he was staring at her. "Will you watch over them?" she asked. He gazed at her knowingly, his eyes shining with magic. She turned and stepped through.

To be continued...

READ THE EXCITING FIRST CHAPTER OF RAVEN AND HUMMINGBIRD BOOK 4!

The house in Alfheim had changed, the understated wood and stone turned into a palace of gleaming glass and turrets that rose so high they were barely visible amongst the clouds. Kat stared uncomprehending, wondering how such a thing was possible.

"It is all due to our son," Val said proudly. "He has a knack with magic that is unsurpassed in recent history." Val put a hand on the twelve-year-old's shoulder. "It is the combination of goddess and Elven blood."

Kat turned to Arwen, afraid for a second. This boy had nearly killed her when he was but a baby. But before she could utter a word, he had moved close and was pulling her into a hug.

"I am so glad to see you," he murmured in a voice nearly as deep as Val's. "I am sorry for how I behaved." He chuckled and pulled back. "A Fae child has no inner restraint unless trained by a member of the Elven race."

Kat stared into the luminous eyes, not at all sure she trusted him, even now. There was guile behind that innocent look he was giving her. She smiled. "It was a long time ago."

"Yes, too long," Val agreed, moving forward to pull her into his arms. "Arwen is much changed. There is no need to worry," he whispered in her ear.

In truth it only been a little over two years, but in that short time her baby had reached his father's height. He looked nearly full grown. Kat glanced at the uninviting monstrosity in the distance, her gaze lingering on the lack of roses, lavender and other blooming plants. The former garden was stark, with nothing in it but strange sculptures that echoed the house design. "What happened to the gardens?"

Val's expression went dark for a millisecond before he said, "Arwen didn't like them. He felt they were an unnecessary addition to a castle that needed no improvement."

Kat looked up at the tapered points that resembled skewers. They were sharp like the tips of bayonets. She suppressed the shudder that went through her body. "It is rather grand, isn't it?"

Val nodded. "Shall we go inside? I have some food prepared and we can talk about why you are here."

Arwen moved to walk beside her, his sidelong glances making her uncomfortable. "I have your hair color," he finally announced. "And your eye shape, I think."

Kat smiled up at him. "Yes. I see it. But your eyes are crystalline blue like you father's."

"All the Fae have eyes like this," he said smiling. He strode ahead to open the door for them.

Kat watched him, surprised by his need to charm her. Those eyes were where the Fae magic lay, their ability to cast spells with a look, something she'd dealt with in the past. It was why she was mother to Arwen.

The inside of the edifice was just as changed as the outside, with copper tables and gleaming glass everywhere. She missed the wooden benches, the enormous fireplace and the homey feeling of the former building.

"Bring in the plate I arranged," Val told his son. "I'll get the drinks." He motioned for Kat to sit at the highly polished metal table.

"Where is Isabel?" Kat asked as she seated herself in an uncomfortable chair. Isabel had served them the last time she'd been here and Kat had been looking forward to seeing the diminutive Fae woman who had done her hair and dressed her when she was blind.

"Arwen and Isabel did not get on," Val answered, turning to a cabinet set into the wall. He came back to the table carrying a bottle and three glasses which he placed in front of her. "This is some of our best Fae wine," he said, pouring golden liquid into her glass. "It's delicious and I know you will like it."

Kat laughed. "What magic does it hold?"

Val chuckled. "It is merely wine, Kat. It might make you feel slightly more awake, but other than that it is benign."

Kat examined the room. The ceiling reached up and up to end in a turret, light cascading downward to bounce off the metal and glass below. She squinted in the brightness and shaded her eyes. "I miss your house, Val. The one that burned."

He nodded as he poured a glass and sat next to her. "I do as well."

"Why did you allow Arwen to change the design?"

The question went unanswered as Arwen appeared carrying a platter filled with meats, cheeses, olives and bread. He looked from one to the other. "What did I miss?"

"Just setting the stage for why your mother's here," Val said, reaching for a piece of bread. "But before we get into all of that, how are things on earth? Is your family safe? How is Bran?"

Kat felt a twinge of apprehension as she glanced at Arwen. The look on his face seemed over-eager. "Everyone's fine at the moment, but the serpent is still up in the sky. Bran left six months ago."

Val frowned. "Why?"

"I…I told him I planned on doing this without him."

"Doing this—do you mean stopping the dark witch?"

Kat nodded, suddenly feeling guilty about all of it. Bran was the person she trusted most in the world. "I don't know why I told him that. Dagda shamed him too. Possibly the combination of things put him over the edge."

Val nodded slowly, looking down at the drink in his hands. He took a hefty swallow. "As I remember, aside from Raven, Bran is without powers."

"Yes, and that's exactly why I worried."

"But yours are back?"

Kat smiled. "I have so much more, Val. Danu…"

Val's eyes widened. "You're in touch with Danu?"

Kat nodded. "I'm also in touch with a life I lived long ago as a druid priestess."

His gaze met hers. "Possibly that's what's bothering Bran—you've outshined him. Men do not normally enjoy that, not even gods and the Fae. It is a hard thing to accept."

Kat nodded. "I suppose it could be that. He expected us to be a team. But how can we be a team when he's so vulnerable? I would spend my time worrying about him instead of focusing on my mission." Kat tasted her wine, surprised by the honeyed flavor. It was just as good as Val had said it would be. "So, Val, tell me why I'm here. Is the witch in Alfheim? What have you learned?" She glanced at Arwen who seemed riveted, his eyes wide with interest.

"Arwen? Can you retrieve my notes from the library?" Val asked.

"Where are they?"

"On my desk underneath that stack of missives I'm been working on. They are handwritten on yellow paper." Val turned to Kat. "This is a busy time in Alfheim. We've barely begun the process of digging ourselves out from under the terrible damage we suffered. Freyr, Alfheim's ruler, has been in touch with those of us who have land. He wants to commandeer our property for various purposes, some of which seem somewhat dubious."

"He's been threatening," Arwen supplied. "Val has been arguing with him, but so far..."

"Arwen?" Val interrupted. "I need my notes please."

Val waited to continue, watching his son rise and head off. Once the boy was out of earshot he leaned toward Kat, placing his hand on her forearm. His eyes narrowed and turned gold, his voice lowering to a near whisper. "Remember that favor you owe me?"

If you enjoyed Kat's Conundrum, please leave a review on Amazon or on the website of your choice. It helps tremendously!

Thank you for reading!

To reach my website go to:
www.nikkibroadwellauthor.com